Forbidden Temptation

(Claimed #2)

Alaina Drake

Published by Accent Press Ltd

ISBN 9781910939697

Published by Accent Press Ltd – 2016

Chapter One

"Come into my office, Dr Lyons." I could barely make out the words that invited me into the Dean of Arts and Science's office. Whether the slurred words were caused by his afternoon Scotch or because his dentures were falling out, I wasn't sure. Regardless, my heels moved across the tiled foyer and into his carpeted office, where my footfall became silent.

"You can call me Jenn if you wish," I said as I stopped in front of his mahogany desk. His wrinkled hand reached out from his suit coat, revealing a spider web of blue veins, and monogrammed cuff links. With an endearing, lop-sided grin, his shaking hand took mine across the desk.

"I do wish. Thank you, Jenn, for coming on such short notice." His open palm motioned for me to sit on the chair across from his desk. The worn leather cushion squealed as it took my weight.

My crossed legs bounced as I sat perched on the edge of the seat. A bead of sweat conveyed my nervousness as it trickled between my shoulder blades. "My pleasure. What did you want to talk about –?"

A wave of his hand interrupted me. "Tell me about your move, Jenn. Are you getting situated in your office? How does it compare to your office in Boulder?"

"Yes. It's lovely. Thank you," I replied, unsure why the Dean had asked me to his office.

"I understand there's a lot more pressure now that you're officially an Associate Professor, so I wanted to offer you any help I could. You're teaching two classes, right?" he asked.

This one is for B, my husband and my favorite belay. Belay on, B.

"Yes. I just put the finishing touches on the syllabus for the senior-level Shakespeare course, the one I'm most excited to teach."

"You finished the syllabus a whole week before classes start? Impressive. Everyone knows professors finish their syllabi the hour before class starts." He chuckled before he continued. "In all seriousness, I'm glad you're settling in. I bet you don't miss working on that dissertation, do you?"

"Nooo ... I do have more free time now." *Where the hell is he going with this?* I was reluctant to believe I had been called into his office for idle chitchat.

His playful grin told me he was toying with me, delaying the real reason he asked me to his office just so he could see me squirm.

Mission accomplished.

Finally, he continued. "I'm sure you're busy getting ready for the start of the semester, so I won't take much of your time." The sarcasm dripped from each measured word. "But I do have a favour to ask of you already, I'm afraid."

"Sure. What can I do for you?" I asked.

"The theatre department is putting on a play, and Lord help them, they think they can do Shakespeare." He rolled his eyes and finished off the amber liquid in the bottom of his crystal tumbler. I chuckled at Dean Andrews's friendly jab at the expense of a rival department. "What they need is a dramaturg with your expertise. They are willing to pay you for fifteen hours of work a week, but I'm not sure you'll be able to help those drama majors with even *double* that time. I always say, 'even if all the world's a stage, not everyone should act.'"

My chuckle morphed into a belly laugh. This old bird was a feisty one. I liked him. "Oh yeah? What makes you think they need so much help?"

The tips of his arthritic fingers waved me towards him as he leaned forward across his desk. I leaned in too, like

2

we were co-conspirators. He whispered, "You know who's directing it?"

"No," I whispered back, although there wasn't another soul in the room to overhear our conversation.

His bushy, grey eyebrows lifted. "Dr Burrows."

"But … I thought … I mean …"

His smile lit as I stammered. "You thought he was brilliant? One of the most revered and respected directors around?"

"Well, yes."

"He is surely respected, no doubt. I count him as a dear friend. But he's *shit* at Shakespeare." His secret told, he leaned back, eliciting a creak from his wooden, high-back chair.

His cuss surprised a laugh from my throat. "How do you know that?"

"He's never loved it. Never truly appreciated the language, the magic. I could tell that the day I met him forty years ago."

"Forty years ago?"

"Indeed. He paid me five bucks to write his freshman literature paper on Shakespeare."

"Wow. Five bucks. You write cheap," I joked.

"Nah. He thought he got the good end of the deal until he got the paper back."

"Oh no."

"He got a D. 'You get what you pay for,' I told him, and he never asked me to write for him again." Dean Andrews winked then turned serious. "Joking aside, I must admit that at first I was hesitant to overwhelm a new professor, but I decided to talk to you first. Do you think you can handle adding that to your schedule?"

Saying "no" never entered my brain. He felt more like my grandpa than the revered department chair who had hired me during the first interview. "I'd love to. What is the play?"

3

His pursed-lipped smirk answered me.

"No way. Let me guess – *As You Like It*."

"Of course it is."

"Of course it is," I echoed him. A large portion of my PhD dissertation focused on the very play.

"As dramaturg, you will be expected to provide insight about the time period and costumes and help Dr Burrows oversee the actors' delivery and characterization. In other words, my dear, you will be the Shakespearean expert who guides the production toward a greater sense of authenticity." He paused, then added, "Or at least you'll keep the thespians from flying the blooming thing into the side of the mountain."

I smiled. "When should I start working with them?"

"Dr Burrows is working with the cast in Westfield Auditorium. I told him I would send you over if you were interested." He checked his watch. "I believe they are in rehearsal, so you can get your first glimpse of the actors if you head there now. I appreciate your willingness to help out, Jenn. You're already proving to be the asset I knew you would be."

"Thank you." I started to stand and excuse myself.

"Before you go, would you be a dear and fetch me that bottle from the counter over there? Help this poor old man out." His eyes twinkled, adding more playfulness to his mischievous grin.

"Sure," I managed through a laugh as I grabbed the half-empty bottle of Scotch from the sideboard. I hoped that if I was ever a dean of a college one day, I'd be day-drinking in my office too.

When I brought the bottle back to his desk, he was finishing a hand-scrawled note. He handed it to me without folding it. "Please give this to Dr Burrows when you see him."

"May I?" I asked, not wanting to assume that the unfolded note was for my eyes.

4

"Absolutely, my dear."

I read the single line:

I'm sending you one of my best and brightest, dear friend, because I have no more faith in thee than in a stewed prune.

I warmed at the compliment and laughed at the Shakespearean insult. "Henry V?" I guessed.

"And that's why I hired you," he praised with an elated smile. "I knew the moment I read your dissertation, Jenn, that we shared a love of the bard. People like us could study his language every day for the rest of our lives and we'd never grow tired. Now your job is to share that love, that passion." His voice changed from philosophical to playful when he added, "Even if it is with drama majors."

"*Especially* with drama majors," I added before I left his office. In the waiting room, I put on my coat, gloves, and hat before stepping into the frigid winter air.

I made my way across campus to the performing arts building housing Westfield Auditorium. Thankfully, my heels met dry pavement, a rarity for Colorado in January. Snow piles lined each side of the sidewalk, and a brisk north wind challenged my heavy wool coat to a duel.

My warm breath puffed its last clouds as I walked up the concrete steps. The rhythmical gallop of Shakespeare's verse welcomed me as I hefted open the heavy wooden door at the back of the auditorium. My eyes fluttered closed as I breathed in the familiar smell of the musty curtains standing guard off stage. Although I'd never felt the need to act myself, the theatre always brought with it a sense of peace that felt like old books smelled.

No one had noticed my arrival, so I felt like a ghost, able to observe without the burden of interacting. To avoid interrupting the rehearsal, I chose a soft, red velvet seat near the back, in a row guarded by the shadows from the balcony above.

Before I had the chance to settle in, my first glance was stolen from me.

No, more accurately, it was demanded from me.

My eyes were magnetized to the figure standing stage right. Although dressed modernly in dark jeans and a tight, white T-shirt, his presence was that of a Shakespearean hero with a dramatic, defined jaw, jet-black hair, and sun-kissed skin.

His voice reached my ears easily at the back of the auditorium, like he was using a microphone. He commanded my attention, daring me to look away while simultaneously promising that I would miss something if I did.

So, of course, I didn't.

I saw his graceful, measured stride that ate up the distance between him and the lucky actress playing his lover. He stalked to her with a hunger in his eyes that promised that even her wildest fantasies were tame next to his. His lips curved and dipped, moulding the beautiful language into music.

I was startled when Dr Burrows called for a pause. "We have a visitor. Please take five," he said to the cast, as he made his way towards me.

I stood and walked down the center aisle that slanted gradually toward the stage. I met Dr Burrows halfway, and he greeted me with a warm handshake that engulfed my petite hand.

"Thank you for coming, Professor Lyons. I've heard great things about your work. We're excited to have you." His hand continued to pump mine in a lingering handshake.

"I'm excited to be a part of the production, Dr Burrows," I replied as I took my hand from his to retrieve the note from my pocket.

"Dean Andrews wanted me to give you this."

Dr Burrows smirked knowingly before he read it. His eyes scanned the single line before he laughed, "Pretentious bastard."

After he tucked the note in his breast pocket, he guided us towards seats in the middle of the auditorium.

"Let's sit here. It will give us a chance to talk in private while they continue. Carry on, please," he said, gesturing to the actors that had reassembled onstage.

Blank verse once again flowed from the stage, but my attention was centered on Dr Burrows's whispered conversation. "Magnetic, isn't he?"

I schooled my face to pretend like I didn't know who he was referring to, but the dip of his chin and the knowing glance over the top of his thick spectacles told me he didn't buy what I was hawking. "You know exactly who I'm talking about. Declan's strong."

I decided to go with blunt honesty. "Without a doubt. But he's too strong."

Dr Burrows turned his face to me, startled. I wasn't able to read his expression, but his eyes flitted right and left, back and forth between my eyes like they were finding something for the first time. "You're right. He's upstaging her. In a scene where Stephanie –" he gestured towards the stage where the girl playing Rosalind stood "should be running circles around him, he's toying with her. Orlando doesn't toy."

"Well, since you're the director, can you make him *not* toy?" I didn't mean it to come out as a criticism, but I immediately worried that it had.

Dr Burrows harrumphed. "Can you whip a donkey to make it go?"

Ahh ... so we're working with a stubborn actor. "Or you could dangle a carrot in front of its nose," I suggested.

Dr Burrows threw his head back in a belly laugh. I wasn't sure why, but I must have said something funny. With a genuine, but sly, smile, he took my elbow and led me to the front of the stage. Before introducing me to the cast, he whispered in my ear, "Mind if I use you as the carrot?"

"Everyone, come downstage, please. I want to introduce you to someone. This is Dr Jenn Lyons. She will be serving as the dramaturg for this production. With a PhD dissertation that focused on this play, she will be an asset to us. Be sure to introduce yourself soon. Thank you for your time today, everyone. We'll see you tomorrow. Same time."

The majority of the dismissed cast talked amongst themselves as they left the stage, but a few remained behind to talk to Dr Burrows. Stephanie, the pretty blonde playing Rosalind, was the first to greet me with a sincere smile.

"I'm Stephanie. I'm sure you've already figured out I'm playing Rosalind. I'm excited to work with you because, clearly, I have a long way to go," she said, defeated.

I comprehended only a small portion of what she was saying as she continued, "... difficult ... manage my emotions ... discouraged ..." I tried to focus my attention on Stephanie as she discussed her frustrations about the role, but my body was distracted by the energy pulsing ten feet away. Declan was having a conversation with another actor while sitting on the edge of the stage, his feet hanging off the side as he drank a bottle of water. His penetrating eyes didn't move from mine when I glanced in his direction. His face remained stoic, unreadable. His eyes never blinked, never flinched, and only after what must have been twenty seconds did he move. His left eyebrow lifted slightly in a challenge I must have accepted because both corners of his full lips tilted in amusement.

I turned my attention back to Stephanie who either didn't notice my distraction or graciously ignored it. "I look forward to working with you too. Don't worry. We have time to get everything polished."

"I'd like to introduce you to Declan," Dr Burrows interrupted when his conversation was over.

Stephanie thanked me again before leaving, and after she did, Dr Burrows guided me to the front of the stage. When we stopped, the other actors dispersed and Declan stood. A full head taller than me, there was no doubt his presence was imposing.

But I already knew that.

From an auditorium away.

For the first time, I was able to see the details in his dark brown eyes, a darker shade on the bottom like they were weighted down by something.

Dr Burrows led the introduction. "Dr Lyons. This is Declan, our Orlando. I need to meet with some of the stage crew, so I'll leave you two to get acquainted. See you tomorrow." The heels of his dress shoes thumped on the wooden stage floor as he walked away.

"Nice to meet you, Dr Lyons." Declan's authoritative stage voice was replaced by an intimate murmur that glided like a kite on a soft breeze. The grip of his handshake was firm but not painful, his smile perfunctory. Since my dad had always taught me that a handshake was the crucial proving ground, especially for a woman in a professional situation, I decided to squeeze Declan's hand a little – OK a lot – harder. I expected his face to register surprise. Instead, what I got was the transformation of his smile from a polite, obligatory one to sincere and knowing. It was such a pretty change that I considered it a reward.

"Nice to meet you too. I look forward to working with you."

I was confused when Declan's response to my pleasantry was a half-hearted chuckle. "What?" I asked.

He took another drink of his water and screwed on the cap before he said, "You don't know me well, do you?

9

You're not part of the theatre department."

I caught the challenge in his voice. He saw me as an English professor, not an actor who loved the craft. Moreover, since I'd never acted, the possibility of taking acting advice from me was rubbing his ego the wrong way. Unhurried, I let a smile cross my lips. His eyes scanned my face and lingered on my smile in the breaths that passed between us.

Declan was the first to break the silence. "What are you smiling at?"

"You don't know me either."

In response to my challenge, his questioning began. "OK. Tell me why you love this play."

This was the crucial moment where I had to prove to him that I was more than competent. I squared my shoulders and met his stare. "I have always considered Rosalind to be one of Shakespeare's strongest leading women. She's intelligent, independent, and witty. And although she believes in the value of true love, she is skeptical of those who act like fools in love. My favorite interactions are in act four when she disguises herself as a Ganymede. In my mind, no character is worthy of the prize of Rosalind –"

I paused when Declan rolled his eyes.

Then continued, "But if there is one, it is Orlando. He's intelligent, honest, charming even."

He crossed his tan arms over his wide chest and lifted an eyebrow. "Good summary, but it sounded like an English professor's lecture. Now, tell me, Dr Lyons, you saw us run act three, scene two. What advice do you have for me?"

Arrogant man. He thought I had nothing. He couldn't be more mistaken. "You upstaged her. Remember the purpose of this scene is to set up the important ones to come. Orlando thinks he needs to be cured of his lovesickness. By the end of the scene, he should be *begging* for her help. And mean it."

"You don't think I wanted help?"

Neither Declan nor Orlando wants help. "No. Because you can't want help if you don't think you need it."

Even though the stage lighting had dimmed since rehearsal, I didn't miss his smirk, but he schooled his amusement quickly. His eyes narrowed in judgment. "And you, the English professor, think you're the one to teach me?" he asked skeptically.

I chuckled at his smugness. His ego truly had no end. A part of me wanted to challenge him further, but, professionally, I knew our first meeting was not the time. Yet I couldn't let him think I was intimidated easily. So I decided to bait the line and throw it in the pond. "Wow. There is one way you have Orlando nailed in that scene though."

I felt the bite almost immediately. "Oh, yeah? What's that?" he asked.

"Rosalind concludes that Orlando is definitely not in love. How does she know he's not in love?" I asked rhetorically. His wide eyes scanned mine for the answer. It was the first flicker of vulnerability he had allowed me to see. *Time to set the hook.* "Because he's too in love with himself. I believe her actual words are, 'You are rather point-device in your accoutrements, as loving yourself than seeming the lover of any other.' *Orlando*'s got that nailed. So in at least one respect it appears we have the part well cast."

If he was surprised that my comment wasn't the compliment he was expecting, his face didn't show it. My gaze locked with his in a challenge that heated the air between us. The silent duel ended when his phone chimed.

Without breaking eye contact, he pulled his phone from his back pocket. His thumb swiped across it, and only then did his eyes scan downwards to what appeared to be a calendar alert. "I have a meeting with my advisor in ten minutes. It was nice meeting you, Dr Lyons."

"Nice meeting you as well." I watched his long legs take the stairs down from the stage two at a time.

His retreating footsteps were drowned out by a familiar click of dress shoes behind me. "You're still here, Dr Lyons?" Dr Burrows asked as he watched Declan walk down the center aisle and leave the rear of the auditorium. He shook his head with an amused grin on his face that told me there was some joke I wasn't getting.

I must have looked at him expectantly, because he explained the cause of his amusement.

"Didn't you see the back of his shirt? His shirts are always entertaining, but today's pretty much summarized Declan to a T."

"No, I didn't." *I surely wasn't looking at his shirt as he walked away.*

"It had a quote on it from George Burns." After a pause, he continued, "'Acting is all about honesty. If you can fake that, you've got it made.'"

In that moment, I questioned how much I could trust the gorgeous, arrogant man who wore it.

Chapter Two

The wide-legged, wool pants ended their crease at the top of my comfortable flats. Paired with a tailored suit coat and a tight bun at the nape of my neck, the look was professional if not a little severe.

Exactly the look I was going for.

After reapplying my lipstick in my small office mirror, I grabbed the copies of the syllabus and my coffee mug. It was one that Nina, my friend and former roommate, got me when I told her I would be teaching a Shakespeare class. "You'll need to play the part of the quirky, weird professor, Jenn," she told me. When I opened her gift, I was greeted by an off-white coffee cup with black lettering that said, "Where there's a Will, there's a way." It still made me laugh as I carried it down the hall and two flights of stairs to the classroom full of students waiting for me.

Nina was right, of course; as the new professor on campus I would be playing a role. As a teacher in front of a classroom, I had always relished the idea that it felt like I was on a stage. All my gestures, mannerisms, and voice inflections were analyzed by the mostly awake audience. Since no students would know who I was, this was my opportunity to create a character – any character I wanted. I could be the eccentric professor who muttered to herself and "accidentally" dismissed class fifteen minutes early. Or I could be the hard-ass that scared away half the class after the first day – there would be conveniently fewer essays to grade that way.

But today I decided to simply be myself, or, more accurately, the version of myself I liked best: poised and confident, exuding control and competency. Putting on my imaginary professor hat, I squared my shoulders and slowed my pace. As I entered the room, the din of casual conversations hushed as twenty-five sets of eyes followed my every step, gauging, assessing. It's possible all twenty-five sets missed the small, almost imperceptible smirk that crossed my lips, the one that relished the heady high of control.

But one set of eyes in the back of the classroom didn't. Because his smirk matched my own. *Like knows like*, it said.

Of course he's here. I allowed my eyes to meet his briefly before I turned into the center aisle and walked behind the lectern at the front of the classroom. "Welcome to Shakespeare II, a lecture and discussion course focusing on Shakespeare's comedies. I'm Dr Jenn Lyons."

And with that I began the first class as *Dr* Lyons. Warm yet professionally aloof, I spent the next thirty minutes discussing the syllabus, the expectations, the assignments and their due dates, and how they would be graded. Most students followed along dutifully while a few asked questions.

My eyes scanned the classroom. There were more women than men, but that was to be expected in the English department. The girls donned their favorite Victoria's Secret yoga pants and the guys hadn't bothered to take off their well-worn baseball caps.

My scanning eyes landed on the magnetic man in the back row. Declan's long legs were casually stretched under the desk that was too small for his large frame. He looked like a caged animal, and the lines creasing his forehead gave him a demeanour that matched. He remained focused on the notebook in front of him, in which he was clearly doodling since his pencil often tilted length-wise so he could shade his "masterpiece". Occasionally his arms would extend over his head like he was stretching to keep himself awake.

Irritation snaked up my spine, particularly at his nonchalance that bordered on indifference, one short step away from becoming an asshole. A very short step.

Then I read his T-shirt: "I'm an actor ... would you like fries with that?" If it was possible, I became even more irritated. His silly T-shirts treated his craft like a pithy joke he could buy at the angry kid store.

But what disturbed me most, despite his personality, I couldn't manage to be unaffected by his broad shoulders that stretched his T-shirts, his formed biceps that led to defined forearms, and his shell of nonchalance that challenged me to crack it to find the real man hiding inside.

Thinking my mind had shifted to inappropriate places given he was my student, I cleared my throat and shifted my attention to the petite brunette in the front row. "Can you begin introductions, please? Say your name, your major, and what year you are. Then finish with something interesting about yourself that will help me and the rest of your classmates remember your face and name."

The brunette, whose name turned out to be Carly, began, and I dutifully took notes on my roster so I could memorize the students' names quickly. A dozen students followed her lead as we wound our way across the classroom. I allowed myself a few glances in Declan's direction despite my best intentions to avoid him. I noticed he didn't seem interested in getting to know his fellow classmates, and he often rolled his eyes when a nervous student would try to make a joke.

So cavalier.

So cocky.

I blinked my thoughts away as another student finished her introduction. "Thanks for sharing, Deidre. Next student, please," I prompted.

On his turn, Declan exuded confidence, even swagger,

displaying no inkling of the first day tentativeness of his classmates. "I'm Declan. I'm a senior theatre major …" He must have said more, but, as I scanned the alphabetized list for his name, I realized for the first time that he wasn't on my roster. He must have seen my confusion, because he clarified. "I go by Declan, which is actually my middle name. The name on the roster should be …" Here, he paused, and for the first time he appeared unsettled. His right leg bounced under the desk, his fingers fidgeted with his pen, and his eyes refused to meet mine. Then he finished, "William Monahan."

The silence in the room filled the empty space of a few seconds before his eyes flicked to mine. "After my father," he needlessly clarified. Now that I got the chance to scan his dark head of hair and those unmistakable cheekbones, I realized he was the spitting image of his father, famous Hollywood actor and playboy Will Monahan. While he didn't share his father's salt-and-pepper hair, he did share his muscular, well-toned body. And his smirk was a dead ringer … for his son who was sitting in *my* classroom.

He cut the tension in the room with a joke that, surprisingly, read humble. "I'm thinking maybe I could add the 'something interesting' to my introduction so you can remember my face, but, now, maybe not so much." The final three words came out hurried, like they were all one word. I added a laugh to the class's rumbling chuckle.

After the laughter gave way to expectant silence, he continued, "I need one more elective class in order to graduate, so I enrolled to help with my current role. This May I plan to graduate with a degree and hopefully make a career of acting."

I clarified for the class, "Declan is playing Orlando, the male lead in the college's spring production of *As You Like It*."

"Cool! We should go as a class to see it," the spunky brunette in the front row interjected.

"That's a great idea," I agreed. "It will be a great way to begin our discussion of –"

Declan interrupted, "– of how bad the actor is who played Orlando." Declan's quick comeback surprised me even though it probably shouldn't have. I couldn't tell in his tone if he was jabbing me for my previous criticisms or if he was attempting to make a joke at his own expense.

The class laughed, but none of them knew the conversation we'd had in the vacant auditorium. I decided to laugh along with them, but it was a stilted, forced snicker that his piercing eyes didn't miss.

Feeling uneasy, I decided to move along, not give weight to the new knowledge all of us now possessed: a veritable celebrity, or at least a celebrity's son, sat among us. The rest of the students introduced themselves and I dismissed the class with the assignment to read *Comedy of Errors* for the next class.

As the students filed out, I righted the classroom for the next professor. After the chalkboard was erased, I double-checked to be sure there was no trash or papers left behind. As I turned to leave, a single folded piece of notebook paper on the floor caught my eye. My first instinct was to throw it in the trash, but something inside me begged to unfold it.

Although what was inside contained no words, it felt like a love letter.

It was a sketch of a woman in a pencil skirt and heels, the same outfit I had worn the first day of play rehearsal. My hair flowed over my shoulders in soft curls, and the proportion and shading, although abstract like a fashion designer's concept drawing, was gracious.

There was something so compelling about seeing myself in that light that made me refold the paper along the creases and tuck it into my pocket. I made my way down the hallway and up the stairs to my office on autopilot while I tried to figure out why I wasn't bothered that one of my students was drawing pictures of me. No, not just one of my students. The gorgeous, haughty actor who wears crappy T-shirts.

I closed the door to my office and sipped my cooled coffee as I walked to the large window overlooking the sidewalks and parking lot below.

Of course, the first thing I noticed was him and his worn leather jacket that would undoubtedly be accompanied by a motorcycle in the spring. His black biker boots that strode with purpose and pace slowed only when he came upon a slow-moving student who was more interested in texting than walking. With a frustrated head shake, he veered off the sidewalk, through a large snow pile, and towards the student parking lot.

My fingers tapped my cup as I studied Declan like he was a Rubik's cube I wanted to solve. Why did he greet the world with an attitude equivalent to a perpetual middle finger? I was having a hard time figuring out how the condescending actor of yesterday coexisted with the student who appeared, dare I say it, sometimes humble today, especially about his family's fame.

I was still trying to figure the man out when he stopped in front of a car parked in the back row. Given that his father was known for his lavish Beverly Hills mansion and penchant for drunk-wrecking expensive cars, I expected Declan to push a key fob that would make a Beemer or Mercedes chirp.

When I saw Declan drive away in a crappy Camry with rust on the quarter panels, a few colored Rubik's cube blocks slid into place. I got a glimpse of the man underneath the armour he chose to wear.

Chapter Three

I spent four hours most afternoons at play rehearsals, but since they were never scheduled on Thursdays, that time was all my own. Today I decided to make the thirty-minute drive down to Boulder's south side so I could work out at the gym I'd frequented when I lived with Nina and Hannah. After working out, I planned on having dinner with them at a local bar.

Although there was a gym on my new campus, I couldn't force myself to give up the membership to this one because whenever I finished running on the treadmill, I got the chance to do what I really came for: the rock-climbing wall.

It was in a large, three-storey room with six inches of padding on the floor. In the middle were two ten-foot boulders with various handholds peppered on their surfaces so climbers could practise without restraints like safety ropes and harnesses. With hundreds of handholds that simulated real-life rock-climbing terrains, the wall allowed me to practise my technique and develop strength in the cold winter months.

Dressed in tight yoga capris, my climbing harness, and a thin-strapped shirt with a built-in bra sweaty from my run, I entered the room. I changed from my running shoes to my climbing ones, which looked like those aqua shoes my mom used to make me wear to the pool in the summers. They were the equivalent of ballet shoes with rubber soles, and I wore them because they helped me maintain grip on the narrow holds.

Due to the danger of falling from these heights, gyms

usually employ a person to serve as a belay, which means that he stays on the ground wearing a harness around his hips and legs. Knotted to his harness is a rope that is wound around an anchor at the top of the wall. The other end of the rope is attached to the climber's harness. As the climber ascends the wall, the belay pulls on his end of the rope to take up the slack. In the event that a climber falls, the belay holds firm on his end of the rope using a belay device, so the climber only falls a matter of feet. In other words, he acts as a spotter and a safety net to minimise the risk on the climber.

But the employee who usually worked on Thursdays was not in his normal ready position when I walked into the room. Jonathan was a person I'd come to trust, and since I'd planned on trying a difficult climb today, I wanted him to spot me. Thinking he might have gotten called away to give a safety training course, I turned towards the front desk to inquire when he would be back.

I only made it a few steps when a voice halted me.

"The employee who is supposed to belay is out sick with the flu today."

"Oh, darn. Thank y ..." My pleasantry was halted mid-phrase. Because I knew that voice.

And those biceps.

And those shoulders.

And when my eyes lifted further, I also recognized that smirk. "What are you doing here?" I didn't mean it to sound rude, but it certainly might have seemed that way.

His throaty chuckle told me he didn't take offense. "Well, I try to make it down here twice a week to climb now that I found this place. Much better than the college rock wall. And since we get Thursdays off, I thought today would be perfect. I could say the same about you. Do you climb?" he asked, quizzically.

"Yes, for about three years now. I like coming here to practise when the winter makes me stir-crazy."

In the short time I'd known Declan, one thing I had learned was that he often provided the swiftest of comebacks, which made the pause that followed curious. He ran his hand through his long hair. "I must admit I didn't see that one coming, Professor." He added the last word as an afterthought, and I wondered why he did so.

Regardless, it served to remind me that I was in tight, revealing workout gear. And although it *should* be perfectly acceptable for me to wear this outfit in a private club I belonged to, I had to remind myself that perceptions are what matter. The college's strict no-fraternization policy was drilled into me during new employee orientation, and I was in no mood to risk my new position.

So no matter the reaction my body was having to the beads of sweat on his forehead and the veins pumping blood into his post work-out muscles, I needed to gracefully exit stage left. "See you at rehearsal tomorrow," I began, before moving a few inches to the right. Declan stepped to his left to block my path.

The proximity of his torso made my nipples bead under the thin material. Horrified by my body's reaction to my student, I attempted to slide left and around him. But his large shoulders shifted and halted my escape again. Then he bent his large frame forward so our eyes met on an equal level. His normal smirk was erased by a genuine smile that revealed straight, white teeth, and most importantly, something playful and endearing.

"Not so fast," he chided. "I climb too, and I'm an experienced belay."

Even though every part of me wanted to agree, I simply couldn't. "I can't."

Before I got the chance to explain, he anticipated my argument and offered his refutation in a whisper like we were sharing a secret. "Look around. There's no one here. It's vacant. And even if there were, we are two adults who happened to need each other's expertise when the gym has a sick employee." He took my hand and led me to the wall without waiting to see if his argument was successful.

Which, of course, it was. Or maybe I simply convinced myself it was successful enough. Because I wanted to see this man climb.

I wanted to see his muscles flex and stretch.

I wanted to see how he moved up the wall. Would it be a graceful dance with the wall or a series of brute force pull-ups that showed no love or respect of the craft?

And, even more bizarrely, I wanted to see how well we could work together. Could I trust the man two stories in the air when I didn't really know him on the ground?

We pulled on our harnesses as he asked, "What grade do you climb?"

All climbing routes are graded on their difficulty on a scale from 5.0 for beginners to 5.15 for world class climbers. I was thankful he asked, because one part of being a strong belay is getting to know the type of climber you are working with. "I can consistently climb 5.10 in the gym, but I'm trying to challenge myself so one day I could climb a real mountain."

I was surprised when his only answer was a lift of a single brow. Then he moved us from the less challenging wall to the far right, where the more difficult climbs were set up. My pride bubbled at his response.

"How about you?" I couldn't help my curiosity.

"Last fall, I got my first outdoor 5.12." If it was possible to say this without bragging, he managed it.

Color me impressed. "Wow." Could the man I met today be any different from the arrogant actor I had met onstage? "Was it around here? Which one?"

"Bolting for Glory."

"Really? Redgarden Wall in Eldorado Canyon?"

He immediately stopped fidgeting with the knot on his harness and looked over his shoulder at me, his face unreadable. After his eyes scanned my face from left to right and back again, his stoic answer was barely a whisper. "Yes. Yes it is."

"What? Did I say something wrong?" I asked quickly.

With a small smile, he reassured me, "No. I'm just surprised is all. Not many women would ..." His voice trailed before he seemed to snap himself from his wistfulness. "You're first, Professor. Up you go."

We double-checked our knots as I rubbed chalk on both hands to help my grip. As I walked towards the wall and grabbed the first holds, I turned to look at him over my shoulder. "Hey, Declan. Eyes up here, buddy," I playfully chastised him when I caught his eyes wandering below my waistline.

Not an embarrassed blush to be had, he simply shrugged like "what's a guy to do?" For the second time today, Declan stirred my pride, but this time, something else simmered and smouldered deep in my core. That feeling was much more personal than professional, so I added, "You can call me Jenn."

His jovial smile turned serious. He stepped behind me so only a few inches separated his front from my back, but despite that small space, I could feel the heat radiating from his body, and for the first time I could smell him, a combination of pure, clean rainwater and agar trees.

His right hand reached around the buckle on my harness and tugged. His hand moving around my pelvis set off fireworks that radiated from my center. "Just checking your harness, *Jenn*."

Yeah, right. "Thanks. Safety first." I couldn't keep the sass out of my voice.

"Safety first," he echoed. Not wanting to encourage more conversation, I gripped the holds a foot above my head.

I began the communication ritual all climbers use. "Climbing, Declan."

I waited for the response an experienced belay would

know. "Climb, Jenn." It told me his full attention was on my safety, so I used my legs to propel me to the next set of holds, which were a longer reach away.

Two minutes later and halfway up the wall, I ran into a tricky portion, which climbers call a crux.

"Well, hello, crux. Nice to meet you today," I joked, and I heard Declan's soft chuckle from below. I reached around behind me to a small canvas bag tied around my hips with first my right hand then my left to rechalk my hands.

Doing so allowed me time to think. If I wanted to complete the route correctly, I had to do a tricky dyno move, a technique I hadn't yet mastered. If my normal belay was here, he would have probably encouraged me to stay on the yellow holds, and I would have followed. But since Declan was noticeably silent (and because I didn't want to embarrass myself in front of a clearly superior climber), I reached left and grabbed a hold not intended for this route. Doing so allowed me to easily ascend to the top.

"Take," I called, which signalled to Declan that I was at the top and ready to rappel down. Declan loosened his grip on the rope, which allowed me to walk backwards down the wall. When my feet reached the floor, he held up his right hand for a high-five.

"Good girl," was his only praise as our palms hit with a slap, but my pulse skyrocketed at the compliment. I hadn't realized how much I wanted to impress him until he offered me that morsel. It made me want to earn it again. Ten times over.

Through my labored breaths, I managed a response. "Thanks. Let's switch."

He nodded as we retied our knots and he chalked his hands. He didn't try to fill the silence with conversation, for which I was grateful, since I was still trying to catch my breath. After scanning the wall for a few seconds, he pointed a few feet to our right where the handholds were fewer and more spread out.

"You mind?" he asked. At first, I hadn't a clue what he meant, but when I saw his arms cross over his torso and his hands grip the hem of his T-shirt, I knew exactly what he wanted to do.

My squeaked "no" did a terrible job of hiding my embarrassment over how much I wanted to see what was under *my student's* shirt.

His crossed arms lifted and extended above his head.

Holymotherofheaventhankyoujesus might have been the first words that leaped into my head but thankfully not out of my mouth, since the breath I had only just recovered eluded me again. Only then did I understand what women meant when they ogled a man's washboard abs. A bead of sweat was making its glorious trek down the center crease and my tongue wanted to lick it before it reached the bulge in his shorts.

Holy hell. What am I thinking? I am his professor. I gawked just long enough to realize his chest was decorated by a single tattoo over his heart. Since the words were in a foreign language, I memorized what I could before he turned his back to me and faced the wall.

"Climbing, Jenn." He clapped his hands together once, spraying a cloud of white chalk dust.

"Climb, Declan."

His knees bent slightly, enough to thrust his body upwards. His hands caught holds above his head that seemed impossibly out of reach. His arms easily took his weight as he got his feet under him. I pulled my end of the rope taut as he ascended with finesse and care. The muscles around his shoulder blades bunched with each hold. Though every move was calculated, there was a graceful beauty to his climb, spontaneity mixed with a reverence I rarely saw from him. That he didn't feel the need to caveman his way up the wall to impress me impressed me more.

He paused occasionally to gauge the route he wanted to take, and during one of those pauses, I felt the need to encourage. "Looking good, Declan. You gonna do the layback?"

"Sure. Be ready." His next move was a strenuous one up a crack that required his handholds to move in opposition to his footholds. I heard him expel a deep breath before all his muscles worked in unified motion. He completed the move quickly as he reached for the next handholds and completed the climb with relative ease over the next few pitches.

"Take," he prompted, and I slowly lowered him to the ground, where he bent to retrieve his shirt and tugged it over his head.

"Awesome climb. It was fun to watch." Seeing that he too was winded, I didn't ask any questions. Instead, I began unbuckling my harness, preparing to head to the showers before I went to dinner.

But his right hand grabbed my wrist. Surprised, I looked up into his now intense eyes. "You're not done." It was a directive, not a question. "I saw what you did. You used a hold that wasn't on the route so that you didn't have to dyno. Either you didn't want to fall in front of me or you didn't trust me to back you up, but either way I'm not having it."

Damn. Damn. Damn. "But my muscles ... not sure ... haven't climbed in a while." Apparently complete sentences were eluding me.

"I gave you a chance to recover while I climbed. You can do it. You're in great shape, and I'm here if you need me."

Suddenly, I wanted nothing more than to overcome the challenge I should have taken the first time. And, without a doubt, I wanted to meet his expectations. "What do I get if I do?" The phrase was innocuous in my head, but when spoken out loud, it sounded like a blatant flirt. *Well,*

26

because it was.

If he was surprised, he didn't show it. In fact, his eyes remained down as he focused on completing the knot on his harness. "What do you want?" he asked.

I stepped closer to gain the attention I wanted like a drug. I pressed a finger to his chest. "I want to know what this says."

His eyes snapped up so I got a good look at the diamond-like facets sparkling in his eyes. They were dark, reflective at best and brooding at worst. "Sure," he bit out, which made me want to tell him to forget I asked.

My muscles were achy from my first climb in a while, making them shake as I attempted to tie the rope onto my harness.

"Here, let me." He gently pulled my hands from the rope and methodically tied the knot onto the harness while I rubbed another layer of chalk on my hands.

"Take a breath. Good," he praised. His more encouraging demeanor had returned. "I've got ya. Trust me. I'll talk ya through it."

With that, he turned my shoulders to the wall and stepped back to tighten the slack on the rope. After another breath, I shook my arms at my sides and reached up.

"Climbing, Declan."

"Climb, Jenn."

I started the climb like I had the previous one. My mind wandered as my hands reached and pulled on the solid holds. This man was so different from the arrogant actor. This Declan was charming, playful. And I *liked* him, despite the fact that, based on my first impression, a big part of me didn't want to. His unpredictability had me questioning my own judgment. Why was I attracted to a man who was so capricious? Could I trust that type of man as more than just my belay? I was snapped from my reflection when I got to the crux, about eighteen feet off the ground. My muscles tensed, causing me to pause.

"Good. Release one handhold at a time and shake out your arms before the next move. Relax back against the rope. I've got your weight. You're going to go over the slope with a dyno. Use your leg muscles to drive rather than lifting with only your arms. Turn your right hip into the wall to make your reach longer."

"I don't think I …"

"Leave your worries to me. Let *me* worry about keeping you safe. If you fall, you fall. So what? This is the place to try something new."

"I've never …" I started.

"Good, then I'll be your first."

I leaned my head forward so I could look at his face under my right arm. He was silently chuckling at his own joke. His playful smile warmed me from a distance. "Haha, very funny."

"Good. Nice to see you can relax a bit. Go for it."

My heart a little lighter and my head more composed, I felt bold enough to try the move. I crouched down on my legs, gathering all the energy I could for the dynamic move that was fifty-fifty at best. I let out a breath, pushed off the holds with my legs, and grabbed the yellow hold I swore was out of my reach. I got my feet under me as I smiled with elation. And relief.

"Nice! Atta girl," I heard from the ground.

"Fuck … son of a –" Sharp ribbons of pain shot through my knuckles and my forearms were screaming at me in agony as I continued up the route.

"Yeah, I bet your grip is worthless after a move like that," he deadpanned. "You good?" He continued laughing while I climbed the rest of the wall with ease, cussing like a drunken sailor. But I would have been lying had I said that I wasn't supremely pleased with myself.

"Take," I said between panting, gulping breaths. He lowered me down to the ground slowly enough for me to catch my breath.

He stepped close enough that we were toe to toe, his chin at my eye level.

Before he got a chance to speak, I decided to ask him the question that had been bugging me on the wall. "Why are you so different here?"

His lips pursed in a smirk. "You mean why was I such an asshole the first day?"

"Something like that."

"Surely you had to know that I wanted to impress you. You are a pretty woman, and obviously smart. But you were threatening to me."

"Ahh … so I was on your turf, and you had to defend it."

His smile warmed. "Something like that."

"So here," I gestured to the climbing walls, "we're on even ground?"

He looked up to the wall that towered above us, deep in thought. His gaze returned to mine, and he bent closer so our eyes were on the same level. "You could say that. Yet you also make the ground under me shift in a way I can't explain."

Surprised at the invasion of space and his declaration, my first instinct was to step back. But before I got the chance, his command halted me.

"Close your eyes." His gruff direction was unhurried and confident, like he knew I would comply.

My chest still heaved between us, and I tilted my chin to look into his eyes in defiance of his order. "Why?" I challenged.

"Because you want to. No," he checked himself, "because you need to. You *need* someone to take control, don't you? You took instruction so well on the wall and your body flushes with praise. My little always-in-control professor likes the delirious excitement of giving up that control, doesn't she?"

Yes. Holy hell, yes. "No."

29

His response was quick and forceful – he wasn't buying the lie I was willing myself (and him) to believe. "Close. Your. Eyes."

God help me, I did. And with my chin tilted upwards, I envisioned his lips meeting mine in a gentle kiss. I felt his breath breeze across my face as I prepared myself for the moment I was sure was coming.

It didn't.

Instead, his lips grazed my ear as he whispered. "That was so fucking hot, Jenn. You put your trust in me, and for that you get a reward."

OK, here comes the kiss. A breathy chuckle puffed in my right ear. "Not that, although I wish to hell we could. I wouldn't jeopardise you like that."

When he continued, it was in a direction I hadn't anticipated. Small puffs tickled my ear. "My mother was Italian. When I was little, she would always sing me a song before I went to sleep, and every night she would smile as she brushed hair off my forehead before whispering in Italian. She would call me her little '*anima inquieta*'." I recognized the words from his chest immediately. Before I got the chance to ask him what it meant, he translated, "my little restless soul."

One more colored block slid into place.

Chapter Four

I got to the bar and grill on Pearl Street ten minutes late, and both Nina and Hannah were waiting in our booth when I arrived. With its dark wood accents and large-handled beer mugs, the bar felt like an English pub.

The girls stood up to hug me when I walked in. "Jenn, we're so glad you could come. We miss you so much. How's the professor's life treating you?"

Before I could answer, Nina piped in. "Yeah, you lucky bitch. How's it feel to be the one giving the grades?"

"Good. I'm busier than I thought I'd be, especially now I've taken on the dramaturg role." I spent the next half hour discussing my new life. My best friends and old roommates, who were both working on finishing their PhD dissertations, listened attentively over two rounds of pale ale. By the time our entrées arrived, the lack of food had caught up to us, and we had begun our ritual of sharing recent dating horror stories. Of course, I had very little to talk about, and, for a reason I couldn't identify, my mind wandered back to Declan.

An hour ago, I had politely excused myself from the climbing room after Declan shared the story behind his tattoo. The instant his lips left my ear, the room got colder. As did he. His stoic, unreadable mask slid into place, a signal that he regretted what he had shared. Telling that story had cost him a piece of his well-guarded privacy. He coolly thanked me for spotting his climb and promised to see me at rehearsal the next day.

I showered quickly, let my hair air dry, and put on minimal make-up since I was running late. While I got ready in haste, my mind was replaying in slow motion the hour I had spent with Declan. I bristled at his claim that I somehow craved losing control. Without doubt, my body had responded to his commands with an ease I wouldn't have expected. But did I *need* that? Surely not.

"OK, girlies. It's time to give up the goods. I'll start." Nina's comment pulled me back to the present.

Hannah leaned forward. "I've waited so long to hear this story."

Nina laughed as she flicked her wrist back and forth. "I'll put you out of your misery. I've been having sex with Tanner since we met them in the bar last semester."

"I knew it!" Hannah said at the same time I almost sputtered beer out my nose.

"What? I feel so out of the loop now I've moved out. How did I not know this?"

Nina popped a fry into her mouth and talked while she chewed. "We've kept it low key. There's no commitment, and there never will be. We're both a good, convenient fuck, one fantastic train stop on our tracks that will someday end in very different places."

"At least it's fantastic," Hannah prodded.

"Definitely. He can go all night. He'll tie me to the bedpost if I ask nicely, and sometimes, if I beg, he lets one of his friends double-team me." Nina casually took a bite of her Reuben as if she had told us she went shopping today.

Hannah and I simply stared, part in awe of this sexually-explorative woman and part scared what would come out of her mouth next.

"You l-l-l-like that?" I asked.

"Hell yeah. Who wouldn't?"

"Um, me?" I offered.

"Maybe you just haven't found your inner vixen yet. Maybe she's hiding under all those suits and ballet flats. Maybe she walks by the lingerie store in the mall and

32

wishes she could tie that bow between her lace-covered breasts. Maybe … she just hasn't found the right muse."

Suddenly an image of a muse in a sweat-soaked T-shirt and climbing harness flashed into my mind.

"Tell me I'm wrong," Nina challenged.

You're not wrong. I decided to deflect. "Why has this started to feel like an intervention?"

"Because you need one," Nina and Hannah said at the same time.

"Look. Let's do an experiment," Hannah said. "Scan the bar. Tell me which guy you would take home tonight if you had your pick."

I looked from table to table carefully, considering the dress slacks at the bar, the dirty jeans in the booth in the corner, and the corduroys standing at the high-top table. I finally decided. "Dress slacks drinking at the bar."

Nina's response was more inquisitive than judgmental. "Why?"

"He looks successful. He's well groomed and attentive to detail. And he looks like a gentleman."

"And he's been scanning his phone for the last twenty minutes," Hannah said. "Ten bucks says that on your date he'd ask for your Twitter handle and take an inane business call that he swears is ultra-important. Not hot."

"Twenty bucks says he prefers missionary and hasn't a clue about the glory of butt sex," Nina added. "See, here's the problem, Jenn. Your man-picker is broken. You've spent your adult life choosing the men you think you want. So you go on date after date with khakis and dress pants when what you really need is ripped jeans."

So true. "Not true."

Hannah might have actually rolled her eyes. "OK, counsellor, I'd like to enter into evidence Exhibit A: Oliver."

Now it was my chance to roll my eyes. "That's not fair. You can't handpick a single exhibit and claim it proves a pattern."

"Wait, what's the story of Oliver? I missed this one. Spill," Nina said through another mouthful of French fries.

Although I groaned in protest, I began the story. "Last November, Oliver and I dated for about a month before he invited me to accompany him to a condo in Vail."

Nina interrupted. "Pause. What did Oliver do? Just curious."

Hannah's belly laugh made me wince as I answered. "A dentist."

"Got it." Nina's scowl spoke volumes. "Continue."

"So we get to Vail, and skied for a few hours in the afternoon. We warmed up in the hot tub. He was built, bordering on sexy, he clearly had money, he wasn't hung up on any exes, and there was no big drama from his childhood I had to fix. He made me dinner, we ate it in front of the fire ..."

Anchoring their elbows on the table, Hannah and Nina leaned in for the "good part". Their words, not mine, because, unfortunately, I knew what was coming.

"He told me he was cold, so I thought that was guy talk for 'come snuggle with me under the blanket,' but he really *was* cold. He donned a sweater, lay with me under the blanket on the couch, kissed the top of my head, and ..."

"Fell asleep," Hannah and Nina finished as they flopped back into the booth.

My forehead hit the table in frustration. "Worst of all, he snored right in my ear. If it's possible to mewl and snort at the same time, he managed it."

"What did you want him to do?" I lifted my head to Nina's surprising question.

"Have sex with me?" Why my answer was a question, I'm not sure.

And why our table went silent, I also wasn't sure.

"Did you hear her answer?" Nina asked Hannah like I

wasn't there.

"Sure did. Nina, how 'bout you ask me that same question, and I'll answer for you?"

Nina mimed holding a microphone. "Hannah, when you're alone in a wooded retreat with Beckett in front of a raging fire, what would you want him to do?" Nina reached the invisible microphone to Hannah's mouth like a reporter.

Hannah's eyes met mine in a stare so intense that my back hit the booth seat behind me with a thump. "I'd want him to strip me. Make me feel vulnerable, defenseless. I'd want him to tie my hands behind my back. Then he would strip while I watched from my knees in front of him. I'd beg to suck him off, but he'd be a gentleman. 'Ladies first,' he'd say. So he'd lick me to my first orgasm, then spin me around so I could get him good and ready. Then I'd be face down on the couch with my ass high enough for him to stand while he fucked me. His fingers would leave impressions on my hips because he would grip me so hard. One of his hands would hold my tied hands tight against my lower back, and although I wouldn't be able to see, I would hear his low growl as he came. That's what I'd want him to do."

My heart was beating so loudly I was sure the entire table could hear it. "I *do* want that," I whispered. "But I want a gentleman too."

"Nothing about what I just described is ungentlemanly. Maybe you need to change your definition of what a gentleman is, m'dear. Gentlemen don't just pay for dinners, open doors, and help change a tyre on the side of the road. They also know what their women need, and meet those needs with a passion that makes her feel wanted like a goddess."

I've never felt like a goddess. "So how do I get that?"

"You start by choosing the right guy," Nina took over. "So, here's your first assignment. In two weeks, we're all going on a triple date. I'll bring Tanner, Hannah will bring Beckett, and you'll bring a date that meets these four characteristics. Number one: he has to have at least one tattoo. Number two: he can't own any khakis. Number three: he has to be a bad boy, a brooder, or a player. And Number four: he has to make your girlie parts tingle."

"Two weeks? That's not a lot of time."

My protest was cut short when Hannah's phone chimed, reminding me how long we'd been at the bar. "Gotta go. Beckett's at home waiting," Hannah said with a wink.

"Sorry we didn't get a chance to chat much about you two, Hannah," I said.

"Yeah, sorry about that," Nina agreed. "How are things going?"

Hannah's wistful smile covered her face with a peacefulness I'd never seen from her before. "Amazing. He's everything I thought I never wanted, yet everything I should have."

For the second time tonight, an image of a sweat-soaked T-shirt flashed into my head.

Chapter Five

I had gotten so caught up in reading student essays that I hadn't realized I'd skipped lunch. Given that I had just over an hour before rehearsals started, I decided to grab a quick lunch at the college cafeteria. It had been eight days since I'd talked with Hannah and Nina at the bar, and my mind was still processing their advice. I replayed their conversation in my head as I grabbed my food from the buffet line. I handed the young man working the checkout a twenty dollar bill, and he handed it back with a frustrated scowl.

"What? Why can't you take my money?" I asked.

He smacked his gum, perturbed he had to repeat himself. "I said that guy in front already paid for you." He pointed to a figure standing ten feet to my left. He was also holding a tray of food as he casually leaned against a pillar, an amused expression playing on his face.

"You?" I mouthed. I hadn't seen him outside of the classroom or practice for more than a week. If I was honest with myself, I would say he'd been on my mind a lot, especially after talking with Hannah and Nina.

His grin stretched across his lips and lit the darkness in his eyes. "Come on, I want to discuss the play with you before rehearsal," he said, loud enough so anyone listening in would hear easily.

I followed his lead to a small corner booth out of the way of the normal dining room, which was clearing from the lunch crowd. I set down my tray across from his as he laid out pages of the script he would be running through today.

"Thanks for lunch."

"You're very welcome."

"What questions do you have about act two?"

"We're not really going to discuss the play, are we?" It was then that I realized that setting the script out on the table was a ruse in case anyone walked by and wondered why we were having a somewhat private lunch.

"I guess not. So what *are* we going to talk about?"

He shrugged as he bit into his sandwich. "We're going to play a little game. I get to ask you five questions, and you get to ask me the same. We both have to answer any question asked with complete honesty. No half truths. No omissions. No deflections."

Despite sirens going off in my head telling me what an epically bad idea this was, I was too curious about him to pass up the opportunity. Maybe that's what he was banking on, because when I nodded my assent, a mischievous grin passed his lips before he checked himself.

He cleared his throat. "Ladies first."

The first question was a no-brainer for me. I'd wanted to ask it since the first week we met. "Tell me the story of your parents." I expected my question to meet with a brooding stare that told me I'd asked something much too personal. Instead, I got the opposite. He grabbed his neck with two hands like he was strangling himself.

"Ouch, you go right for the jugular, don't you?" he choked out.

I couldn't avoid laughing at his over-the-top reaction. "You actors are so dramatic."

"And apparently you professors can only speak in prompts. 'Tell me about your parents' is not a question, but I'll let it slide."

My pursed lips smiled as I blew steam from the spoonful of soup. I enjoyed this playful, easy-going side of him. I'd met the brooding, arrogant actor who challenged

38

me. I'd met the easily distracted student who often made jokes at his own expense. And I'd met the controlling belay who heated my core. I couldn't tell you which mask was the real Declan – if there was one – but this one surely put me at ease. My inability to reconcile them did not.

He turned serious as he continued. "My mom, Adele, was born in Italy. She married my father when they were young and she was pregnant with me. From what I remember, she had long, dark, beautiful hair. My grandmother tells me we were close, but I have limited memories of her. She died in a car accident when I was six. Since then, my dad has tried to marry his way through Hollywood, upgrading each wife as he moved from D-list, to C, to B, and finally to the A-list celebrity you know today. Except each new wife was worse than the one before; each one wanted a piece of Hollywood's up-and-coming star, and he didn't have a problem doling out those pieces like he had a never-ending supply. None, of course, could measure up to my mom, and as I'm sure you can tell, his choices have … soured him in my eyes. We rarely talk now, and while it bothered me at first, I enjoy the freedom from the paparazzi and the fame I never wanted."

There were so many follow-up questions I wanted to ask, but I knew I had to be judicious. "So why did you go into acting?"

"You mean 'Why did I go into acting if I hated my father so much?' That's what you really wanted to ask." I tore off a piece of my cinnamon roll and chewed while I waited for his answer. He took a slow sip of his drink before he began.

"The truth is, I've always wanted to act. I think I was called to do it from a young age, not because my dad dragged me to casting calls before I could walk, but because I always enjoyed the art, the ability to become someone else for a while. But, like all teenagers, I rebelled against what I thought my dad wanted me to be. After I graduated from high school, I spent two years blowing off all the casting calls I could before some buddies and I thought it would be fun to backpack around Europe for a summer.

"A summer turned into four years of backpacking and smoking more weed than Cheech and Chong. When the long-haired hippie-nomad lifestyle finally lost its allure, I grew up, came back to the US, and enrolled in college as a theatre major. Although I'm not proud of those four years, they served their function: they taught me that forging a new path just to thumb my nose at my father didn't make me happy, either. Acting made me happy, and I had to come to the realization on my own that I could love the craft of acting and not end up like my father. I could follow my father's path without matching his footsteps. You see, he doesn't enjoy the craft. He enjoys the fast cars and fake tits. I want to be a stage actor where I can devote myself to performing art, even if that means I don't drive a Ferrari. And I'll be able to look at myself in the mirror every morning."

Although the narrative really didn't surprise me, his ability to reflect did. My next question bolted from my mouth. "So, how old are you?"

His lunch finished, he leaned back in the booth and stretched both arms horizontally on the seatback. *Don't look at the biceps. Don't look at the biceps. Ah, fuck it. There's that tingling in the girlie parts Nina was talking about.* The motherfucker grinned. Whether it was from my impetuous question or my blatant gawking, I'm not sure. Probably both. "Twenty-eight."

My eyelids descended slowly as I blew out a breath. "Oh, holy hell." It was so much easier to not want him when I thought there was a possibility of a six-year age difference. My head thudded the heavy wooden pillar behind me and I stared at the ceiling.

He chuckled at my anxiety. "Let me guess; you're

twenty-eight too? Never mind, I don't need to know. Not one of my questions, by the way. Speaking of, let's turn the tables." That made my eyes peel back to him, where he was drumming the fingers of his right hand against the heavy wooden table. He tilted his head to the side as in deep thought. "Tell me about *your* parents," he echoed.

"Not as exciting as yours, I'm afraid. My parents are still married. They live in a small suburb of Dallas, where my dad is an optometrist and my mom keeps his books. They work together all day, eat every meal together, sleep together, and do it all again the next day. They've always encouraged me to do anything I wanted. When I went into English, I didn't get any of the 'what are you going to do with that degree?' lectures. I guess you could say I'm a product of an utterly uneventful, yet loving, childhood."

I took a drink of Coke to wet my mouth and prepare for the next question, which I thought would follow my line of inquisition. Why I wanted to become an English professor was one I could nail with my eyes closed.

"Do you like sex?"

The sip of Coke backed up into my nose, making it sting. "Excuse me?" I was finally able to sputter.

"You heard me." Unmoving, he acted like he would wait a lifetime for my answer. He was amused, entertained by catching me off-guard. I felt like one of those toy mice cats swat at a few times to amuse themselves with before moving on to something more interesting.

"I'm not sure that's a question I should be answering. You're my —"

"Come on," he huffed.

I lifted my chin to his challenge. "No." After a pause, I added, "You said no lies, so there's your honest answer. No, I don't like sex."

"So you think Orlando should defer more to Rosalind in act two even though he doesn't really learn that lesson until act four?"

41

I didn't understand the question until I looked over to see Ingrid, a junior theatre major playing Celia, walk by. If she saw us, she didn't show it. With her ear buds blaring music and her fingers texting on her smartphone, it was likely she hadn't registered our existence at all. But Declan waited until she was around the corner before he asked another question.

"Why not? And, yes, I understand this counts as question number three. My fault for asking a yes/no question."

His joke cut the tension at the table, but I couldn't make myself comfortable with this line of questioning. "Declan, I can't. I'm your professor."

"I understand the situation. Trust me, I do. I wouldn't do anything in public to jeopardize your position. But we both know what I want to do with you has nothing to do with being in public. We both have good reasons to maintain discretion. You would lose your job and I wouldn't graduate. But you can't deny the heat between us. I want to unpack your layers just as much as you want to figure me out. I want to know how the stuffy, formal English professor and the flirty, sexy rock climber can live in the same body. How can you look at me with those heated eyes at the gym then treat me with cold precision during rehearsals? Now, tell me. Why not?"

"Because I can't turn my brain off long enough to enjoy the moment," I spat out. Embarrassment and frustration made me sound angry. "I keep thinking about what I have yet to get done that day or what's on my to-do list for the next day. Or, even worse, I keep thinking about how I wish he would clip his toenails or do something different to make it feel better. And before you ask, I'll tell you. No, I don't orgasm during sex, and I don't know why I can't simply tell him what to do differently. I. Don't. Know. And that's the truth."

"I know it is."

I waited for him to say something else, but he didn't. Instead, he sat forward in the booth and stretched his long legs underneath the table. His eyes didn't leave mine as his right foot found my left and his left found my right. With his booted feet between my ballet flats, he pushed outwards on my insteps so my legs separated and were widened under the table. Each foot might have moved only six inches, but the distance didn't really matter, because both his legs and his eyes were opening me, making me more vulnerable than I had ever been.

"No lies." His feet continued pressing against mine as he asked his next question. "Do you want me?"

More than I should. "Yes." My answer was immediate and clear, and I hoped to be rewarded with a playful smile or even a smirk. But I was rewarded in a different way. His eyes darkened with his feral, possessive stare. I had pleased him, which made pleasure bubble in me.

I hadn't planned on this being my fourth question, but feeling so open, I had to ask. "Why are you pursuing me? Is it because I'm your professor and a forbidden challenge? A mountain for you to climb and conquer before you move on to the next challenge?" It was more a rant than a series of questions, and I decided to allow him the choice of which one he wanted to answer. "I don't do casual sex, Declan. That's not how I'm wired. And I won't pursue anything with a man who wants only that."

"You are a treasure, not a challenge, and that's something I intend to teach you. Having sex with you will not be a lesson in conquering, Jenn, because you will not be conquered. Even if you were to let me dominate you during sex, which is something I think you *are* 'wired' for, you still wouldn't be conquered. Because deciding to give yourself to me is the ultimate act of control. I am pursuing you because I want you to see yourself as I see you." He paused so my heart could catch up and I could remember to suck in a breath. Then he continued, "And while I have

43

no qualms against what you call 'casual sex,' I respect your needs. We won't have sex until you're ready."

While my brain and a few other parts were sizzling, he casually checked his watch. "We need to get to rehearsal. You can go in first. I'll wait a few minutes."

I was touched at his prudence. I believed him when he said he was looking out for me. "But you have one question left."

One corner of his mouth tilted upward. "I reserve the right to keep it and use it any time I want. Do you want to do the same with your last question?"

"No."

"Ask away then."

"Do you own any khakis?"

Chapter Six

A few days later, I was preparing to lead a lecture and class discussion on the first half of *As You Like It*. Before I left my office for the seminar, I checked my student drop box that hung outside my door. The drop box was a place where students would turn in late essays or assignments if they had to miss class. I rifled through the various printed pages, sorting and prioritising. When I got to a small, sealed Manila envelope, I paused, then opened it.

Inside was a white sheet of computer paper with handwritten words. I opened it, giddy like a high-school senior hoping that the letter stuffed in her locker was an invitation to prom. It said:

I would love to meet your friends. Thank you for asking.

I couldn't deny the excitement that sparked through my chest when I read his acceptance. Last week during our lunch conversation, Declan had showed uncertainty when I had asked him to meet my friends on our triple date. I tried to assure him, "We'll be in Boulder at least a half hour away from campus, and my friends won't know you're my student." Although I wasn't sure if those were the reasons he was reluctant to agree, I made the arguments anyway, and he asked for a few days to think about it.

It had been more than a few days, and since we had not exchanged phone numbers, he couldn't have called or texted me his response. Before I folded up his letter, I noticed something else on the paper. What was at the bottom of the letter was curiously intimate, although it was just a series of numbers. His phone number was scrawled across the bottom, and as I saved it in my phone, it felt like our relationship was crossing some invisible threshold.

I glanced at the clock and realized I was going to be late for class if I didn't get going. As I walked down the stairs, I reviewed my notes for the class lecture I had outlined for today on Orlando's penchant for hanging love letters to Rosalind on the trees in the forest. Clad in my pant suit, ballet flats, and a smirk, I strode down the hallway to the classroom with Declan's letter in my pocket.

This lesson was going to be fun.

I began the class with a short lecture on the play. "Today, we are going to focus on the first half of the play. In act two, Orlando tries to woo Rosalind with love notes that he writes and places on the trees in the Forest of Arden. In one of them, he calls himself 'her slave' and says he would die without her. But the one most interesting to me is in scene two, lines 86-93." My eyes scanned the room and landed on Declan. He bit his bottom lip to try and contain his smirk. He had known exactly what he was doing when he placed his letter in my drop box. "Declan, can you read those aloud for us?"

As he leafed through the text to the correct page, I added, "Consider this practice, yes?" The class chuckled, since he most likely had these lines memorized already.

Today he was wearing a black T-shirt under a fitted, grey Henley that hugged his arms and broad back. His black leather jacket hung from the back of his chair, and his black boots were haphazard and untied.

He began:

"'From the east to western Ind,
No jewel is like Rosalind.

46

Her worth being mounted on the wind
Through all the world bears Rosalind.
All the pictures fairest lined
Are but black to Rosalind.
Let no face be kept in mind
But the fair of Rosalind.'"

"Thank you. Now, here's the crucial question. Rosalind is motivated in part by these love letters to disguise herself as a man and teach Orlando about how to love in act four. Yet many ask, 'why?' These love letters on the surface seem quite romantic. What woman doesn't want to be called a jewel, a *treasure*?" As I emphasized the last word, echoing what Declan had called me at lunch the previous week, I couldn't help but let my eyes slip towards him. He was trying to temper his grin by biting his cheek, but his eyes remained firmly fixed on me. He knew exactly what I was doing.

"What woman doesn't want to hear a man say that no other woman's face will be 'in his mind' other than hers? So, I ask you, why does she feel the need to educate when his poems are quite romantic?" I already knew the answer, but I wanted to know what the students thought. More specifically, what one student thought.

When no one answered, I asked a follow-up prompt that I knew Declan would feel compelled to answer. "Does she not believe his interest is sincere?"

I wasn't disappointed when he chomped the bait. "No. She knows his interest is sincere. Orlando doesn't jest. He's too *honest* for that. The poems, while seemingly romantic, are too romantic for Rosalind."

Yes, you're right. "Too romantic? Do tell. I gotta hear this," I said, playing coy, which made another round of laughter roll through the class. I crossed my legs at the ankles as I leaned against the lectern. With my arms also crossed, I waited through the silence.

He continued, "Rosalind is skeptical of the unrealistic love in literature that wouldn't stand the test of time in the real world. Orlando says he would die for her, but he doesn't know her well enough to say it, so it feels inauthentic and unrealistic. He's simply repeating lines he's read but never felt. That's why he needs an education."

I let Declan's words swirl around in silence for a few moments. "Nicely done. I'd add one thing. He also needs an education because, although he might be *honest*, he often dons a mask, which makes the other characters question what they see. What is real and what is not?"

We were having a private conversation between the two of us in the middle of a crowded room, as if we were speaking a different language.

When I asked the question, the muscles around Declan's jaw clenched before he spoke. "Orlando's not the only one wearing a mask, though. Rosalind has to pretend to be Ganymede – a man – in order for her to educate him."

Some students murmured their agreement, but I wanted to push a bit further. "Surely. But is that a commentary on Rosalind's character like it is with Orlando's? Or is Shakespeare making a comment about the time period in which it was written? Would a woman be able to educate Orlando like she did? The play's final speech suggests this theme might …"

"Perhaps," Declan interrupted. "Or maybe *Rosalind* just feels more comfortable in her layers." He was accusing me of donning a mask just like I'd done with him. It was an accusation that hit its mark somewhere deep in my chest.

As much as I wanted to continue the debate, I knew a contest of wits to determine who was more egregious in their armour-building was one neither of us should want to win. An uneasy weight pressed on my shoulders.

"We'll continue with this thought later." I dismissed the class for a five minute break.

While I normally stayed behind to answer student questions about missing or late assignments, I had to retreat to the restroom to secure my armor. I walked down the hall to the restroom, entered a stall, and closed the door. I took a few cleansing breaths in the empty room before footsteps thudded on the tile floor outside.

"You're never going to believe this. Guess who I just ran into," a woman's voice in the stall next to mine said. I could hear the murmurs of another voice talking back to her on her phone.

"No," she said when her friend apparently guessed wrong. She spat the next words out. "*Declan*. I just saw him in the halls, but when I tried to start a conversation with him, he blew me off. Told me he didn't have time to talk. Not now. Not ever."

Her friend must have sympathized, because she said, "I know, right? You'd think with how many times he's used me for sex he would have the decency ..." She didn't finish that thought before she went on. "And you know what he just said to me? 'It was just sex. We were convenient fucks for each other.'" She twittered on, but I'd had enough. If Declan Monahan was a Rubik's cube I was trying to solve, a few more blocks had slid into place after hearing this conversation.

I washed my shaking hands and walked back to the classroom, cussing at myself for forgetting the type of man I'd invited to meet my friends.

He's a player. I don't do players. I do stable men who respect women rather than use them. I'd much rather have boring, comfortable sex with dress pants or khakis. I vowed to myself that I would cancel our triple date and have nothing further to do personally with Declan Monahan.

As I walked back into the classroom, I forced my heart

rate to slow. I slipped into professor mode again and, given the conversation I overheard, decided to change the focus of the class to a scene in act two.

"OK, let's back up one scene to act two," I said to get the attention of the class once again.

"Whoa. What happened to our discussion of act four, Professor?" Declan playfully interrupted, clearly oblivious to the anger boiling in my veins.

"There're lessons in act two that need to be learned," I sniped.

The class hushed at my abrupt tone, and Declan scowled before lowering his eyes to the notebook in front of him.

I repeated, "Let's look at the end of act two. Jacques, although a minor character, serves an important function. While Orlando spouts overly-romantic notions, Jacques is the eternal pessimist. So cynical is he that he declares:

'All the world's a stage,
And all the men and women merely players.
They have their exits and their entrances,
And one man in his time plays many parts,'

"He goes on to discuss the seven stages of man, but the four lines I read are the most interesting to me, and the most often quoted. What are your thoughts on why? Why have these lines resounded so much?"

As multiple students offered explanations that were interesting but not compelling, I allowed myself a peek at Declan to gauge his reaction. His scowl had deepened to a grimace. *Good. Let him stew on it.*

Other students asked clarifying questions or offered disagreement, and I allowed the discussion to flow without my interruption.

The period was about to end, so I decided to offer my opinion and leave them with something to think about as they left. "One reason I've found these lines so powerful is that, to me, they're scary if they're true. If we are all constantly acting on a stage, how do we know if the people we interact with on a daily basis are authentic? Maybe they're just pretending to be who they want to be while hiding who they truly are. If people can flit through our lives with continual exits and entrances, and if a man in his lifetime plays many parts, how do we ever trust?"

I stared at the man I'd never trust after what I'd overheard in the bathroom.

I almost left the questions alone, but since my speech didn't convey the message of the play, I decided to offer a pleasant bent that could take the sting out of Jacques' musings. "Don't be disheartened. Jacques' speech was meant to contrast with the authentic and real love depicted between Orlando and Rosalind, and since they get their happily-ever-after, one message of the play is that real love can overcome many things, including life's pessimism."

But not when it comes to Declan.

"Thank you for your time today, everyone. See you next week."

The classroom emptied quickly. I took the stairs to my office and sat behind my desk. I closed my eyes as I rested my head against the chair, exhausted by the discussion. Anger at the layers I'd uncovered in Declan vaporized my exhaustion, fueling my resolution: I'd never let Declan see Jenn's layers – only Professor Lyons'.

Chapter Seven

In a moment of renewed anger later that night, I used the phone number he gave me to text him:

Won't be able to go on Saturday. Have to cancel.

He used the number from my text to call me back a minute later. He must have sensed my customary "hello" was colder than usual, because he asked, "Why do you need to cancel? Have you changed your mind about hanging out?"

I made sure my "yes" was measured and curt.

"Why?"

"I'm busy."

He huffed. "Now tell me the real reason."

Fine. "I believe it was the words 'Declan' and 'we're just convenient fucks' in the same sentence that turned me off a bit." He sighed on the other end of the line as I shifted my tone from sarcastic to serious. "I actually let myself believe that we could somehow find common ground. As you told me before, you're OK with casual sex. I'm not." *And I'm your professor. I let myself forget that.*

I noticed with his next comment that he didn't deny the conversation in the hallway had happened. "So you overheard me talking to –"

"No," I interrupted. "In the women's restroom, I heard a girl talking on her cell phone to her friend. Look, Declan, I think we should just –"

Now it was his turn to interrupt me. "Let me explain before you make any judgement. Please." My silence gave him permission to continue. I thought he'd proceed to tell me who the "clingy" girl was, so his next words surprised me. "If my father taught me anything, it's that relationships are nothing more than a business transaction. Both parties negotiate for what they want."

That was an explanation that was supposed to make me feel better? Not in a million years. "Wait. Hold on. That doesn't make sense. You would think that if you've spent your entire life seeing how terrible casual sex can be you would want the opposite. Something real and lasting, based on love."

"Not at all. I've unfortunately seen the benefits of a well-negotiated business transaction. Wife number three had a hell of a pre-nup. Where my dad went wrong, though, is that he can't call a spade a spade. If he wanted casual sex, that's fine by me. But the problem is that he wrapped it up in a nice package and tied it with a marriage bow and pledged enduring love. The true crime was allowing his latest fling to masquerade as eternal commitment. A joke. A charade. A lie. *That* is what I'll never do. I'm being honest with you when I say that the conversation you overheard was from the perspective of a woman who wanted more than we agreed on. I never told her I wanted anything more than sex. I couldn't have been any clearer."

This was supposed to make me feel better? It only served to turn me off. "Ahhh … what a gentleman you are. At least you told her you were using her up front."

"And she was using me, too. While you might not like the idea of casual sex, you have to believe that I was honest with her. I never lied or misled her, just like I've never lied to you."

"OK. Let's say I believe you. That still doesn't help us. I won't have no-strings sex with you, and that's all you say you're capable of."

"No. I said that it was all I was interested in. There's a

54

very easy solution for this."

"Which is?"

"We take sex out of the equation. We simply go out on the date on Saturday with your friends, and we have a good time. No pressure. No sex landmines."

Despite my disgust, a feeling of disappointment surged through my treacherous body. "You're OK being friends without any sex?"

"Hell no. I want to fuck you senseless against a wall in your office. But I won't do that if you can't trust me."

Damn it all, the picture he painted was so ... enticing. I couldn't help the fact my body wanted what my mind said I shouldn't. He continued, "So, we'll build a friendship first, starting on Saturday. Then you'll be the one to tell me when and if you want more. But I need to hear from you that you won't hold this conversation you overheard against me."

"Don't worry. I'll let it go."

Declan felt the need to clarify. "I want you all in or not at all."

I knew my answer before I said it. "I'm in."

Declan's Camry was clean on the inside, and soft rock music played quietly on the radio as we drove the thirty minutes down the Diagonal Highway to Boulder.

My nerves rattled if I allowed myself to think about what I was doing. I was on a date with my student, a guy I was so attracted to that I wanted nothing less than to ask him to pull over to the shoulder so I could straddle him while cars whizzed by. But he was also the guy who could so callously walk away from someone he'd been intimate with. The moments of heat between us were in constant conflict with the cool realities, making me feel unstable, fickle. I hated that feeling, and, to top it all off, if we were discovered, I'd lose my job.

I sat in the passenger seat and smouldered in silence,

worrying myself into regretting the invitation.

"What's going through your mind? I can practically hear your brain working itself into a frenzy."

I had hoped that I had disguised my worry well enough, but since I clearly hadn't, I slumped into the seat, defeated, and rested my head against the cold window in frustration. If I was going to do this, I needed to be all in, as Declan had suggested. There was no point in taking on this huge risk for both of us if I was going to be a melancholy bore the whole time. "Sorry. Just worried is all."

"I know, Jenn. I do. I kicked myself so many times for convincing you to come tonight. I told myself I should protect you from this. Just walk away. We could get together after I graduated if that's what we wanted. But … I can't stop."

Against all the sirens warning me away, I answered honestly, "Me neither."

His eyes briefly flitted to mine to check the honesty of my response as he drove down the highway. He must have found the truth I had intended in my agreement, because a contented, gentle smile drifted across his face as he reached his right hand across to rest on my left thigh. His hand was more comforting than sexual as I absorbed his heat through my jeans.

We talked through the rest of the car ride and arrived at my old apartment twenty minutes later. It felt odd to ring the doorbell at a place I'd once called home.

Nina answered the door seconds later. "Welcome! Welcome!" she greeted. "Come on in. You're a little early."

"Yeah, we planned ahead and left Longmont early, thinking that the seven inches of snow we were supposed to get would make for a slower drive. But seven inches turned into a dusting."

"Wouldn't be the first time I was disappointed when I was promised seven inches," Nina deadpanned.

Caught off-guard, Declan coughed next to me. He recovered quickly and reached out his hand to shake hers, which she accepted. "Nice to meet you, Nina."

Her eyes narrowed, but Declan didn't flinch at her blatant stare. "Do you have a tattoo?" she asked.

Declan first glanced at me as if he was trying to determine if I had told Nina the personal story of his ink. I shook my head slightly to answer his silent question. Satisfied, his attention turned back to Nina. "Yes."

"Do you own any khakis?"

This time, Declan smiled at Nina's inquisition. "No."

Her gaze lingered for a moment before she apparently found what she was looking for. "Nice jacket," she said over her shoulder as she led us to the living room. And with that, Declan had earned Nina's approval.

Declan shrugged at me as if saying "that was a little weird", and followed Nina to the living room. Over a few beers, Declan asked polite questions about Nina's dissertation work and listened attentively to her responses.

"That's the lovebirds," Nina said when the front door opened and closed. Soon, Hannah and Beckett walked into the living room as they took off their gloves and coats. Nina handed them both a beer and, hand in hand, they walked over to the couch to greet me and introduce themselves to Declan. Tanner arrived five minutes later, and with the group complete, Nina called a cab to take us downtown.

All six of us crammed ourselves into the minivan cab, the three girls sharing the back bench seat. "Oh, he's a smooth one. I approve," Nina whispered.

"And those arms," Hannah hummed. "You'll have fun climbing that one."

I smiled, warmed by my best friends' approval. Ten minutes later, the cab stopped in front of The 912 Grill, a restaurant and bar known for its locally brewed beer and the outdoor ice skating rink attached to it. A large corner booth was reserved for us and we all shoved in, which meant that my thigh was pressed against Declan's, and his right arm snaked around my shoulders possessively. One of his fingers drew lazy circles on the top of my shoulder as we all perused the menu. Goosebumps rolled in a wave across my shoulders and up my neck at his delicate touch. While my first reaction was to shy away from a touch that was a bit more than "friendship building", I couldn't deny the peacefulness his touch brought, like it was anchoring me in the middle of a choppy ocean.

Decision made, I closed my menu and looked up to find four pairs of eyes narrowed on Declan's touch. Hannah's eyebrows raised in surprise. It wasn't that Declan was doing anything inappropriate; it was just that I had never been with a man who was so physical around my friends. The dentist, the accountant, and the architect had all kept their hands to themselves.

Tanner, who sat next to Declan, began a conversation after we placed our dinner orders. "So, Nina didn't get a chance to tell me much about you. What do you do?"

"I'm an actor," Declan answered.

"I can see why," Hannah joked, which was followed by a laugh when Nina elbowed her in the ribs. "What? He's hot as hell," Hannah whispered to Nina, although the entire table overheard her.

Beckett simply rolled his eyes as the waitress brought our beers. "What my girlfriend is *trying* to say is that you do look familiar."

Oh shit. Oh shit. Oh shit. Had Beckett's path crossed with Declan's somewhere? Declan must have been worried too, because he quickly deflected. And he deflected with a whopper. "I might look familiar because a lot of people say I look like my dad."

"Who's that?" Hannah leaned in.

Declan picked up his beer and casually took a sip before answering. I could tell he didn't want to name drop.

"Will Monahan."

"Ho-ly shit." Nina's three syllable curse broke the silence. "You do look like him. Are you going to act in Hollywood too?"

"Nah, not my scene. I'd rather do live theatre. I would love to work for a travelling troupe like the Colorado Shakespeare Company. Do live shows outside in the summer and travel during the winter to do shows across the country."

Thankfully, everyone seemed to accept his answer. Maybe they were still trying to comprehend the fact that a Hollywood star's son sat at their table, but, regardless, I was grateful that the conversation soon shifted to Tanner's latest court cases. As a high-profile lawyer, he always told the funniest stories about courtroom battles between bitter exes.

I pretended to listen, but all I could think about were the wide shoulders and defined jaw that sat next to me. It was like a sculptor had asked my body what her ideal man looked like and made him just for me. Heat flooded between my legs as my body filled with the sweet rush of endorphins.

The rest of the dinner passed quickly, and thinking the date was over, Declan began saying the customary good-byes. Oops. I must have forgotten to tell him about the second half of the date. Declan was surprised when Nina told him what we were doing next. "Not so fast, Dec. Now we get to drunk skate."

"Drunk skate?"

"Yeah. You know, like ice skate after you've been drinking. And if you fall, you have to do a Jäger shot."

"But then the person who falls a lot will get even more drunk …"

"Yep, and then he'll fall even more. That's the idea. An amazingly vicious and hilarious cycle, at least if you're not him."

I expected Declan to bow out. Who wants to make an ass out of himself in front of his date's best friends? And it had been kind of sprung on him at the last minute.

I held my breath, because even if he didn't realize it, this was an important moment for us. His willingness to make a fool of himself, to put his ego on the line, in front of my friends was crucial. Although I couldn't deny the appeal of the bad boy, brooding, motorcycle-riding, control freak actor in private, I also needed the playful, gracious, humble … gentleman.

"Damn. I'd have brought my skates had I known we were going to do this."

His enthusiasm surprised me. "You have ice skates?"

"An old pair, yes. In my rebellious teenage years, I went through a stage where I thought I was going to be the next Wayne Gretzky. It pissed my dad off to no end, so I signed up for every league I could."

The six of us paid for our skate rentals and bundled up in heavy coats and gloves. We locked away our purses and shoes in a rental locker and found the guys waiting for us in the carpeted area by the rink door. Tanner and Declan had seemed to hit it off well throughout the night, and since Beckett and Hannah were glued at the hip (and a few other places) all night, I was thankful Declan had someone else other than me to talk to.

The ice rink was about 120 feet long, and packed with skaters. Electric blue lights were strung high overhead, casting an ethereal glow over the ice. One of my all-time favorite places for people watching, I enjoyed the whoops and jeers as somebody took a dive, only to be helped up by her giggling friends. The white powder shavings on their asses, the evidence that gave away who had fallen, always made me chuckle.

Hannah wobbled onto the ice first while Beckett shook his head and held her elbow while she flailed. She had always been the flailer.

Nina and Tanner cautiously stepped onto the ice, but their dynamic couldn't have been more dissimilar. While Tanner's intelligence and ridiculous physique made him attractive, his gracefulness was not one of his best qualities. He inched along the boards at the edge of the rink as Nina giggled beside him. "Fuck off," he said when she poked fun at him.

Declan held the rink door open for me and motioned towards the ice with an outstretched palm. "M'lady," he said with an overly dramatic bow.

I stopped in front of him so our chests hit with a bump. "Ahh … a proper gentleman. It's hot as hell on you, bad boy."

"Finally some sass. If I would have known that all you needed was three beers to give me hell, I would have fed them to you long ago." He stepped onto the ice confidently and skated backwards with his hand stretched towards me. I inched my way to him, thinking I'd better join Tanner along the outskirts.

He caught me looking at the boards. "No. No. No. Hold my hand. We'll go down together."

I hope not. In more ways than one. "We better not. Jäger and I aren't friends."

I took his hand anyway as he chuckled. We started skating counter-clockwise around the rink. Well, he dragged me and I shuffled my feet. Soon, my body seemed to magically figure out how to balance on the thin blade despite the alcohol making my head spin, and we soon picked up speed and settled into a rhythm.

He started a conversation as we took a break along the boards a half an hour later. "When you're in class, why do you insist on wearing those terrible pant suits? They hide that amazing body under there."

Ouch. That one stung a little. "Because I'm afraid I won't be taken seriously otherwise. It's a way for me to establish my credibility, I guess. It makes me more confident."

"Well, I hope there will come a day when you come into class in a skirt that brushes your knees. Maybe add some killer heels, too. Your hair down across your shoulders like it is now. And maybe you even wear stockings under your skirt held up by a garter belt." His hand inched up my hip to my ribs, only to retreat and repeat the same path. "That's what I think confidence looks like. And it'd be hot as hell on you."

His words threw gasoline on my already smouldering fire stoked by his soft touch. I wanted him to move his hand between my legs to rub my center with the same brush of his fingertips.

Whoa. Where had that come from? Just friends, remember.

I gripped his biceps as I let my imagination run wild. His hand was between my legs again, but this time, I pretended to push his hand away, like I was protesting his touch though I really craved it. He'd then take my hand away and tell me, "Jenn, I'm going to touch you, and you're going to let me."

"What do you want, Jenn?" His voice brought me back to reality.

At my pause, his gruff voice encouraged, "Tell me the truth. What were you thinking about?"

"I was thinking about how much I wanted you to touch me." He seemed disappointed by my answer, so I added what I was really thinking. "I didn't want to tell you what I wanted you to do, OK? I wanted you to do to me what you wanted."

His eyes darkened as he turned his body. His broad shoulders leaned towards me, and his attentive eyes dared mine to look away. "You wanted me to take my pleasure and the responsibility of yours."

His lips were an inch from mine. "Yes. Ever since that day on the climbing wall, that's all I can think about."

"I can do that for you. I will." He leaned forward even more, so I closed my eyes. "But not now. Not here. I promised you more. I promised you friendship first, and I won't let you down, as much as it kills me to stop right now."

My eyelids clicked open, and my eyes focused on the pained smile slowly backing away. "Thank you. You're right," I said.

He held out his hand. "Let's go skate some more." I again took his hand in mine, and my pride smiled when he readjusted his pants.

As our feet glided over the ice, neither of us felt the need to fill the space with chatter, so my mind wandered. Before tonight, if I'd thought I could pour water on the flames burning between us and effectively put them out, I might have. But after tonight, I knew I couldn't. And I desperately didn't want to. He had been charming and charismatic, and despite the opportunities, he'd kept his promises.

For the first time, I had found the gentleman my mind required and the bad boy my body desired.

Behind us, a loud whoop followed by a thump made us both pause our strides and turn. Tanner was lying spread-eagled on the ice while Nina held her stomach in laughter. Skaters veered left and right to avoid tripping over him. As Nina went over to help him up, Tanner moved his arms and legs back and forth. "No problem here. I just felt the need to make a snow angel. Right in the middle of dozens of people." Declan's snicker matched my own, and we skated over to help Nina heft Tanner off the ice.

"This oughta be good," Declan said when Nina grabbed his left hand and I grabbed his right.

Declan acted like he was in on a private joke. "What?" I said. "What oughta be –?"

"Come on down here with my pride, Nina," Tanner said as he pulled Nina down to the ice with him. I lost my balance for a split second and followed Nina to the ice with a screech.

"Oh, hell," I cursed when my elbow hit the ice.

"Shit. Sorry, Jenn. I didn't mean to get you too," Tanner said sincerely, although he was still laughing.

I rolled onto my back to see Declan standing above me, no longer chuckling. He was laughing so hard that his laugh was silent, and despite the throbbing in my elbow, I chuckled with him.

He reached a hand out to help me, and I decided I'd try the trick Tanner pulled on us. Yet when I yanked on Declan's hand, he didn't move. Not even a flinch. "Nice try, babe," he said, to which I replied with a mock glare.

"Thanks, man," he said to Tanner as Tanner finally got to his feet. At first, I couldn't figure out why Declan would thank Tanner for pulling me down, but with his next comment it became clear. "Let's find you that shot."

He smacked the frost off my ass with one hand before he took my hand to guide me from the ice. At the bar, he ordered and paid for a Jäger shot. "Bottoms up, babe." He watched as I brought the shot glass to my lips and tipped it back, emptying it in a single swallow.

"Nice." His eyebrows, that edged towards his hairline, told me he was impressed.

Gah. Why do I have to be so affected by his praise? It's like he has rewired me. "Thanks. Let's go get you a shot." I took his hand and led him back to the rink. As we entered, Beckett and Hannah were exiting.

"She fell," he explained with a grin. "Time to drink up, dear." Although Hannah schooled her face into a mock pout, I could see the twinkle in her eye when she looked at the man she loved. Seeing the two of them together so happy and in love made me realize how much I wanted that for myself some day.

Back on the ice, I decided to try to break Declan's confident façade. "OK, Gretzky. Let's see you skate on one foot."

And, of course, he did, although he occasionally waved his arms frantically like he was about this lose his balance. His confident smirk told me it was definitely an act. Then he skated back to me like a puppy waiting for his next instructions. By this point, the alcohol's warmth had spread past my stomach and to my chest and neck. It was admittedly a lovely buzz.

"Hmm … let's see you do a jump and land on one leg like figure skaters do."

And he did. It was only a half-rotation, but it was a half-rotation more than I could do. And he landed on his feet, damn it.

"OK. Now, let's see you do one of those really fast spins where you go faster and faster as you bring your arms in."

"Now you're just playin' dirty. You're trying to make me fall."

"Duh."

He went over to a vacant corner of the ice that was much less crowded since the rink portion of the bar was about to close. He skated in an arc and then brought his feet together, ankle to ankle. His arms pulled in awkwardly, but he did spin a bit faster. He wasn't Brian Boitano, but he wasn't on his ass either.

As he finished his spin, the toe pick on one skate caught the ice and his arms circled in the air as he tried to catch his balance. But it was too late, and he landed with a thud on his back.

Worried, I skated over to him. Two playful eyes shined back at me, and it was then that I wondered if he had fallen on purpose. I offered him my hand to help him up, and like an idiot, I had forgotten the lesson I learned from Tanner. He tugged on my hand and my ass landed on his lap. Even if I had braced myself, I doubt I would have been able to stay standing. I was no match for him.

65

He was sitting up now with his legs stretched out in front of him. I made to playfully slap his chest, but he anticipated me and caught my wrists. The moment of stillness actually had a sound as our eyes met. His begged for permission as his hands left my wrists and grabbed my neck underneath my hair. He paused long enough for me to nod the agreement I felt in every cell of my body.

He pulled my lips to his with a ferocity that made me suck in air through my nose. Our pursed lips locked for a second before I felt his mouth open. I followed his lead, parting my lips so our tongues could stroke gently. He used his hands to tilt my head to the side to deepen the kiss. I could taste the hops on his tongue as we explored and joined. He pulled his mouth away too soon, but as one connection was broken, another was formed. His eyes mated with mine in a moment more intimate than any sex I'd ever had. I was now warm in places that had nothing to do with the Jäger shot, and this was an even lovelier buzz.

Then he broke the spell. "Let's go get those shots."

As he got to his feet and helped me to mine, I couldn't tell if he was happy with the kiss or if he was upset he'd pursued something he'd said he wouldn't.

We went back to the bar, and he did his Jäger shot. His throat worked to swallow the liquid, and he ordered a water to chase it. At my inquisitive look, he offered, "I have to drive us back to Longmont tonight." After a pause, he joked, "You know, you don't have to get me drunk to have me. I'd do you stone-cold sober in the car in a random parking lot if it wasn't for the promise I made to you."

So there was my answer.

We'd been playful until this point, and I had loved this side of him. But when he said it that way, I couldn't look him in the eye. "I know, and I'm thankful for you respecting my feelings on this."

He tipped my chin up with two fingers under my jaw.

66

"Hey. Something's bothering you. Tell me. Please."

A few people bumped into us as they walked awkwardly around the carpeted bar in their skates, but little could distract me from the man in front of me. "Since the last time we talked, I've been thinking about you. Honestly, there are times like tonight and when we were rock-climbing that I wanted you so much it scared me. Those times made me *hate* that we agreed to be just friends. Then there were the other times when …" I didn't finish that thought out loud.

Declan didn't say anything, so I continued. "I've just noticed how different you are in different settings. And I can't forget the T-shirt you wore on the first day I saw you. The one with the George Burns quote on it. And then the class discussion on layers and masks paired with overhearing your jilted ex. There are times I can't help but worry who the real Declan is. Do you feel like you have to act with me? Do you wear a disguise with me?"

"I don't think there's a real Declan any more than there is a real Jenn. We *all* play roles. We *all* have our disguises and our defences. Some are just more authentic than others. And I can tell you that I haven't felt more at peace with myself than I have tonight. But you don't have to worry that I'm purposely dishonest with you. I'll never lie to you."

During his speech, his hand moved from my jaw so his fingers grabbed the nape of my neck and his thumb rubbed a small circle on my cheek. His body was telling me he was sincere.

"Thank you for that." I stepped closer to him so our lips almost touched. "Knowing that you aren't putting on an act when you're around me makes me want to be more than friends."

His eyes heated, and the dark weight that normally settled at the bottom of his brown irises lifted. "I have something to ask you. Two weeks from now is spring break. We don't have a lot of time off because play practices run during the break, but we do have the Friday night off. If I rented us a cabin in Estes Park for the night, would you come with me?"

Although I wanted nothing more than to hole myself up in Estes with him, I couldn't readily agree. "It's so fast, Declan. I'm not sure."

"I'll keep my promise. No sex unless you green-light it. We can get to know each other better away from the fear of being found out."

My body remembered the heat of the kiss on the ice, and it wanted more. "I'd love to go. Thank you for asking."

Chapter Eight

If the next two weeks proved anything, it was that we were unable to pretend any longer with each other. And it was getting harder to pretend around everyone else. We rock-climbed in the Boulder gym at least two times a week. I would marvel at his gracefulness and he would praise my growth, most of which he orchestrated. "Now, do the same climb without using any yellow holds," he'd say after I completed a climb. And back up I'd find that he'd chosen the yellow holds because they made me complete a difficult move I hadn't yet mastered.

"You'll need this move if you're going to climb outdoors. You want to sometime, right?" he said as he untied the rope from our harnesses.

"Definitely," I tried to regain my breath. "Especially since I'm getting more confident."

His simple response was a proud smile.

Other days, we'd find some stolen time to have a quick lunch before play rehearsals, which were still proving difficult. Since I'd started working with Stephanie, she had improved, and her confidence was growing. But Declan's intolerance for her occasional ineptitude often turned into what felt like a criticism of my tutelage. Like many naturals, he was impatient and judgemental, which added tension to the set.

Thankful that the tension was forty-five minutes away in Longmont, the drive to Estes Park felt more like an escape than a vacation. And we knew exactly what we were escaping from.

We pulled up to the small, wooden lodge around

dinnertime on Friday. I stayed in the car while Declan got the keys for our rental cabin. The cabin was situated under a large rock formation next to a small river. Given that it was detached and in a secluded alcove, it was private and intimate.

"This is just what a Colorado cabin in the mountains should be," I said. Weathered logs formed the outside structure, but inside was more modern with contemporary electrical and plumbing fixtures. While the small kitchen welcomed me from the foyer, the bedroom down a short hallway loomed like a shadowed secret, clouding my thoughts with worry. *Is this too fast? Are we ready for this?* We hadn't slept over at each other's houses yet, and our physical intimacy had been limited to a few passionate kisses.

Declan's arms snaked around my shoulders from behind. "I can't wait to get you out of that head of yours."

He nibbled my ear and pulled on the belt loops of my jeans. He tugged me down the hallway, leaving our suitcases at the front door. He turned up the heat on the thermostat before we stopped in front of the king bed that dominated the room. Control emanated from him, gentling my roaring heartbeat.

"Will you do something for me?" He didn't wait for my answer as he pulled the bedspread off and threw it on the floor. He then pulled back the heavy blankets to expose the fitted sheet. "Climb in here. Just lie here and drift. Think about nothing specific but what you sense. What sounds are there? What do the sheets feel like? What does it feel like to simply be present?"

I sighed. He knew me well. I toed off my shoes and climbed in as he tucked the covers around me. "I'll be in the other room." He left without a second glance or a kiss to the forehead, both of which I craved. I rolled onto my side and took a few cleansing breaths. Soon I was aware of the softness of the sheets pillowing me as I floated. A small animal must have landed on the roof from an overhanging tree because I heard a thud followed by the pitter-pattering click of small claws. The evergreen scent in the room made it feel like all the windows were open despite the fact that it was much too cold outside for that to be true.

I'd always had a hard time turning off my brain. The lists, the worries, the stresses of the day always dominated my thoughts if I lay still. I had been stretched thin with obligations and endless grading for the last two weeks, which left me weary. For the first time in a long time, the anxiety gave way to contentment.

I'm not sure how long I lay there, but what brought me back to the present was the clanking of pans in the kitchen. I lay still for a while listening to the bubbling of boiling water and the sizzling of meat, and when my stomach growled from the scents wafting down the hallway, I got out of bed, free of tension.

I halted at the small corner of the hallway where I got a good view of the kitchen. Declan was cooking dinner. He must have brought some supplies in a cooler I hadn't noticed earlier. He sipped a beer between turning the chicken breasts and stirring the pasta. The reduction sauce bubbled in a saucepan, and he brought a small spoonful to his lips to test it. Seemingly satisfied, he stirred more without adding any ingredients.

"You gonna stand there for ever?" he asked without turning around.

I yelped. "How did you know I was there?"

He turned around then and a tender smile welcomed me further into the kitchen, where I sat on a stool next to the refrigerator. "How was your rest?"

I noticed he didn't answer my question. "Great. Thank you. I didn't realize how much I needed it until you mentioned I should lie down for a while."

He stepped away from the stove and squared his

shoulders to me before he spoke. "You're welcome. I like giving you what you need, especially when you don't realize what it is."

Pure lust catapulted me from the stool, and I tackled Declan so he landed with a thud on his back. For the first time, I instigated a kiss that didn't start with the pecking niceties. Our teeth clanked together while I bit his full bottom lip then circled my tongue with his. Our legs were as entwined as our lips, and my hips began rocking against his erection with a need that surprised me. I held his head down on the wooden floor by gripping his long hair. He groaned under me and his hands squeezed my ass and pulled me up and down, creating a friction between us.

He tore his mouth from mine by turning his head over his left shoulder. Then his eyes returned to mine. "Way to go. I didn't think you had that one in you. I've waited a long time to see that. It must be hell burying it as deep as you do."

The vixen inside me decided to play with him, so I leaned down to whisper against his lips. "When you bury it deep, I assure you it won't be hell."

His eyes lit at my forwardness before he scowled with worry.

"What?" I asked.

He audibly sniffed. "I hope the dinner isn't burning."

I had totally forgotten about the food, so I dashed off him and began stirring the nearest pot. He joined me, stirring and draining the pasta while his hips brushed against mine in a touch both erotic and wholesome, like we'd done this for years. The dinner of blackened chicken fettuccine Alfredo was saved and we sat at the small wooden table. He popped the top on two more beers, and we drank and ate in silence until a question nagged my brain so incessantly I had to ask it.

"How many women have you been with?"

"Oh, hell." He took a long draw from his beer as he

rolled his eyes. "I should have known that question was coming. Guys don't keep a tally. I'm not sure, and that's not because it's so high. I've just never cared to count like each is a notch on my belt. Best guess? Between ten and twenty. How do you feel about that?" he added after I didn't say anything.

I placed another spoonful into my mouth and chewed to buy myself some time. "I'm glad that you're more experienced," I said, suddenly realizing it was true. "You know what you like and you know better than I do what I need. But then it makes me feel wholly inexperienced."

"Why? How many men have you had sex with?"

"Two."

His face registered no response. *I have to learn how to do that.* "Let me guess. Missionary position with a khaki-clad dentist? Never mind, don't answer that. You said before that you didn't orgasm with sex. Have you ever?"

"Oh, I can come with my purple vibrator under the covers if I'm in the right mood. But, no, I've never come with …" Fuck, I couldn't even say it.

"Good old-fashioned penetrative sex?" he finished as he raised an eyebrow before taking a long draw from his beer. He broke our eye contact as he took our empty plates to the sink. "You know that's normal, right?"

"Huh?"

He leaned back against the sink and crossed his ankles casually like we were discussing the weather. "Most women don't come from just penetration. And if you can't, you're not broken." He returned to the table, grabbed my hand, and led me to the bedroom where he took off his shoes and lay down under the covers. I followed him, laying my head on his shoulder and outstretched arm. His hard bicep flexed under me, curling me towards him. My leg bent over his torso as his hand repeatedly brushed through my hair from root to tip as we talked. He continued the conversation looking at the ceiling while I watched the rise and fall of his chest.

"The most important sex organ is the brain, and if your brain isn't engaged in the present, you probably won't come. Even then, there's nothing wrong with you if you take some time and work before you let go. I bet that if you put your trust in me that I could bring you to that top. You would enjoy the ascent far more than if you had to rush to the finish line. It's not a race. It's a climb. Let me lead you on that climb."

A tear leaked from the corner of my eye. He must have felt it because his hand reached around my face and under my eyes to test for others. "Why does that make you emotional?"

"Because I was convinced I was broken. I thought every woman had a screaming orgasm during sex, and although it felt good, I could never do it. To know that I'm not defective ..." I trailed off, then added, "I want you to lead me."

I said it so softly that at first I thought he hadn't heard me, because he didn't say anything. "Declan?"

"I just want to be clear what we're doing here, Jenn. You'll follow my wishes. You'll let me lead you, but if you ever want to stop, you will simply say 'stop', and, no questions asked, everything halts." His matter-of-fact tone added a hint of warning as he continued. "But it will not be missionary, and it will often not be gentle. You'll maybe hate what we do turns you on, but that's part of figuring out who you are. You'll pleasure me, and I'll make sure that pleasure is returned in spades, but your job will be to learn how to be the master of your own head. I can help with that, but I can't do it for you."

My body flushed with goose bumps. "I understand."

"OK. Then we're going to lie here just like this. You will close your eyes and concentrate on matching your breathing to mine. You'll hear my heart, but you will hear nothing else, see nothing else, feel nothing else other than what I tell you to. You will lie here as long as *I* wish us to."

I nodded against his chest, and my head rose and fell with his deep breaths. I closed my eyes, but, at first, I couldn't control the galloping of my breath, and mine certainly didn't match his. My jaw tensed against his chest as I tried to remember what underwear I had on and if they matched my bra. Were my legs shaved? Fuck, what if I suck at this?

But I desperately wanted to follow his directions, so I concentrated on his scent, the feeling of his warm palm on my temple, and his hardening length under my thigh. A freedom sprouted from somewhere in me I couldn't name.

Finally, he moved out from under me so we were side by side facing one another. Each of his palms cupped my cheeks as he pecked my lips and retreated. "Now you're relaxed."

"Yes. Thank you."

"Good. Now strip me."

Happily. We both sat up so I could take off his shirt then his belt. I unbuttoned his jeans and rasped open the zipper, brushing his solid erection as I slid them down his legs and threw them on the floor. A flood of lust left my skin overheated.

"Everything, Jenn."

I hooked my fingers under the top of his boxers and slid them down and off as well. I was too curious not to reach over and test to see how hard he was – to be sure that he was as affected as I was. His erection was granite hard under velvety softness, and I stroked it twice before he groaned, "Fuck. Yes."

I pulled tentatively a few more times until his hand grasped my wrist and made me pump harder. "Just like that," he instructed as he took his hand away. I gripped harder and was rewarded with more curses and labored breath.

"Enough. Enough," he said. "Arms over your head."

I followed, and since I was sitting up, he easily stripped off my shirt and unhooked my bra. The cool air breezed over my exposed skin, leaving me feeling vulnerable and unguarded.

"Turn over on your stomach." I did so, thankful that I felt a little less exposed. He arranged my arms so my elbows, bent at ninety degree angles, were in line with my shoulders. My palms were flat on the mattress, and he turned my head so that I lay on one cheek without a pillow. He reached under my hips to unbuckle my jeans, lower the zipper, and slide them down and off my legs. When his weight didn't return to the mattress, my breath audibly hitched.

"I'm going to get something. I won't be long. Show me you trust me and what we're doing. Don't. Move." I heard his jeans zip on, and then I followed his footsteps into the kitchen where I heard the sound of a metal bowl or pan clanking. Then the front door opened and closed, and I was left with an eerie silence.

In that silence, I was able to work myself into a frenzy. *What am I doing lying naked and alone in a cabin with a man I don't really know? Why am I allowing him to tell me what to do? Why am I wet as hell but embarrassed by it? This is not the type of man I should want. I'm not even sure this is the type of woman I want to be.*

I bolted upright on the bed, but froze when I heard his voice from the doorway. I hadn't heard him come back. "Lost your headspace already, huh? Already convinced yourself this wasn't for you? That this is somehow perverted and wrong? That you shouldn't like it?"

"You left me here ..." I started to protest.

"And you didn't trust me," he interrupted. "But you will. Your chance to choose, Jenn. End it right now or lie back down."

It was a directive, but not a harsh one. In fact, there was

some vulnerability in his voice that told me this was an important moment for him. He added softly, "There's strength in submission, Jenn."

My brain fought what my body had already decided as I lowered myself back to the mattress and waited.

And waited.

And waited.

Whether he was giving me time to reconsider or bolt or get back into the right mindset, I wasn't sure. But finally I heard the zipper rasp again and felt his weight bow the mattress as he climbed up to straddle my hips, careful to keep his weight from resting entirely on me.

He rubbed up and down my spine with a firm touch, but he took his touch away abruptly. "You're tense again, so I'm going to help you get back to where you were. We're going to do this right. You're not going to move or say anything unless it is to say 'stop'. You'll let me do what I want because it pleases me."

At the risk of being reprimanded for talking, I felt the need to communicate. "I want to please you." God help the war raging inside me, but it was the truth I couldn't deny.

He leaned down and brushed the hair off my ear before he murmured, "I know you do, sweet girl. And soon I hope to be able to give you more peace about that." He took my wrists above my head and tied them together with a length of climbing rope he must have got from his car. "But for now, just know that if all this came easily to you, there would be no appeal to it. I don't want to restrain a pushover. I want to bind something unattainable. Wild. Like wind. Like fire. Just know that when you let me restrain you, I know that I'm harnessing a goddess."

"Declan ..." My heart was bursting with something for this man, and I whimpered.

He sat up once again and tapped my lips twice. "No more. Just feel."

I closed my eyes and focused on my breathing. Soon

77

the only touch I could feel was his flat, open palm on my back between my shoulder blades. He pressed lightly at first, then harder. "Quiet your mind."

The pressure of his hand was hard enough that I felt myself fading and softening into the mattress as it centered me. "I can feel you thawing under my hand, Jenn."

A peaceful smile slid across my lips. It was a euphoric and tranquil moment, one when I no longer fought myself or my desires. I could feel my desire wetting the sheet under me as I tried to press my clit against the mattress.

"Still," he ordered when I squirmed. "I'll take care of you. Sometimes the slowest climbs have the highest peaks. You know that."

I trapped a screech in my throat when, without warning, I felt a cold, wet blob on my lower back. It slid off my back in rivulets on each side, adding more wetness to the sheet. Just as I was about to let my curiosity get the best of me, he said, "Snow."

He placed more splashes of snow along my spine, down my thighs, and on that sensitive spot on the back of my knees. Each melted away, drawing lines of pleasure across my heated skin.

"How does it feel?"

"It kinda burns."

"Yeah. Isn't it funny how something so cold burns as it melts?"

Like me.

"Yes." I couldn't help the whimper that followed that begged him for more, for release.

"I know, Jenn. Let's do this."

He mounted me so his erection pressed into my back. He reached his hand underneath my stomach as he leaned forward, splayed on top of me. "Spread your legs. Wider. Good." His lips bushed against my jaw. "Now, I'm going to show you how far from broken you really are."

His fingers moved lower. His first two fingers found

my burning clit. He circled then pressed, circled then pressed. Each pass used a different pressure than the last, some gentle, some hard, and soon my hips moved into his pressure, begging for more. The length of his body Velcroed to mine was not enough weight to suffocate but enough to remind me I wasn't in control. And I couldn't miss how his hips rhythmically drove into my lower back so I could feel his erection jump and twitch.

Then the two fingers that had always been pressed together separated into a V and rubbed each side of my clit and lower and back up.

So close. "Please. Please. Please."

I both heard and felt his whisper. "I bet no one told you that the nerves that run to your clit also run on each side and much lower, did they? Can you feel the blood rushing to your clit?"

"Yes. Yes. Yes." My chest was heaving now, pushing my back against the rock of his torso. His skin was heated against mine as we shared a thin layer of sweat that made our bodies slide easily. His heat, his power, and the woodsy scent of his cologne circled me, narrowing me on the moment and nothing else.

His voice was deep and unflappable when he spoke again. "And it makes you close, yes?"

Don't lose it. Don't lose it. This is the part when I always lose it. I could only nod.

His fingers returned to my clit and rubbed firm circles in one direction then the other. "You're afraid to chase it because this is when it always goes away." It was a statement and a question, whose heavy breaths blew across my back. With a single finger, he traced my vertebrae, momentarily distracting me from the pulsing between my thighs.

He continued, "You know that the clit retreats just a little right before an orgasm?" I tried to close my legs for more friction.

"Stop," he ordered. "I can't rub you like I want to you do that." He used his knees and feet to force my kne wider. My legs protested the stretch before they settl into his pressure and took with it any bit of restraint I ha left.

He grunted in my ear as I felt him thrust his cock against my lower back. "Fuck. What you do to me," he panted through labored breaths.

His fingers on my clit pressed down with more force than I'd ever thought to use. My thighs vibrated as the skin on my chest prickled. I felt the wave coming.

"I'm so proud of you. So fucking proud."

White light flashed across the room as I exploded with a scream that sounded distant to my ears. My stomach muscles convulsed one, two, three times before the energy radiated down my legs and out of my curled toes.

"Wow," was all I could say as I came back to myself. "I'll follow if that's where you lead." Then I shifted so the cold, wet sheets brushed against my skin. "Bad boy, you got the sheets wet. We can't sleep on these."

His lips brushed mine in a soft, reverent kiss. Then I felt them smile against mine. "Silly girl. We're not sleeping."

Chapter Nine

He kept his promise. We rested little and slept even less. Declan woke me in the middle of the night with his tongue and lips. But it was when his teeth grazed my most sensitive part that he showed just how much I wasn't broken as I shattered into pieces. And since Declan hadn't had any "relief" during our previous session, I insisted on returning the favor.

"You don't have to, Jenn. We're not keeping score."

"I know, but I want you to feel good. It can't be comfortable."

"Oh, we're way past uncomfortable," he joked as he lay back on the bed and propped up his head with a bent elbow behind his neck. His triceps and shoulder muscles bunched along his bent arm, zinging my core with an electric shock of lust. I wetted my lips as I snaked down his torso. His hard, heavy erection lay against his stomach before I gripped it. At the smallest touch, Declan groaned, "Suck it, Jenn. I can't wait much longer."

My flat tongue licked from base to tip before I took the head into my mouth. I moved slowly up and down, even though I could only take half of his length without gagging. My hand squeezed around the wide base and pumped quickly, matching my mouth's faster rhythm.

"Oh, fuck. Yes," he hissed through labored pants. His propped arm shot out from under his neck, and his head hit the mattress without a sound. Although I couldn't see his face any more, I imagined what his face would look like as he chased his release. I felt his hand softly guiding me at the back of my head. His hips rolled a gentle rhythm

beneath me that matched mine.

"Close. Close," he chanted, and I felt him harden impossibly further against my tongue. He pulled me off with a pop, took himself in his hand, and tugged twice before he groaned out his release that landed on the ridges of his abs. His eyebrows pulled together as if he was in pain, but his face relaxed into a gentle smile when his hand eventually stilled.

I loved watching the man lose his control for a few seconds, but, if I was honest, I wished he had come inside me. "But I wanted ..."

"It's too soon, babe," he interrupted. "We didn't talk about that yet, and that's not really something that you just spring on someone." His hand intertwined with mine. "I'll take you up on it next time."

I awoke the next morning with our legs tangled together like the crawling vines on old mansions. We showered, checked out of the cabin, and spent the day walking around quaint downtown Estes Park. The wide sidewalks and ornate storefronts made me feel like I was taken back in time. We browsed the tourist trap knick-knack shops where I bought a T-shirt.

I learned a few things about him that day, most of which I found comforting. He shared my dislike of saltwater taffy, and helped me polish off ten dollars' worth of chocolate brownie fudge and a bag of caramel corn. We munched as we walked, and while our hands were normally full of treats or coffee, we did find the occasional moments to hold hands. It was something we hadn't dared to do near campus, and being able to do it so freely zinged me with the same feeling I had in middle school as I stole hidden kisses under the football bleachers.

With what I'm sure was a goofy grin, I made Declan walk around the famous rock museum, which he grumbled about at first. After our tour of the Native American art exhibit, we found an eatery that advertised the best pizza in Estes. I learned that day that Declan liked just as much cheese on his pizzas as I did.

"Thank you for bringing me here. It's exactly what I needed." The cheese stretched from my mouth on a foot-long string when I attempted to take a bite. When I pulled the mushrooms off my slice and placed them on the side of my plate, Declan snatched them and piled them onto his uneaten slices.

"You're welcome." He paused to lick the grease from his hands. "It was exactly what *we* needed. Speaking of need, touch me. Reach your hand under the table."

I hesitated.

"Now, Jenn. You've been walking around in those tight jeans all day teasing me, and I can't do anything about it since we've checked out. Reach under the table. No one will know. Only us. And it makes it even sexier that they're all sitting a few feet away and haven't a clue." His head jerked to the dozen other customers who were sharing pizzas in booths, whose tables were also covered with white and red checkered tablecloths.

My hand feathered against his jeans and along his inner thigh. I traced the inseam down to his knee and the strategically-placed hole that was most likely there when he bought them. I used the tip of a fingernail to trace the circumference of the circle. As my finger circled around and around, my body relaxed into his heat, his strength. I remembered what it felt like to circle a more intimate part of his body, so I moved my hand up along his inseam again.

Holy Lord, he definitely dresses to the right. There was no doubt which way his manhood strained against his zipper. I felt the rock-hard length of it twitch at my touch, and he shifted his feet under the table as if in discomfort. The muscles along his jaw line tensed a few times before he grabbed his beer mug and drained it. He reached for my hand, pulled it away, and set it on my lap. "Actually, I think that just made it worse," he said as he readjusted himself.

I laughed as I ate another bite of pizza. Declan had also ordered some lasagna, a house specialty the waitress insisted he had to try. At first, I thought he had ordered it just to be nice, but he had eaten a lot of it, surprising me with the amount of food he was able to consume. He'd asked me once at the beginning of the meal if I wanted some, and I declined, but now everything, including his pasta, looked good. He must have seen my roving eyes, because he chuckled and asked, "You want a bite?"

"Sure. Thanks," I agreed as I reached my hands across my plate to the lasagna I thought he was trying to hand me. But a small shake of his head stopped me, and it was then I realized what he wanted. I followed his lead and lowered my arms. As he lifted a forkful, my mouth opened in a move I thought would be awkward or embarrassing. But his face as I chewed the food he had offered made me feel like there was nothing shameful about the act. In fact, I had pleased him, and as bizarre as it sounded, I relished it. Even after last night, I hadn't come to understand that feeling yet.

"You like to follow as much as I like to lead," he whispered. "It looks good on you."

Emboldened by the beer and the attraction zinging between us, I green-lighted him. "Lead on."

A frustrated growl told me he wished we were alone, which reminded me that we had an audience. He chewed another bite before he continued, "I have a question to ask you."

No good conversation ever starts like this. "Suuure."

"Remember when we talked on the phone about my father's relationships?"

I nodded.

"Do you remember when I told you that relationships

for me were akin to a business transaction?"

Painfully, yes. I nodded again.

"They always have been, but after last night, I can't pretend any more that you're nothing more than a well-negotiated contract."

I'm pretty sure you never were for me.

"You've gotten under my skin. I can't explain it. I often don't want to feel it, but I do."

I found my voice for the first time since he started this conversation. "Me, too, Declan. I want to be more than friends. Can we change the equation?"

"But I want you to know I have no frame of reference for this. I've never experienced a healthy relationship, so I'm afraid I'll screw this up." He looked away through the window for a moment before his attention turned back to me. "Even though I can't promise you forever, I can promise you have the best of me now."

"I want the best *and* worst of you now. I want the romantic, charming Gretzky and the moody, mercurial actor. That's what makes you Declan, and I'll take that over any whispered promises of forever that neither of us will be likely to keep."

He reached for my hand across the table and stroked the knuckles with his thumb. "Thank you for understanding, Jenn. I want more, but I'm not sure how to get it."

"We'll make it together."

"Yes. Speaking of, I have a proposition for you."

Holy mercy. How much more can my heart take today? "Proposition?"

He pulled a small stack of paper from his back pocket and unfolded the sheets in front of me. "I've been doing a lot of research, and I've watched you climb for the past month. You're really improving, so once the weather turns good, I think you're ready for a real climb."

I stared at the picture in front of me. My brain felt like

it was short-circuiting. I couldn't seem to connect the dots. "Wait. What?"

He cracked an amused smile. "I want to climb with you."

"What the fuck did you just say?" I'm not sure who was more surprised at my rare curse. "You climb 5.12s. I'm not in the same universe as you."

"The 5.12 climb I completed was a top-rope climb. You know those are easier. I want to lead climb you up that." He pointed to the picture.

Now that my brain had finally caught up, I was able to recognise the picture. It was one of the most iconic climbs in Colorado. "The Maiden?"

"Yep."

"What grade is it?"

"5.6. Tricky, but certainly within your abilities. You're climbing much higher grades in the gym now, but since you haven't climbed outdoors, this will be a good challenge. And I'll be there to belay you up it."

"You've lead climbed before?"

"Yep. And I've climbed the Maiden twice, so I know it well. You can do it."

"I've always wanted to climb the Maiden, but I could never find someone to top."

"Oh, I'll top you." He had the gall to smirk.

"Don't I know it."

"So, in all seriousness, what do you think?"

"I think I would love to. Let me do some more reading on the climb, and then we can plan our workouts to prepare for it."

I was rewarded with a reaction as close to giddy as Declan got. "Awesome. I look forward to it."

He paid the bill with a smile stuck on his face. Then he checked his watch and frowned. "We better be getting back. We have a long day of rehearsals tomorrow."

His plummeting mood bled into mine, and I was

reminded just how far from reality we were in Estes. "Ugh. Back to civilization."

Chapter Ten

I had reached my limit. Declan's bristling form stood his ground defiantly next to Stephanie, who was left to cower in his shadow. There was no denying his skill. The electricity of his calculated movements and the mesmerizing gallop of his delivery were nothing short of genius. But the man was also infuriatingly stubborn, and had little patience for the imperfections of others. And he lacked the insight to see that his bulldozing of the scene when it went sour didn't fit with Orlando's character. That meant I would often play peace-keeper among the cast alongside Dr Burrows.

With opening night three weeks away, tensions were running higher than ever, and sensing an impending meltdown, Dr Burrows called for a ten minute break. Actors and actresses scattered in multiple directions off the stage like someone had announced there was a hundred dollar bill hidden somewhere in the auditorium. Declan stomped off stage right, throwing a drop curtain out of his way as he left.

"Declan, I need to talk to you …" Dr Burrows shouted, but Declan's stride didn't stop as he left the stage.

While the sensible part of me told myself to leave him alone, I was furious. Wanting to give him a piece of my mind, I motioned to Dr Burrows that I would handle it. He nodded his approval.

I followed Declan off stage and down a hallway. I found him leaning against the painted cinderblock wall with his head tilted up. One knee was bent so he balanced on one foot and rested the other against the wall. His hands were clenched at his sides, and he appeared to be taking deep, calming breaths.

Too bad I didn't take any of those. "What the fuck was that, Declan?"

"Excuse me?"

"You can't browbeat Stephanie into perfect acting. So what if she doesn't do it the way you want her to? You were cast as Orlando, not Rosalind, and as much as it might pain you to hear it, Orlando is not the star of this show. This is not *Hamlet*. This is not *Julius Caesar*. This is the story of a woman, and you are the supporting actor."

"Are you questioning my ability to act? I know who Orlando is supposed to be."

"Then why don't you play him?"

"Because Orlando can't follow a woman who can't lead. Stephanie's no Rosalind."

"That's not the issue."

"What the fuck is it, then?"

I should have let it go, but I couldn't. "*Orlando's* not the problem. The issue is that *Declan* can't follow a woman's lead."

He bounded from the wall and stalked to me so his breath blew strands of my hair as he spoke. "Where is this coming from? You embarrassed about what you allowed me to do to you over the weekend, sweetheart? Wish you had led?"

Asshole. Asshole. Asshole. His pedantic tone churned my annoyance to the violent side of pissed off. "Quite the contrary, honey." I stepped forward so my chest bumped his. "This is not about Estes. This is about what happened on that stage. Dr Burrows and I are trying to help you and the other actors make this the best show it can be. And you bulldozing a scene doesn't help. You *will not* do that again. Hear me?"

He didn't answer, so I felt the need to add one more thing. "And if you *ever* disrespect my authority within this cast again by reminding me of our personal dynamic, I can guarantee you there will be no more Estes. And don't forget I have pull with Dr Burrows. It would be a shame to go to all of this work …" I let my threat vibrate between us.

The humming florescent lights above us tinted his skin yellow as we stared each other down. "You wouldn't dare," he whispered.

"Wouldn't I?" I challenged. "I won't be manipulated. And you better get comfortable real quick with the fact that when it comes to this play, I'm in charge."

Flames might have been coming out of my ears as I turned away, my heels clicking furiously on the concrete floor.

"Wait, Jenn. Wait."

I kept going until his hand grabbed my wrist and tugged. "For God's sake, stop."

He tugged a little harder. I whirled around so forcefully that our chests banged together. He took two steps forward so he had my back pinned against the concrete wall. A single breath later, his lips collided with mine so violently that the back of my head would have hit the wall had his hand not been cradling it. He controlled the kiss with his lips, his tongue, his hand. I met his intensity to reinforce my point. I tugged a fistful of his hair with one hand while I forced his lower body towards mine. My teeth tugged at his lower lip when he tried to pull away, which made him growl and force open my mouth with his tongue until we were stroking, giving and taking, with long lashes.

My breath no longer became my own as I inhaled what he gave, returning it to him with equal fervour. It felt as if we were breathing life back into whatever had been born in Estes, and we were trying to figure out if it would survive in this separate world.

This time he was successful at his attempt to pull his mouth away. He closed his eyes and gained his breath as he leaned his forehead against mine. "I'm sorry. I've got a lot of things on my mind. You. My dad. This role. I'm struggling, and I know it. When every fibre of my being isn't Orlando, I doubt my ability to act this character. But nothing excuses what I said to you. Please forgive me."

"I'm sorry too. I should have come to you to talk about what was bothering you, but I didn't. I came here to pick a fight out of my own frustration. It's over now. We'll move on. But you have to tell me something. What about your dad has you troubled?"

He pivoted so that his back was against the wall, his shoulder next to mine. He stared at a point across the wall with blank, defeated eyes. "He's coming to the show."

"That's awesome, isn't it? I'm sure he wants to be supportive."

"Yes, but when I haven't seen him in years, I wonder what the first meeting will be like. And I'll be acting a part in front of him that I'm uncomfortable with. Although everything inside me says I shouldn't care what his opinion is of my ability, I can't. Even though I hate the man he is, I respect the actor he was. He was a genius before he sold out. I watched his early films so many times I still have them memorized. I have a lot of thinking I need to do about this role, Jenn."

The truth steamrolled into me with the subtlety of a locomotive. Now I understood why he'd acted the way he did the day we met. "I get it now," I whispered.

"Get what?" His eyebrows lifted in question.

"Why you were so damn prickly when we met."

He allowed a small smile. "Your criticisms hit too close. Stephanie is struggling and knows it. The same is true for me. But where we diverge is in her willingness to put her pride aside to ask for help. Admitting that I'm struggling is not something I'm good at, especially to a pretty professor." The smile finally lifted to the corners of his eyes. "Surely you know that my initial skepticism of your abilities was my mask for my own insecurities. I wanted to impress you so much."

"I was, and still am."

"But you saw through me to the raw, insecure core. And that threatened me."

"And it still does," I said, gesturing towards the door to the stage. "Exhibit A: what happened today."

His eyes lowered to the ground. "Like I said, I have a lot of thinking to do."

"I'll leave you to it, but before I do, I need one more." He smiled as my lips connected with his in a slow wave of a kiss that rolled with accepted apologies. I pulled away as Ingrid, the actress playing Celia, rounded the corner and cleared her throat. Her face registered no reaction to what most assuredly would have been a surprising exchange. I started to panic when I couldn't read her reaction.

"Dr Burrows has called everyone back to places," she instructed.

"Thanks," we both said as Ingrid walked back through the stage door, and, thankfully, her flowery perfume and the click-clack of her heels gradually faded away. Before we followed her back, a worried expression clouded Declan's face. "We have to be more careful, Jenn. That was too close. All it takes is one slip. One time. And you would be out. I won't do that to you. I care about you too much for that to happen."

My heart sped as he reminded me of the gravity of the situation. There would be no second chances for the career I had worked years to attain. "I agree."

"I'm going back in." He leaned in to kiss my forehead, but stopped himself short. I saw his disappointed grimace as he turned the corner that led back to the stage.

I leaned against the wall and tried to control my erratic breathing. When had I become so cavalier? When had I started making such rash decisions? I'd never been one to let my desires override my self-control. A heavy weight pounded in my chest as my eyes filled with tears.

Knowing I had to address the full cast after rehearsal today, I wiped them away and re-entered the stage.

The rest of the rehearsal went comparatively smoothly. The director insisted that play rehearsals on Tuesdays would always end with a short lecture on a topic of my choice. The lecture was aimed at helping the actors gain more insight to their characters, Shakespeare's language, or the themes of the play. Today I had planned a fifteen minute lecture on one of the major themes of the play.

"Take it away, Dr Lyons," Dr Burrows said.

The cast sat in a semicircle on the stage while I stood front and center. "Thank you. Today I want to discuss one of the most important elements of *As You Like It*. The play is known as one of Shakespeare's most famous pastorals. Understanding what a pastoral is will help each of you create a character arc that changes with each setting. A pastoral is a story that involves the main characters leaving urban or court life to reconvene in a country setting. The woods or countryside, which in our case is the Forest of Arden, allows characters to regain a sense of balance lost when they were living in civilization. Moreover, the forest allows the main characters to gain a greater sense of self-understanding."

Declan's eyes burned with intensity when I glanced in his direction. It must have been obvious that I had prepared this lecture after we'd come home from Estes.

"And ultimately the characters are able to achieve love because of the freedom from constraints they experience in the real world. In short, attachment is achieved from their exile."

I tore my eyes from his stare, trying to maintain my composure in front of the cast. "But one has to be careful not to assume that Shakespeare's message here is that civilization is bad and nature is good. Remember that

94

Shakespeare's married couples return to the court in the final scene with a sense that all has been righted as it should be. They realistically can't flee civilization forever, but leaving it for a while allows them to return to it and thrive."

Declan nodded his understanding of the message meant just for him. While many times before I had cherished these stolen moments in public settings, now they exhausted me. I was tired of hiding us like we were some dirty secret. *Well, you are.* I finished the lecture, agitated and exhausted, then opened the floor for questions.

"So what does that mean for each of us?" Ingrid asked.

"Each of you should be aware that your character will act differently in every setting. In the court, you will act according to the constraints of proper societal expectations. Your mannerisms will be more purposeful, your language and tone more measured and proper. In the forest, there should be a lightness, a playfulness to your spirit. You're allowed more physical touch and emotional communication than would have otherwise been acceptable. But in the all-important final scene in the court, you will return a combination of the two. You will respect the propriety polite society requires, but you will do so with a balanced spirit and a sense of being renewed. Think about this theme in the coming week and how it can inform your character's actions in various scenes."

I paused for further questions, and when none were offered, Dr Burrows dismissed the cast.

"Thank you, Dr Lyons. See you tomorrow, everyone."

I need air. I tried to gulp it in as I escaped through the back of the auditorium. I ran from the theatre to the green space outside the student union where I collapsed on one of the benches, troubled by the harsh words we'd used in the hallway and the continual need to watch our backs. Our kisses had been foolish, but in that moment, I couldn't have made myself care, which troubled me now even more. I was exhausted by the charade we had to play in the theatre and the classroom.

And I found myself looking forward to our next exile.

Chapter Eleven

The first of April always brought with it a sense of exploration, of new beginnings, this year more than ever. I trained with extra focus over the next two weeks. I spent evenings studying professional guidebooks on climbing The Maiden so I would know what to expect. Declan pushed me harder than ever, too, but he often praised how physically and emotionally ready I was. "This is something you're ready for," he'd say as we shared a bottle of water after our workout. "And I can't wait to be there to see you do it."

"I wouldn't want anyone else with me," I'd reply. And we'd leave the gym, reluctantly heading back to our own apartments near campus.

So I was prepared when Declan called me Wednesday night. "The weather forecast for Friday looks favorable. No rain. Mid-sixties. The ice and snow have melted off and if we go during the work week, we'll have the place to ourselves. It's too crowded on weekends, so I think Friday should be the day."

Well, at least I thought I was prepared. Now that I had a specific date for our climb, my muscles tensed with anxiety.

"Jenn? You there?"

"Oh, yes. Sorry. Sure, Friday sounds great. I don't teach on Fridays, and rehearsal is cancelled for the actors while the stage crew puts final touches on the set. What time do you want to meet?"

"I'll pick you up at ten. Any earlier, it will be too cold to enjoy the climb. I'll double-check all the gear and ropes we'll need are in good condition and packed."

My "thanks" must have sounded distant.

"And, Jenn, your job is to stay out of your head. You're ready."

We ended the call. I put in a leave request online for Friday and packed all the gear I'd need for the hike and overnight camping we planned to do after we finished the climb. The hike to the mountain from the nearest access point was over two hours each way, so we couldn't expect to hike there, climb the mountain, descend, hike out, and drive home all in one day. And, truth be told, I was looking forward to roughing it in the wilderness for a night with nothing but Declan and a tent.

I spent the next days emotionally yo-yoing between "I'm so ready for this" and "what the hell am I thinking?" Declan probably anticipated that, so he would often text me encouraging pictures of a woman climbing a mountain or a shadowed figure standing on top of a mountain backlit by a yellow sunset. I would look at those photos when I started to doubt and imagine what reaching my own peak would be like.

I couldn't sleep much on Thursday night, although I told myself I needed it. So on Friday morning, when I woke up an hour later than planned, I was equal parts frustrated and wired.

Declan rang my apartment call button at 9.50, and I buzzed him up and unlocked my door so he could come in as I scurried around my apartment like a squirrel trying to find all his nuts before a big snowstorm.

He sauntered in, casual as he pleased, with one hand in his pocket and the other holding the apple he munched on. He leaned against the door jamb of my messy closet as he followed my movements with amusement.

"What's so funny?" I asked.

"You. You're so hyped and we haven't started the hike yet. You're gonna have an adrenaline crash."

I stuffed my backpack with the final last-minute items I needed and blew out a frustrated breath. "I know. I can't help myself."

When he sat next to me on my bed, I thought I was in for another lecture on getting in the right mindset, but yet again, he surprised me. Wordlessly, he took a bite of the apple and offered me the next one. By now, I knew better than to take the core from his hand because one of his favorite things to do was feed me. So I leaned into his shoulder, opened my mouth, and took a bite when he brought the sweet fruit to my lips. He smiled as I chewed and leaned sideways to nudge me with his shoulder as he said, "Let's do this."

We drove the half-hour to Boulder, found a restaurant for a light lunch, and continued driving south, to the South Mesa trailhead. We parked his Camry and double-checked our climbing gear and supplies.

We found the Mesa trailhead and hiked along an easy dirt path. When the trail allowed, we walked side by side, and although we rarely touched, I felt more connected to him the further we climbed, as if I was able to absorb his calm confidence.

Instead of worrying about the climb, I focused on enjoying the peaceful hike. The cloudless, blue sky was iridescent, and the buds on trees promised the start of something new. The rocks crunched under our hiking boots as we finally made our way to the first landmark of the hike. We turned on to another trail at an abandoned stone water tank. A few hundred feet further, we passed an old rock quarry and followed a narrower dirt path designed for climbers' access. The path dissected two tall pines that acted like a gate of no return. Once I passed nature's gate, The Maiden's steep east ridge dominated the horizon.

"There she is," Declan said, pausing to take a sip of water as we looked at the rock standing proud in front of us.

"She's beautiful." A sandstone rock formation jutted out at a forty-give degree angle with the horizon.

"Yes, she is." I pointed to the top of the cliff. "It looks like Pride Rock in Disney's *The Lion King* – you know, the one where that weird monkey holds Simba up to introduce him as the next king of the pride?"

Declan laughed. "Never thought of it like that, but you're right."

He led us down the pathway to the south so that we could place our extra gear at the base of the mountain where we planned to descend. In the case of The Maiden, while it is possible to descend the way we came up, the real appeal of the climb is the descent from the West Overhang. After climbing to the summit, we planned on rappelling off the highest point to a small area called The Crow's Nest. The rappel was 110 feet down, and a free rappel, meaning we would be dangling in open space, completely exposed, with only the rope and knots for security.

When we got to the place we would descend to, we noticed two other packs already placed there, which told us that some climbers had already started ahead of us. We placed our packs alongside theirs and retrieved the climbing gear we needed. We buckled our harnesses, changed into climbing shoes, put on our helmets, and loaded onto our harnesses all the necessary ropes and steel hardware we would need to climb and rappel.

As each piece of gear and climbing equipment went on, my body recognized the familiar routine. And it was that familiarity that made me keep my nerve.

Standing at the base of the massive sandstone peak, I felt disoriented when I looked up. The sheer rock face made me feel miniscule, reminding me of the profound respect a climber must have for the rock. It might be climbed, but it is never conquered.

"Come here." Declan wrapped his arms around my shoulders in a tight hug. His even breathing metronomed in my ear as I laid my cheek on his shoulder. My nose brushed across his throat so I could smell his sweat mixed with the woodsy cologne. My eyes closed to the peacefulness of the moment. His soothing words mixed with the occasional cardinal warble and the wind whistling through the pines created a chorus that centered me.

"You worried?" he asked.

"I'd be lying if I said I wasn't."

"You know, a little worry is good. Any climber who isn't reminded of his own mortality as he takes the first step is a climber that dares the rock to teach him that lesson. But too much worry taxes your muscles and you won't be able to perform. The whole appeal of rock-climbing is that it is inherently dangerous. Embrace that danger and enjoy it. I won't let anything happen to you."

One arm stayed on my shoulders as we walked slowly to the side where we would begin our climb. We saw that the climbers before us would not be done for a while, so we rested on a nearby boulder and ate a protein bar. By the time our wait was over, I had become desensitized to the enormity of the challenge. That thirty minute wait we hadn't planned on was the most convenient of gifts. But it also meant that we had to focus on completing our climb in an efficient manner before the sun set. It was clear there would be no one who could climb up after us safely in the daylight.

When we saw the climbers were clear, we uncoiled the rope to connect us together. We tied the rope onto our harnesses using a figure-eight knot and safety-checked each other's.

For the two weeks since Declan had proposed this climb, I had imagined what this moment would be like. What would he say? The simplicity of what really happened trumped all my imaginings.

He kissed my forehead and spoke against it. "See you at the top."

After those perfect words, he turned and began the comforting ritual of communication.

"Climbing, Jenn," he said.

"Climb, Declan," I answered, which communicated I was aware he started his climb, and was vigilant for falling rocks or tangles in the rope.

The Maiden climb is traditionally broken up into five pitches or stages. The first pitch is a forty-foot climb on a steep west face. The afternoon sun baked our backs, and I could see Declan's shadow follow him as he climbed. It was always much more dangerous for the lead climber in these instances because Declan was not on belay. Unlike at the gym where there's a pulley at the top to run the rope through and down to the belay, this natural rock doesn't allow for that type of protection.

The only protection he had were chocks: inch-long anchors made of steel and shaped like cowbells. Attached is a small loop of steel rope. About every ten feet, or whenever the rock allowed, Declan placed a chock in a small crevice. He inserted the small portion of the cowbell shape down into the crack, so if he were to fall, the rope would tug the chock further into the crevice and the wide part of the cowbell would hold his weight.

After placing the chock, Declan attached his lead rope to its loop with a carabiner. Each chock would most likely prevent him from suffering a fatal fall.

Declan's holds were sure and purposeful, elegant and natural. I watched the way he used the rock's natural curvature to his advantage as he tested a hold. He would dismiss some and look for another, safer hold. I tried to memorize his choices, which was another advantage of going second.

At the top of the forty-foot wall was a small summit where Declan stopped his climb. At that point, there was a fixed bolt lead climbers use to anchor themselves to the rock with a carabiner. I watched Declan bolt himself in and prepare the belay device.

"Belay on, Jenn," he yelled.

"Climbing, Declan."

To confirm that he heard me, he replied, "Climb, Jenn."

My body relaxed into the comfort of the familiar for the first twenty feet. The wall wasn't entirely vertical, so I could rest a lot of my weight on my legs with minimal stress on my arms. I'd need that strength later.

My job was to remove the chocks Declan placed as he climbed. I paused after the first twenty feet to regain my breath. Because I was smaller, I couldn't follow the exact holds Declan had used, so I had to find my own route. I checked a few side holds, but I wasn't confident in them. Starting to feel frazzled and indecisive, I expected to hear Declan's instructions or encouraging words as I searched, but I was thankful that he let me struggle a little, which demonstrated his level of confidence in me.

I soon found a small ledge perfect for my smaller hands and used it to start the second half of the first wall. I reached Declan minutes later at the top of the forty-foot wall. I used a carabiner from my harness to clip into the bolt.

"Off belay, Declan," I said, to tell him that he was no longer responsible for my safety.

"Belay off, Jenn. Nice work by the way. Your form was great."

"Thanks for letting me suffer a little," I said between heavy breaths. "I needed that – to know that I could figure it out on my own. This is so different from gym climbing because the holds aren't marked with brightly colored tape. It'll take me a while to get used to it."

"You're welcome. That's why we're starting at an outdoor 5.6. Climbing here is a very different challenge to gym climbing." He tilted his head to the right. "This next pitch is easier. Climbing, Jenn."

"Climb, Declan." He began to downclimb from the small peak we had rested on. We successfully downclimbed pitches two and three, stopping to belay and clip into bolts as we went.

Pitch four was notoriously the most difficult of all the stages of the climb, so we paused to rest for a good ten minutes. We sat hip to hip with our knees bent for support in front of us. Perched on the side of the peak, we were able to see for miles across the green hills and flat grasslands that gave way to roads, buildings, and bridges. So far removed from civilization up here, it felt primal, savage. We had to rely only on ourselves and the trust in our partner in order to literally make it out alive.

Declan looked over his shoulder at the horizon to check the sun. "I'm not sure how long the next pitch will take us, so we better get started." We re-chalked our sweaty hands in preparation.

"Trust yourself. And trust me." Declan checked our harnesses and turned towards the rock. "Climbing, Jenn."

"Climb, Declan."

This pitch was the most difficult because it wasn't a straight climb upwards. Instead, Declan went diagonally up the peak, following the traditional route. Going both sideways and upwards at the same time limited handholds and made for some tricky foot placements, especially if the holds required Declan to stretch off balance. As the second, I had to watch carefully to be sure the rope didn't get caught between his legs. If it did and he fell, he could be yanked upside down and smack his head against the rock.

Once again, Declan took his time checking and testing holds, dismissing some before accepting them as the only possibilities, something that made my heart jump with nerves. Halfway through the pitch, Declan passed a single small tree that dared to grow out of the sheer rock. I pictured myself clinging to that small tree when I got there, wrapping my arms and legs around it for the small respite it offered.

The next part of the climb was the most exposed, with fewer opportunities to use chocks or clip to a fixed anchor on the rock. This was the most dangerous part for a lead climber. He paused for a moment, and I could see his chest rise and fall with a deliberate breath. His shirt was soaked through with sweat, and his arm muscles bulged so much it looked like they were testing the seams of his shirt armholes. He traversed left around an edge, shimmied up a corner crack, and climbed a narrow ledge from which he could belay me. The maximum effort he used on the last move told me he had cranked it. It either meant he was getting tired or he wasn't completely confident in it. As his right foot hit the ledge, he completed the move, but his foot hold slipped. He still had a strong grip of the rock, though, so the slip was more of a minor blip rather than a serious fall risk. But seeing any falter in Declan made my heart thump in my throat. If he had a problem, how was I supposed to do that?

He gained solid footing before he clipped into the anchor and prepared to belay. "Belay on, Jenn!"

"Climbing, Declan!"

The first half of the pitch was surprisingly enjoyable. My mind seemed to forget that the steep drop-off meant more dire consequences than the padded gym floor, so my body relaxed into the holds. I focused on the choices of small handholds.

Choose. Step. Pull.

Choose. Step. Pull.

The repetition of this series of movements let my mind wander into a climber's high. It was the first time I had experienced that type of peaceful relaxation, similar to the feeling I got when I practised yoga. Although I was completely aware of my surroundings, I had the sensation

I was floating outside myself, hyper-aware yet numb at the same time. My legs carried the majority of my weight, so my arms felt rested when I got to the tree.

My confidence soaring, I passed the tree quickly. My hands were sweaty on the sun-warmed rock, which made the removal of some of the chocks difficult. The holds were increasingly deceptive. Some promised safety then gave way with a small tug, making it difficult to trust any of them. This was a danger I'd never experienced in a gym. With every step and pull, I second-guessed my choices, and my frustration grew to the point where my movements, that were once calculated and deliberate, were now unplanned and hasty. I could feel that frustration growing inside me like an ulcer, but I was helpless to tamp it down. It had a mind of its own that festered and peaked, making me feel like I had to scream and vomit at the same time.

"Up rope! Up rope!" I shouted, wanting to feel the rope tugging at my harness. I'm not sure Declan could have pulled the rope tight enough to stem the panic attack that was threatening.

"I'm right here, Jenn." Declan tugged on the rope twice, lightly enough to let me feel the tug on my harness but not hard enough to pull my hips off balance. "You're at the crux. Look at your knuckles. They're white. You're gripping too tight."

When I looked at my hands, I was surprised by the bloodless tips. I willed my hands to loosen their grip, but the nerve that communicated between brains and hands had been severed. My hands didn't feel like my own. "I can't."

"A tight grip means a tight mind. Let go for me, Jenn. Start with your shoulders. Good. Now your forearms. Yes. Think about each finger. First, your thumb. Does it really need to grip there or do your legs have your weight?"

"My legs." My thumbs were the first to give up their

death grip. The others followed seconds later.

"There. Now you're ready. Go again."

"But I saw you. You had to crank it here. If *you* had to, there's no way I can do it."

"I *chose* to crank it. But your hands and feet are much smaller than mine. You can use holds I couldn't. You're more flexible, and your core is strong. Don't try to go the way I did. Find your own way."

I took advantage of my momentary boost in confidence. I surveyed the possible holds. If I stretched on my right leg, my left hand could barely reach what looked like a solid hold. Even though stretching that far made me vulnerable to losing my balance, I decided it was the best option. My arms and legs moved in an instinctive rhythm.

Foot.

Hand.

Foot.

Hand.

I launched onto the small ledge before my feet knew they were there. My mind registered a full second later that I was standing next to Declan on the belay ledge. I clipped a carabiner on to the fixed bolt.

"Well, fancy meeting you here," he welcomed, stripping me of the tension of the last five minutes.

I kissed him then mumbled against his lips. "Off belay, Declan."

I felt his lips breeze across mine. "Belay off, Jenn."

Our foreheads rested together as I slowed my breathing. My hands wound around Declan's narrow waist as his large palms kneaded the muscles around my shoulders. "The last one is all mental. It's nowhere near the climb you just did. The hard part is that it's so exposed."

I already feel exposed. "If you're ready, I'm ready."

"Yep." He turned towards the rock one last time. "Climbing, Jenn."

"Climb, Declan."

The holds on this pitch proved closer together and more obvious. The only tricky part was the transition to the upper east ridge, but Declan bounded over as if had completely forgotten he was a foot away from the sky. Soon, he reached the top, communicated, and I began the pitch.

"Climbing, Declan."

"Climb, Jenn."

I climbed at a forty-five degree angle to the horizon so that whenever I lifted my head slightly, all I could see was the distantless blue sky. The lowering sun made the orange sandstone rock under my fingers more rust colored as it cast long shadows along the ridge. Declan was right – climbing the top edge of the rock was mentally exhausting. Instead of climbing a vertical wall like I was used to, I balanced on a tightrope with sheer cliffs on both sides. Like an ant crawling up the spine of a buffalo, I edged methodically forward.

Declan's shadowed figure stood like a finish line at the peak. His legs spread wide for balance, he gradually pulled the slack of the rope as I ascended. Although most of my attention was focused on the holds, I glanced up a moment as I rested. His peaceful, serene smile backlit by the setting sun warmed me like nothing else. He was proud of me, and more importantly, I was proud of myself.

At the transition to the upper east ridge, I considered my next move. "No yellow holds," Declan said from above.

Of course, there were no colored holds, but I smiled. He knew the last move over this ridge would require a single move, and during our training, he'd forbidden the yellow holds to force me to practise it.

Elated now I was so close, I felt like egging him on. "Ah, that's not much of a challenge. What about no green or yellow holds?"

His eyebrow raised in surprise. "A little cocky, are we?

Go for it."

I retrieved his last chock and put it in my pocket instead of on my harness. Then I easily pulled over the last ridge and scrambled to the summit where I attached to the bolt.

"Holy heavens, yes!" I screamed so the whole world could hear what I'd done. I extended my arms to the side and tilted my head up to the sky, allowing the setting sun to bake this feeling into my skin. Like Rose at the front of the *Titanic*, in that moment I was invincible, bigger than the world.

I expected to be tackled into a Declan hug when I reached the summit, but since it hadn't come yet, I opened my eyes. I watched him as I unbuckled and removed my helmet, setting mine beside his on the rock. He stood a good five feet away on the flat summit with his thumbs hooked on his harness and a tranquil, thoughtful smile on his face like a father gets when his daughter goes off to prom. His happiness and pride were painted across his face, but so was his reluctance to intrude on this deeply personal moment for me. He was a voyeur to my triumph, and not wanting to interrupt it, he was content to be a part of it from a distance. The sun cast a yellow glow to his skin, and the vision of Declan standing on the summit as he watched me was burned into my soul like a Polaroid picture.

But I wanted him to be a bigger part of it. More than ever before, I needed his touch to ground me on the top of the world. My small "thank you" whispered into his chest seemed so paltry.

"You're welcome. It was beautiful to see. You were high, weren't you?"

"Yeah."

"The first half of the fourth pitch?"

I nodded.

"I could tell. You know you're addicted now, right?"

I turned in his arms so that he held me from behind as

we looked out over the landscape. I understood why everyone used to think the earth was flat. I swore I could see the edge of it along the horizon. "Only if you'll share my addiction."

"I'll climb with you any time." His teeth grazed my ear, and I felt his erection press against my ass. "But there's something else I'm more addicted to."

I pushed my hips back against him. "Please?" I asked.

"Please what, Jenn? What do you want?"

Blood rushed from my taxed arms to my core, igniting a need in me that amazed even me. I'd never wanted like that before. "You. Please. Please," I begged.

"But you can't say it? What you want is nothing to be ashamed of. I hope there will come a day when you learn to ask for what you want, that you *take* what you want. You're beautiful in your triumph, but you'll be the most beautiful then."

Before I could plan my response, he sat back on the rock and took me with him so that I sat between his legs, cradled in his arms. "You really want this?"

I nodded.

"I need to hear you."

"Yes."

"You on the pill?"

"Yes."

"You good with no protection?"

If I had trusted him with my life for the last hour, I could trust him with this. "Yes." In a moment of rare boldness, I added, "Top me, Declan. Please. Lead me like you did today. I need it."

The sharp edges of the summit dug into my back when Declan flipped me over and mounted me. Before I had the chance to yelp, he held my hands immobile above my head.

"Now we're getting somewhere." His eyes turned fierce as he fiddled with something on his harness out of my line of sight. I tried to sit up to see if any hikers along the ridge would be able to see us, but his weight held me down. I knew we were the last climbers of the day, but I couldn't avoid the worry.

My wrists were tied together with a short length of climbing rope as he talked. I could feel the racing pulse in my wrists beat against the restraint. "You worried about someone seeing us?"

"Yes."

He leaned down and fiddled with something else above my head. He whispered in my ear like there was an audience waiting on our every word. "So what if there is? Pretend there's a hiker just over that ridge. Do you think he'll touch himself while he watches? Will he be able to hear when you come?" Then I heard the metal clink of a carabiner attach to a bolt and realized that my hands were now attached to a bolt fixed into the summit.

He bit my ear before he murmured, "Belay on, Jenn."

Although my panties were soaked and my nipples beaded painfully in my sports bra, I instinctively struggled against the restraint. Of course, it didn't budge at my attempts, pumping a new course of adrenaline through me. I tugged at the restraints again as Declan sat up and straddled my knees. "It feels good to struggle against it, doesn't it?"

"Yes."

"You thought about why?"

"I don't want to think about why."

"Because it makes you feel like a little bit of choice has been taken from you. Your mind knows you fully consented to this. But tell your body that. Isn't it funny how when you're grounded, your body gives you permission to fly?"

I pulled a few more times, and each tug sparked an electrical current to my core. He loosened my harness and pulled it down, along with my climbing pants and underwear. The cool air drifted across my exposed skin as Declan unhooked his harness and pulled down his hiking shorts. His boxers followed, and he took himself in one hand while his other slid up my leg and cupped my wetness.

I rocked my hips in invitation. He watched his fingers circle me before two of them disappeared into me. He studied my face for a reaction as he circled his fingers then bent them to rub my G-spot. My hips bucked involuntarily and he withdrew his fingers as he leaned forward. His lips took mine in a passionate kiss that twirled and circled. Slow then fast, slow then fast, his tongue controlled the pace as I felt his cock nudge my opening. As we kissed, he lifted and bent one of my legs so my foot was flat on the rock.

"I can't wait any longer." When I felt the head of his erection penetrate me, I closed my eyes. "This is the first of many, Jenn. Memorize everything about this moment. Feel the rock scrape your back. Feel the rope chafe your wrists. Hear the clink of the bolt holding you down. Remember what it feels like when I hit the end of you."

And he did.

I felt him nudge a spot deep inside me, stretching me and filling me in a way I had never known. "Oh, fuck. Hold on." He stopped moving, fully settled inside me. His head dropped so his forehead rested against my collarbone. His pants heated my skin as he exhaled. "You feel so good."

I opened my eyes and looked at the wide blue sky through strands of his dark hair criss-crossing over my face. The small wisps of clouds that occasionally dotted the sky were tinted pink from the setting sun. Finally his hips pulled away and started a slow, steady rhythm.

With one hand, he turned my chin so that I looked over my arm to the edge of the cliff and the horizon beyond. He laid his left cheek on my right one so we could both look at the sun burning a bright orange streak across the sky. His hips continued their purposeful rhythm, but he'd often change angles and depth as his cheek stayed glued to mine.

Declan trailed soft kisses up my neck and along my collarbone. His touch was soft but my senses were so attuned that I felt his long eyelashes blink against the skin on my neck.

We didn't say anything in that moment.

At least with words.

And it lasted a long while before he cemented a lesson I'll never forget. "You climbed a fucking mountain. There's nothing you can't do."

The beauty and tenderness of the moment bubbled out of me with a whimper. I felt a tear drop from the corner of my left eye. He lifted his cheek from mine, so I turned my face to look up at him. His face was placid as he smiled down at me and used his thumbs to wipe the tears from under my eyes.

"I want to do it all with you," I confessed.

"We will. Whatever we have to do, we'll find a way." He held himself still as he groaned. I felt him pulse inside me. I used my inner muscles to squeeze him. His eyes screwed shut and dropped his forehead to my breastbone. "Jenn, I'm not sure how much ..."

The tenderness of the moment combined with the intensity of his thrusts kindled a new wave of want. "I'm there, Declan. I'm there."

He lifted his eyes to mine as he pushed my bent knee to my chest. He surged into me two times before he ground his pelvis against my clit. That unexpected pressure combined with his words got me to the peak. "Let go for me, Jenn."

"Declan. I'm coming. I'm coming!" My screams were loud enough that I didn't have to imagine them echoing through the canyon. My hands clenched above me in the restraints as my toes curled and flexed in my shoes.

"Ah, fuck." Declan thrust twice more, rubbing my spine against the jagged rocks before he levered his upper body off mine with both arms. He arched his back, tilted his chin up, and closed his eyes as he roared his release. The picture of his agonized face in ecstasy reminded me of a wild, untamed wolf howling to the moon.

He collapsed on top of me and reached a hand above my head. I heard the click of the carabiner.

"Belay off, Jenn."

Chapter Twelve

"We really should be getting off the rock before it gets dark," Declan said while we pulled on our clothing. We reattached our harnesses, tied the figure-eight knots, and pulled on our helmets. Declan rigged the rappel devices and ropes. I used two chains of quickdraws to anchor us to the bolts at the cliff edge so if one failed, we would have another available. Since this would be a full rope-length rappel, Declan tied two ropes together with the flat overhand knot at the anchor. We worked together seamlessly as twilight threatened to make the already scary rappel even more so.

Since I was the weaker climber, I went first, so I stepped to the edge of the cliff and turned around, preparing to lean backward and begin the rappel. Declan tugged me off the cliff by the front of my shirt. "Whoa. Two things. This is such a long rappel that you need to knot the end of the rope to be sure you don't rappel off the end of it. And just for my sanity, back up your rappel device by running the brake rope around your hip. This will help you if you lose the grip on the brake rope."

His conscientiousness melted me. I stepped forward into him, completing the extra safety steps, and kissed his cheek. "See you at the bottom."

With my feet on the edge, I bent my knees, leaned backwards, and let the rope slide through the rappel device until my legs were perpendicular to the cliff edge. When my legs left the rock, I swayed gently and let gravity take my weight. Since the cliff was concave, the farther down I went, the farther away the edge of the rocks were. I dangled off the rope, controlling my slow descent with pressure from the brake rope. The sliver of remaining sun cast my larger-than-life shadow on the adjacent rocks. Foot by foot, I lowered from the height that had made me a new woman in so many ways. It was funny how this time I was flying, literally suspended in the air, but I felt more grounded than I had in years.

My feet crunched the rocks below at the end of the 110-foot rappel. I bolted into the safety anchor and Declan began to rappel. He reached me at the Crow's Nest in minutes, pulled on one end of the rope to release it from the bolt above, and stowed away the ropes. Then we downclimbed off the gradually sloping south side.

It was nearly dark when we got to our packs. Luckily, we'd planned on staying in a designated overnight camping area a short distance away, so we hiked there using the flashlight to guide our footsteps. The forest was silent minus the rocks crunching under our feet and the occasional owl hooting its hello through the trees. The night air had chilled considerably, but without a breeze, we would be comfortable sleeping in the tent, curled in the same insulated sleeping bag.

The camping area was vacant when we arrived. It was a small clearing surrounded by towering pines whose shadows were shortening thanks to the rising half moon. We assembled the tent within fifteen minutes, filled it with our gear, and zipped it closed. The tent was cozy inside, but what made our flashlight-lit powwow more intimate were the small acts of homemaking we completed alongside each other. Declan unrolled the two-person sleeping bag while I unpacked a small cooler with sandwiches, apples, and water.

These simple acts allowed my mind to relax. No longer feeling the need to be hyper-aware, I let down my guard. So what surprised me was that my hands started to shake and jitter when I asked them to zip up the cooler. They shook more violently when I attempted to open a sandwich bag. Suddenly unnerved, my voice wavered when I called out. "Declan?"

He crawled over immediately, sensing my unease. "What's wrong?"

At least that's what I think he said. I couldn't be sure. My head had started to pound and my stomach was turning in circles.

"Oh, hell." He sat down behind me and wrapped his legs and arms around me.

"What's going on?"

"Adrenaline crash. I knew this would happen."

I couldn't control my shaking muscles like I was hypothermic, but my skin was clammy and warm.

"First, we're going to eat something. It's been too long. Your blood sugar could be low."

"Yuck. Nothing sounds good." I pushed away the apple he tried to bring to my lips.

"Eat it, Jenn. I mean it. The middle of the wilderness is not the place to have a hard crash." He brought it to my mouth again. I bit it reluctantly, but when the juice burst into my mouth, my stomach growled for more. I grabbed the apple and took two more big bites before I drank half a bottle of water. Declan followed my lead and began eating in silence next to me. There was something so affectionate about sharing a meal with him after what we had experienced. Slowly, my muscles stopped twitching and my stomach begged for more food.

It was only then that I noticed something I had missed before. A trail of blood had dried down Declan's left shin from his knee to his ankle. Some bright red blood still oozed from his knee. "Declan, you're bleeding."

Continuing to eat, he didn't even look at it. "Yeah. It's just a little scrape. Happened when my foot slipped on the ledge."

That's not a little scrape. "How the hell did I not see

this before?"

He shrugged. "Your mind was prioritising, noticing only the things it needed."

I launched into protective mode, unable to finish eating until I'd taken care of him. I found the first aid kit in my pack, opened it, and ripped open the small package of antibiotic wipes.

"Really. It's fine. You don't need to ..." His protest was cut short when I swiped the cloth over the cut. He hissed, but didn't say anything else.

"Wow. That hurts like hell. Why aren't you cussing?"

He raised a single eyebrow as if to say, "Dude, I'm a man. I can take the pain."

"All done." I packed away the bloody cloth and pulled out a large square Band-Aid.

As I was about to open it, he snatched it from my hand and shoved it back into the kit. "Nuh-uh. That's where I draw the line. I don't need a Band-Aid."

I smirked at his tough guy side as I finished my sandwich. Protesting the lack of sleep the night before and the odd adrenaline rushes throughout the day, I yawned, overwhelmingly tired. Although I had all the intentions of having more sex in the tent, my body had started to shut down.

"Time for bed." He pulled at the hem of my shirt, but I held my arms down like a toddler protesting night-night time.

"But I wanted to ..."

"Later. We're both tired after a long day."

"Yeah. Yeah. Pretty soon ..." What came out next was one of those comments I should have run through my head again before blurting it out. I meant it as a joke, but it tornadoed around the cramped tent, leaving tension in its wake. "... one of us will have a headache. We sound like an old married couple."

Declan had pulled off his shirt and begun unhooking

his shorts. But at my last few words, his eyes darted to mine and his hands stilled. In silence, we stared at each other. I would have given anything to know what was going through his mind since his indecipherable face gave nothing away. But he dodged the issue of "married couple."

"Here, let me take out my dentures before we climb into bed, dear," he said, miming taking out his teeth and falling awkwardly into the sleeping bag with his arm outstretched. He patted his shoulder like he was fluffing a pillow for me.

I laughed off his attempt at levity. I finished stripping off my dirty clothes and climbed in next to him. I zipped up the bag and turned off the flashlight before I tucked my head into the cushion of his shoulder. My neck fit the curve of his shoulder like two puzzle pieces.

He kissed my forehead as I snuggled in. "I'm proud of you, Jenn."

I didn't remember falling asleep.

The promise of "later" was fulfilled in the early morning hours before daybreak. Declan had turned on the flashlight, which cast shadows on the roof of the tent. The single light illuminated half of his face above me when I opened my eyes from a deep sleep. His fierce, penetrating gaze caught my attention instantly. He had already crawled on top so I could feel his heavy erection against my leg.

"I need you," he confessed.

I revelled in my power to affect this man. "I need you too."

His hands lazily travelled the length of my naked torso as a pecking kiss gave way to a possessive one that crested and swelled like ocean waves. There was no hurry or pressure in his touch. His fingertips feathered over my ribs before they traced over my belly button and to my hip bone. I lifted my hand to his erection. My fingers barely touched it as they encircled the base. I rubbed up and down lightly a few times before squeezing more firmly. After only a few firm pulls, he broke the kiss and pulled my hand off.

"We're going to try something else tonight." He placed my right wrist palm up next to my right shoulder and did the same to my left. He patted each twice to signal I was to leave them there. He lifted his hand in front of my face so I could see his pointer finger pressing against his thumb like he was pinching a grain of salt.

"See this little string?"

There was little light in the tent, but I knew there wasn't any string there.

I nodded.

"Words."

"Yes. I see the string."

"Good. This little string is going to tie down your wrist so it can't be moved." He mimed tying a string around my right wrist so well that my mind double-checked to be sure there wasn't one there.

"And this string," he held up another empty hand, "will keep this wrist from moving." Again, he mimed tying, this time my left wrist.

He levered up to inspect his work as much as the restrictive sleeping bag would allow. "Beautiful. They should hold perfectly."

With that, his head disappeared under the top of the sleeping bag, and I was left staring up at the roof of the tent. His tongue circled one beaded nipple before he sucked it into his mouth. One, two, three sucks later, he licked his way to the other side, repeating the same torment. My hands begged to slide into the bag to grab his hair. They pleaded to ghost down his back so I could leave scratch marks up his back.

But I willed them to be still as I thought about the restraints at the top of the mountain. It was so much easier when I could pull on them, their firmness reminding me I wasn't in control. Now the imaginary restraints weren't taking away my choice to move.

I was.

Two fingers eased into me. Their leisurely path circled inside me, frustrating me.

"More," I demanded with a tilt of my hips.

"Slow climb. Slow climb," he repeated with his lips against my nipple.

I huffed my impatience and decided to break his strings, but I heard a command from inside the sleeping bag before I could even attempt to. "Don't even think about moving them."

"How did you ...?"

His head came out from under the bag. "I know you by now." His fingers continued to circle while his thumb pressed smaller circles against my clit.

"I want ..."

"What do you want?"

Why must I always say it? "I want to come."

"Someday I'll get you to talk dirty to me. That's it?"

Fine. "Twice."

"Greedy little thing," he teased as his head disappeared again. He added a third finger to scissor inside me while his mouth took my nipple in strong, rolling sucks. The rhythm of his mouth and fingers matched, creating a cadence that ebbed through my body. My hips rolled to his pattern and my clit pulsed in response. He kept my nipple in his mouth as he drew his head away from my body, tugging at my chest in an odd combination of pain that radiated pleasure to my core. His mouth popped off at the same time his thumb pressed my clit firmly.

"Oh, oh, oh!" was all I could scream as my peak hit with a force that startled me. My skin buzzed after the third and final wave, and I was surprised when I opened my eyes to see his. He had watched me while I came, the

121

exposure unnerving me.

"That's one. Thanks for not busting my strings." He mimed untying them as I realized that my hands had never moved, even when I came.

"Turn over on your side." He spooned behind me so that I felt his erection against my ass.

"Hmm … sleeping bag sex," I mused. I had wondered how this was going to work, because the width of the bag didn't allow for much leverage if he got on top.

He lifted my top leg under my knee and placed my thigh over the top of his. He scooted closer so his engorged head entered me easily. I whimpered with the stretch as he entered me in one quick thrust. He must have heard me because his hand instantly pressed and rubbed against my clit to distract me from any discomfort. The penetration was so much deeper at this angle than during missionary on The Maiden, so this was the first time I realized how big he really was.

"So deep," he murmured against my back as he kissed a line from between my shoulder blades to the nape of my neck. His hand left my clit to grab beneath my knee and pull my leg as far up as the sleeping bag allowed. This new angle allowed for stronger thrusts that hit a spot deep within me. He rocked slowly at first then thrust so hard a few times that I could hear our skin slap together with the force. His hot breath became labored against my neck.

Declan changed the angle one last time as he bent my knee so it rested on the sleeping bag in front of me. He pushed my knee up so it almost touched my breast. With each push and pull in this new position, his erection rubbed against more of my over-sensitized skin. My backside was more exposed in this position, a fact I fully realized when one of his fingers snaked between our bodies and rubbed the outside of my tight hole.

I flinched. "Decl …"

"If you don't like it, we'll stop. But you might love it."

I'm not supposed to like this. I'm not supposed to want this. "OK."

He continued his long, rhythmic strokes that were slowly making me climb the next peak. His finger circled so long I almost begged for him to push in, but finally the tip of his finger penetrated my ring. He hardened further inside me as his finger slowly entered to the knuckle. "You still with me?"

"Yes. Yes." My skin had broken out into goose bumps and my nipples peaked. His finger moved and pressed against the thin layer of skin separating the two penetrations.

"I can feel myself in you. Feel you pulse, getting ready to come."

My hand moved to my clit and rubbed firm circles in one direction then the other. I moaned in warning. *I'm close. I'm close.*

He pressed his chest against my back as his rhythm became hurried. "Don't you fucking go without me. Don't you dare."

"I can't hold it. Please," I sobbed. Although my mind wasn't able to focus, the irony of the statement wasn't lost. The girl who once thought she was broken was now a woman attempting to hold back an orgasm.

"You will." His finger pumped and stroked with more force now, making me feel fuller. "I'm going over, and I'm going to drag you with me. Feel how full of me you are."

Including my heart. The thought tunnelled through me, and I was shocked that it didn't bother me in the least.

Three hard thrusts later, he roared as his erection hardened and twitched, hammering a new rhythm that gave me no choice but to follow.

"Declan. I'm coming. I'm coming," I bawled into the steamy, humid air. Tide after tide surged through me as white spots dotted my vision. My jaw clenched shut as the last waves ebbed away. Declan turned me over to face him.

Overcome with something I couldn't name, I buried my face into his smooth, sweaty chest and sobbed.

"Sweet girl. That one hit hard, didn't it?" He stroked the hair at the back of my head as I nodded and for the first time didn't ask me to answer with words.

He gave a voice to my some of my tears. "You liked it, but you didn't want to like it."

He let me nod my agreement.

Chapter Thirteen

"So you just packed up in the morning, hiked off the mountain, and went home?" Nina asked.

"Well, yes, but we also went for a big breakfast before driving home."

Hannah and Nina were riveted by the end of my play-by-play account of what had happened the previous weekend. For the first time in a long time, I had the story to tell.

"Damn. That was so hot, I'm sweating," Hannah said, flapping the front of her T-shirt against her chest. "And I can tell you're really happy."

"I *am* really happy, and I noticed this week there was a spring in my step. The confidence I gained climbing with Declan bled over to my day-to-day professor duties. I hadn't expected that, and I have him to thank for it."

"Does he have a brother? A best friend?" Nina asked.

I could hear the unguarded happiness in my laugh. "I don't know about a brother, but he's with his best friend now."

Nina leaned forward. "Really? Call him. Have them meet us here for lunch."

I shook my head even though her enthusiasm was endearing. I certainly wouldn't have minded seeing him. Hell, if I was honest, I missed him. "First, this is our *girls'* day out. Since I don't live with you any more, I miss you two. And, second, he's with his climbing buddy, Pierce. From what Declan says, Pierce is a master climber, and they're tackling Escape from Alcatraz today, so they're busy."

"They're what?" Hannah said. She asked Nina, "Am I the only one wondering what the fuck she just said?"

I laughed again. "They are climbing Escape from Alcatraz." I enunciated clearly, but since they weren't climbers, it meant nothing to them. I explained further, "It's a difficult 5.11 climb in River Wall, northwest of Boulder. All you need to know is that it's hard as hell, but super cool because a river runs below it, so when you climb it, all you see below as you climb is water."

"Whatever you say," Hannah said. "And by the way, I miss you too. But you changed the subject before I got the chance to ask what I really wanted to know. It's obvious when you two are together that you're attracted to each other, but do you love him?"

It was the same question I'd been asking myself for a week. "I don't know. Is that silly for a grown woman to say?"

Hannah shook her head. "Nope. I couldn't point to a specific time I fell in love with Beckett. It was instant attraction but the most gradual climb to love."

"If I had to come up with an answer, I would say that my heart is already involved. We talk every day. I miss him when I'm not with him. And I'd be heartbroken if we decided not to see each other any more."

"Yeah. When I almost lost Beckett was when I realized what I really wanted," she said, "That's when I realized I loved him."

Hannah's wistful face contrasted with Nina's look of antipathy. Why Nina was always so prickly when it came to relationship and commitment, I had no idea. I made a mental note to ask her later. Nina swiftly changed the subject. "And I miss you too. Ansley's awesome, but she's not you."

Now it was my turn to be lost. "Who's Ansley?"

Nina and Hannah shared a glance before Nina answered. "We had to take on a new roommate when you left. You know we're just poor grad students. You understand, right?"

Logically, I did, but I couldn't help feeling like I'd been replaced. "Of course. What does she do?"

"She's studying ballet at the university. She's graduating soon, and from the way it sounds, she's going to join Colorado Ballet right away. She's not really into the bar scene like us, but we get her to go out every once in a while. She'd have come today, but she's in rehearsal."

Hannah changed the focus back to me. "Speaking of rehearsals, how's the play going?"

"Well, the cast is finally getting along. The female lead is starting to come into her own, but she'll never be able to act like the male lead can."

"We should come see it. When is it again?"

No. No. No. They can't find out who the male lead is. "Oh, you don't need to." I realized from the silence that without the full story of why I didn't want them there, my comment was sure to have sounded rude.

"Sorry. I didn't mean it like that. Of course you can come to support me if you want to. It runs for ten days, and opening night is in two weeks. That's why I told Declan he had to be careful today. We couldn't afford –"

Oh shit, shit, shitty shit. I took a drink of water, hoping to hide my tell behind the glass.

I failed.

Nina's eyes narrowed on me as she sat forward. "Why does Declan have to careful? What does he have to do with the play?"

I saw the moment when Hannah connected the dots. "Holy shit, Jenn. Please tell me he's not in the play. He's a student, isn't he?"

My forehead hit the table in front of me and I mumbled into it. "He's in the play. He's Orlando. But it gets worse." I decided to rip the Band-Aid off. "He's *my* student."

The gasps around the table made me lift my head. Their

127

unblinking eyes were as wide as golf balls. I'm not sure I'd ever seen Nina this surprised. "Fuck, Jenn. When I told you to find a bad boy, I just wanted you to swim in the deep end of the pool, not fucking deep-sea dive in the Mariana Trench."

"I know. I know. This is a colossal mess. We tried to fight against whatever 'this' is, but we couldn't. We're keeping it a secret until he graduates in a month, and then it won't matter."

"But if you're found out, you'll lose everything, Jenn," Nina said.

"There's no warnings or do-overs. You know that," Hannah added.

Given that my friends were usually up for almost any casual hook-up, their expressions of fear added fuel to my own. I had been able to push it to the back of my mind since last weekend, but now my worry had reignited. "What should I do?"

"Call if off for a month." Nina's reply was immediate. It made me sick to even consider it. Hannah's distressed look told me she understood how painful it would be to take that advice.

"I *know* I should. I'll think about it." *Not in a million years.* "I really will."

"That was almost convincing," Hannah said.

"That'll happen when the devil shits an ice cube," Nina agreed.

Laughing loudly at Nina's one-liner, I almost missed the familiar ring tone. I pulled my phone from my purse to see Declan's name on the caller ID. I swiped to accept the call and put the phone to my ear with a goofy grin. "Hey. That was a quick climb. Must have gone well."

"Jenn? Is this Jenn?"

"Yes. Who is this?"

"This is Pierce. Declan wanted me to call you. I'm driving him to Boulder Community Hospital."

I don't remember pressing the "end call" button, but I must have. "I gotta go."

"What? What's wrong?" Hannah asked.

"That was Pierce. He's taking Declan to the hospital." I shoved a twenty on the table and scooted out of the booth.

"Wait. Do you want us to come with you?"

"No. Not yet. I don't know anything. Pierce said he'll see me in the lobby, so let me talk to him first. I'll call you when I know what's going on."

"We're here for you, honey," Nina said as she squeezed my shoulder.

"Thanks. That means a lot. I'll let you know."

I dashed out, ran to my car, and drove the twenty minutes to the hospital on autopilot. I was in too much shock to cry, although the floodgates were sure to open soon. Stopped at red light after red light, I pounded the top of the steering wheel in frustration. Then I reasoned with God. *Please let him be OK. I promise I'll go to church more. I'll donate to the homeless shelter. I'll do anything.*

Then the climber in me went through the scenario. River Wall was eighty feet high, and a fall from even half that distance would be fatal. Was Pierce a crappy belay? Did a fixed bolt give way? Declan was always so safety conscious, but even the best climbers died in freak accidents.

My hands were shaking on the wheel when I pulled into a parking space. I took the stairs down to the emergency entrance two at a time, my brain conjuring the worst "what ifs?" and my heart speeding with fear. I sprinted into the lobby out of breath from the combination of the run and bone-deep worry.

Then I realized I hadn't a clue what Pierce looked like. However, it didn't take me long to spot him as I scanned the waiting room. A tall, well-built man in hiking gear sat on the edge of the lobby chair with his elbows on his

129

knees. His hands gripped his hair as he stared down at the dirty carpet. What scared me most was that he was rocking forwards and back in nervousness or frustration.

"Pierce?" I said when I stood in front of him.

His head shot up as he stood. "Yes. Are you Jenn?"

"Yes. Declan's ..." I'm not sure why I hesitated, and I hated that I did.

"Girlfriend, I know. He told me about you."

It warmed me to know Declan had told him about me. About us. But what we were doing in Boulder Community Hospital was much more important. "Is he OK? What happened?"

Pierce sat down on the lobby chair and motioned for me to sit next to him. My wired muscles protested, but I followed anyway. What I really wanted to do was burst through the doors and order to see him.

"They just took him back, so I don't know exactly what's wrong, but I think he'll be fine."

"What happened?" I repeated.

Pierce groaned as if was reluctant to tell the story. "When we got there, the rock was packed. You know there's like thirteen climbs on the rock, and they're spread out enough to allow for simultaneous climbs. So, we got to Escape from Alcatraz, and thankfully we were first to choose it. We decided I would go first so Dec could see my holds. He was going to belay from the ground."

"And? Go on." I was getting impatient.

"We put on our gear, and you know Dec, he double-checked everything. While we were getting ready, we saw these two yahoos setting up on the route next to us. They had no business climbing Redneck Hero. I mean, it was a fifty-fifty chance one of these guys was going to take a serious fall. And the idiots weren't wearing helmets."

"Shit."

"Yeah, shit. I bet you can guess what happened after that."

My shoulders slumped. "Declan gave them his helmet."

"Well, first we tried to kindly tell them that maybe they should try an easier route first. But they weren't having it, so Dec at least convinced them to have the climber wear his helmet. It wasn't a perfect fit. Dec has a big head." He smirked at his own joke.

"Ha ha. Go on."

"The guy took it, of course, since Dec can be so persuasive." *Don't I know it.* "I *knew* it wasn't a good idea, and I told him so, but he wasn't having any of it. He said he'd wear my helmet when he climbed. So I was about halfway up the route when my foot slipped, and instinctively, I grabbed for anything I could reach. It happened to be a hold I had previously tested and determined wasn't reliable. The boulder gave way and took some smaller rocks with it on the way down."

"No. No. No." It was my turn to rock with my hands in my hair. "You know in the spring time there are more rollers. You *know* this. River Wall is notorious for them."

"I know. I should have listened to my instinct." I could tell he felt responsible, so I instantly felt bad for jumping on his case. Accidents happen. "But I yelled 'Rock, rock, rock!' like we're supposed to. He said he didn't hear it because the river was running so loudly. The spring run-off from the winter snow was incredible this year.

"Thankfully, he must have seen some of it coming, because he ducked just in time to miss the big boulder. If he hadn't, I'm not sure what would have happened."

I felt nauseous thinking about it.

"But when he ducked out of its path, he got hit by some of the other falling rocks. They weren't huge, but you know it doesn't take much."

"So he got hit in the head?"

"Yeah." He gauged my reaction as he added, "It wasn't pretty."

The bile tasted awful. I swallowed, trying to wet my

dry mouth and throat. I finally got the courage to ask, "Did he lose consciousness?"

"I don't think so. By the time I got down to him, other climbers who had seen what had happened were tending to him. He was pretty dazed, but beyond that I couldn't say." Pierce put his hand on my shoulder as I leaned forward. "You should know, he was pretty bloody. Cuts on the head really bleed."

I held up an open palm. "Stop. I can't take any more. Just give me a minute."

"I'm sorry, Jenn. His safety was my responsibility. I'll do whatever I can to help."

Silently, I continued to rock forward and back, deep in thought. I remembered what Hannah had said earlier at lunch.

When I almost lost Beckett was when I realized what I was missing. That's when I realized I loved him.

Even though Hannah had lost Beckett in a very different way, I could relate. In the last hour, I hadn't thought about the play, the rehearsals, or who would take over Declan's role if he couldn't perform. All I could think about was the man who'd become my best friend, my climbing partner, my lover.

"Congratulations on The Maiden, by the way," Pierce interrupted my thoughts a while later. "He told me about it. He was so proud of you."

Pierce was doing everything he could to make me feel better, and I hadn't been as concerned about him. Hell, he'd known Declan much longer than I had. I turned to give him a hug. "Thanks for calling," I said as I pulled away.

"He told me to. He said you'd worry."

"He's right."

About an hour later, I didn't recognize his name when the nurse called into the waiting room. "Who's here for

William Monahan?"

"We are," Pierce answered for us. We walked side by side to the nurse waiting at the door to the back rooms. Sets of eyes followed us, most likely recognizing the famous name. His father's name. "We're Dec's friends."

"Ah, yes. Declan. Follow me this way." She led us down a white hallway that reeked of antiseptic and rubber gloves. Her rubber shoes squeaked on the polished tile until she stopped in front of room four.

"Go on in. The doctor will be in to talk to you in a few minutes." Her casual smile didn't raise any warning signs, but I was scared of what I would see when I walked in. Did he want me here? He didn't like me tending to his small cut in the tent. He didn't like appearing vulnerable in front of me, and combined with a possible head injury, I hadn't a clue what would greet me behind the closed door.

"Let's go, Jenn." Pierce's light touch on my shoulder guided me into the room.

Strangely enough, the first thing I noticed was the hospital-issue white T-shirt he was wearing. It wasn't one that he would have owned. *He needed a new one because the other was covered in so much blood.* My imagination ran wild.

Then I noticed he was asleep. His pale face as he lay reclined on the hospital bed faced towards the window like he had been looking out when he dozed off. The IV in his left arm ran to a bag of clear liquid, and, thank the Lord, there were no beeping machines to freak me out more than I already was. From the doorway, I could read the blood pressure monitor's encouraging results.

Declan must have not been very deep in sleep because his eyes opened as he turned his head in our direction. His eyes seemed to focus well, and his speech wasn't slurred. "Hey, Pierce."

"Hey, man. You're looking a lot better. I brought ..." Pierce nudged me forward.

"Who is this pretty little thing?"

Chapter Fourteen

He doesn't remember me. I stood still, horrified.

And Pierce was laughing. Fucking. Laughing. "Dec. That was really cruel. Look at her. She's going to pass out."

Declan was laughing too as he reached his right hand to me. "I'm sorry, Jenn. That *was* really cruel. I had to fake amnesia just to see what you'd do. I'm glad you're here." The fact he was laughing as he said it didn't make his apology sit well. I was glad to see his humour, though, which meant his injuries couldn't have been severe. Right?

I stalked over to his bed. "William Declan Monahan, I don't know whether to slap you or kiss you."

He tapped his finger to his bottom lip. "Hmm ... tough decision."

I raised my hand, and he flinched away playfully because we both knew I wasn't going to hit him. Instead, I leaned in for a kiss. The peck reminded me where we were and why. His lips were dry and chapped. There was dried blood around his hairline that had been missed when the rest of his face had been cleaned. He smelled like sterilized bandages, and he didn't turn his head in my direction, making the kiss awkward and short.

I still loved it anyway.

"Don't ever do that to me again," I whispered against his lips.

"I will never fake amnesia again," he joked, so I gave him my patented teacher-glare. His jovial mood turned pensive. "I know. It was stupid. Really stupid. I'll be fine for the play. Don't worry."

"I'm not worried about the play." I wanted to tell him more, especially after my talk with Hannah and Nina, but with Pierce in the room and his recent injuries, it wasn't the time or place. So I sat next to the bed, holding his hand. Pierce left the room to take a phone call, but it was most likely to give us some privacy. For a few minutes, he lay back and smiled at me while we chatted, but soon his eyelids drooped, and I let him wander into sleep.

For the next hour, I watched his long eyelashes flutter against his cheekbones. His steady, even breaths lifted the thin, white sheet and his tan arms and hands were free of any scrapes or cuts. I ran my fingers back and forth over his knuckles, circling each one with my fingertip before moving on to the next. Soon, his hand was wet with tears I hadn't realized I was crying. I was thankful that Declan was asleep so I didn't have to offer an explanation.

Sure, I was crying because of my relief that he was apparently OK after what could have been a fatal accident.

Those were happy tears.

But I was also crying because I was beginning to realize the depth of feeling I had for this man.

I guess those were happy tears, too, but they were edged with pain and vulnerability.

Later, Pierce came back in, sat in a chair next to the window, and scrolled through his phone while Declan slept. Everything in me wanted to crawl into bed next to him and pillow my head against his shoulder. I needed to wash him so he smelled like my Declan.

An eternity later, the doctor finally came in. He checked Declan's vitals, which made him wake up. "Good to see you took a nap. Hi, Declan. I'm Dr Nova, and I took charge of your care today."

"Yes, thank you. I remember."

Dr Nova smiled. "Good. I thought you would. Given the lacerations to your head and the nature of the injury, I ordered a CT scan of your brain, which revealed you have a mild concussion. The various lacerations on your scalp took ten stitches. The good news is that I think you'll make a full recovery, and I am discharging you this evening. Let's do one final check before we get you out of here. First, do you have someone who can stay with you for the next twenty-four hours?"

"Yes." My response was immediate, and Declan didn't show any surprise or objection.

"Good," said Dr Nova. Then he asked Declan, "Do you want them here while I do the exam?"

"Sure. They can stay."

"Fine. The nurse said that the vomiting has stopped, but do you feel nauseous?"

Vomiting? Nobody told me he was vomiting.

"No."

"Good. Do you have a headache? Scale of 1 to 10?" The doctor tilted Declan's head up so he could shine a light into each eye.

"Yes. About a 7."

Now I'm going to be the one to vomit. He said "mild concussion" right?

"That's to be expected. We'll get you up and walking soon, but are you dizzy or do you have blurry vision?"

"Not sitting here."

"Good. You might find that you are sensitive to light, you might have balance issues, or find yourself more tired than usual. Given your excellent physical condition, I think your recovery time will be a short one, but everyone's timetable is different. Some people feel fine hours later while others have what is called post-concussion syndrome that can last for months. The most common complaints during that time are headaches and blurry vision. You might also feel like you can't concentrate as well as you used to. The biggest thing is don't try to do too much too fast. Get back into your daily routine gradually, and listen to your body when it tells you

you've done too much. No strenuous physical activity for a few days, and I recommend not returning to rock-climbing for at least a month."

Then Dr Nova turned his attention to me. "In the next twenty-four to forty-eight hours, you will want to monitor him for symptoms that suddenly appear, reappear, or worsen. If he resumes vomiting, has difficulty speaking, sudden memory lapses, or one pupil much bigger than the other, you'll want to bring him in quickly. Expect that he'll be tired, he'll have a headache, and he'll probably be cranky. But I suspect, given the CT scan, that everything will be fine. I'll give you a prescription for some pain medication, but he can take over the counter pills instead if he chooses. Let him sleep as much as he wants, and don't feel the need to wake him up. Any questions?"

"What about the stitches?"

"Ah, yes. Keep them dry for twenty-four hours. You can then wash his hair gently, but don't scrub. Be sure to keep them as dry as possible. Look for any signs of infection or if he starts running a fever. Declan, do you have any questions?"

"No. I think we're good. Thank you, doctor."

The doctor left the room, promising discharge papers in the next hour. Pierce and I left the room while the nurse helped Declan get changed.

Pierce turned worried eyes on me in the lobby. "Are you sure you don't want me to watch him? I feel responsible."

I placed my hands on his arms to reassure him. "I'm sure. It was an accident. If you want to help, maybe you can take in his prescription and get some groceries for us for the next couple days. I'm sure Declan has nothing in the kitchen. And if you could get me a toothbrush, that would be great."

He looked relieved to help. "Sure. I'll do that now and meet you at the house later." He left while I waited for the discharge papers. After more than an hour, they arrived, and I drove my car around to the front to pick him up. They brought Declan to my open car door and helped him from the wheelchair to the passenger seat. He moved gingerly but steadily. I reached over him to secure his buckle as the nurse closed the door. His smile was genuine, even though I could tell it was killing him to have me see him like this.

"Pierce is meeting us at your house with pain meds and some groceries. I'll stay with you over the weekend, and then we'll see how you're doing before making a decision about the rest of the week."

He turned his head towards me as it lay against the head rest. "This will be the first time you've been to my place."

"Wishing you'd cleaned?" I joked.

"Nah. Don't mind the stack of porn on the kitchen table." He was so poker-faced, I didn't know if he was serious. His chuckle told me the truth. "Man, you're gullible today."

"And you're cruisin' for a bruisin'."" We continued like that for the rest of the drive, both of us trying to add levity to what could have been a terrible situation. We skirted around any serious emotions in favor of trying to revive the playful banter that was the norm for us.

I pulled up to Declan's apartment ten minutes later, and Pierce was in his car waiting for us. He came over to Declan's side and watched him carefully as Declan got out and walked to the apartment complex's entrance. Declan punched in the code and opened the door. We had to go up one flight of stairs to reach his second floor apartment. He gave me his apartment key and motioned me through the door, so I led the threesome up the stairs.

Halfway up the stairs, I heard a murmured "fuck". I turned around to see Pierce steady Declan's swaying body. Declan grabbed the handrail for balance while his eyes begged me not to say anything. Pierce's eyes swung to mine to gauge if I had seen Declan's stumble.

Declan was a prideful man, and if this was difficult for me, it must have been torture for him. I decided to let it go, but a part of me wanted to march him back to the hospital. I quickly turned the key in the lock and opened the door. Pierce flanked Declan down the hallway and straight into what I assumed was Declan's bedroom.

"Thanks, man," Declan said as he lay down in bed and pulled the sheets over him.

"No problem. I'm going to get the groceries and meds from the car. Anything else you need?"

Declan's eyes closed and his breathing was labored like he was trying to get on top of the pain. "No. Just my girl."

Steady, my racing heart. Pierce left in silence as I toed off my shoes and gently climbed in next to him. He lifted his arm so that I could snuggle next to him. I knew we needed to talk, but he seemed to be in a lot of pain.

I reassured him. "Sleep. I'm not going anywhere."

Chapter Fifteen

Although I hadn't intended to, I must have fallen asleep.
When I woke, no light was coming in through the curtains.
I extricated myself from Declan's hold as smoothly as I
could. Hungry, I went searching for some food and found
a note from Pierce.

*You were sleeping, so I decided to head out. All the
food is put away, and the toothbrush, deodorant, and extra
clothes are on the couch. Sorry, I didn't know what kind
you used. I hope I got the right sizes. There are some
movies too. Call me if you need anything.*

He ended the note with his phone number, and I texted
him a quick thanks for his thoughtfulness. I began cooking
dinner as quietly as I could, but soon, I heard Declan
stirring in his bedroom.

I found him sitting on the edge of his bed, elbows on
his knees. "You OK? It's time for some pain meds."

"Just Advil. I don't like the other stuff. It makes me
loopy."

I brought back the bottle of Advil and a glass of water.
He took the pills and drank the entire glass. "This wasn't
how I pictured our first night together in my apartment to
be."

"I'm just glad there is a first night." I couldn't help my
voice wavering.

"Oh, Jenn. Come 'ere." He held out his arm so when I
sat next to him, his arm flexed as it pulled my shoulder
flush to his chest. "Don't cry. I'll be fine. We get to play

nurse for the next few days."

"Very funny." I slapped his shoulder. "Doctor said no physical activity for a while. But I will enjoy taking care of you. Do you want to eat dinner in the kitchen or have it in bed?"

"I'll come out. Thanks for staying, by the way." He followed me through the hallway. We passed the living room on the left and turned right into the kitchen. He sat at the table, his eyes distant and his head hung low, while I plated the soup and toast and placed the food in front of him.

"When do you think we should call Dr Burrows?" he asked without meeting my eyes.

"Let's see how the night goes. I think you should let the understudy take over for a few days, and maybe in the middle of the week you can try to get back on stage."

"But we only have two weeks." He tested the heat of the soup against his lips before taking a spoonful. "Dinner tastes good. Thank you."

"You're welcome. But let's not worry about the two weeks." I squeezed his hand across the table. "Orlando is getting stronger. I can feel you let go sometimes, and those moments are becoming more frequent."

"Let go?"

"You've begun to let go of the control you like to have over a scene. I see you reacting more spontaneously to things the other actors are doing. That give and take makes your character stronger. There's no doubt you're a gifted actor – the most talented on that stage. Take confidence in that."

"Your confidence in me makes me believe it."

I've thought that a few times myself.

He continued, scowling. "But I still struggle with act four. My dad will be able to spot those weaknesses a mile away."

"Wow. I'm surprised. I didn't know you were thinking

142

about your dad so much."

"I didn't think I would care this much, either, but I do. I wonder why he's coming sometimes. Will he judge me as an actor, or simply be proud of me as a son?"

I placed my hand on his leg in silent support.

His warm hand covered mine. "It's sad to say that I don't know my own father well enough to simply be happy that he's coming."

I didn't know him at all, so I couldn't offer much insight. "We'll make sure you're ready. Let's just focus on recovering first."

He smiled warmly and his eyes skimmed the room as he asked, "So what do you think?"

I hadn't taken the opportunity to look around since I'd been so worried about him. He watched me as I scanned the small apartment. It was surprisingly clean and clutter-free. The eggshell-white walls were bare except for the occasional framed photos of Declan and his climbing buddies on or in front of a rock formation. His sunglasses and tan made him look years younger, and even though he wasn't filled out in his younger pictures, I could tell there was an Apollo body under all the gangly limbs. Other than those pictures, there weren't any family photos, which made me sad. His widescreen television perched on the large wall in the living room in front of a modern black leather couch. There was a sense of humility in his possessions, especially given the money I'm sure he had access to. It was like he was trying to prove how different he was from his father's ostentatious reputation.

"It's you," I said simply. "I like it. Now let's go test out that couch and watch one of the movies Pierce got us." Declan started to take his mainly empty dishes to the sink, but I waved him off. "Don't worry, I'll get them later. I want you. On. The. Couch."

"Easy, woman. You know I don't take commands well," he joked. "But you can pull that voice out any time you like. It's hot. Damn, I wouldn't have thought I could get hard today," he said, adjusting himself in his pants. "It's going to be impossible not to take you the next few days."

He lay down gingerly on the couch while I put in one of the movies without looking at it and tried to decipher his array of remotes that looked like they could run the space shuttle with their buttons.

He laughed. "Here, give them to me." He navigated the controls with ease as I snuggled into his side.

As the opening credits began to roll, he grunted, "Really?"

"What? Pierce bought it. If you don't like it, don't blame me."

"Did you look at what you were putting in?"

"No."

It was then that I heard Declan's voice on the television. But it wasn't his. It was Will Monahan's. And it was his latest action movie. "Oh, hell. Sorry. I didn't realize …" I got up to change it.

"Wait. Don't. I should watch it before he gets here."

"You haven't seen it?"

"I made a point not to."

Curious, I asked, "But you want to now? Wait, why would Pierce choose this movie when he knows you're not close to your dad?"

"Well, firstly, Pierce and many of my friends around here don't know Will Monahan is my dad. I prefer it that way. And yes, I want to see it now."

"Why?"

"For the same reason I'm nervous about him coming to see me. Maybe I'll be able to see through him when he pretends."

It wasn't more than twenty minutes into the noisy car chase scene and Declan had fallen asleep. I lay still next to him and watched him breathe silently. I couldn't help but compare the man in my arms with the one on the screen. Their voices were eerily similar, even their mannerisms, but Will didn't have the commanding presence Declan had on stage. Will's grin was magnetic, for sure, but there wasn't a light in his eyes, and if it had ever been there, it had flamed out long ago.

Later, Declan sucked in a deep breath next to me as he woke. "Damn. Sorry, I fell asleep." He started to sit up and groaned.

"You OK?"

"I think I need some more pills."

I checked my watch. "Sure. Has it gotten worse?"

He walked to the hallway while I went to the kitchen for more pills. "No. About the same." When I looked over my shoulder, I saw him walking with one hand sliding along the wall for guidance.

My heart jumped in my chest, worried that maybe I was missing something. I wondered how much his pride was making him hide symptoms from me. I followed him into his room where I gave him some pills. He took them quickly and lay back on the bed.

"I know we have things to discuss, but I can't tonight. I promise we'll have the conversations tomorrow," he said.

I kissed him on his lips as he closed his eyes. "Tomorrow," I agreed, and I went out to clean the dinner dishes, wash my hair with Declan's shampoo, and happily brush my teeth with the wrong toothpaste.

I managed to sleep that night with one eye open.

Declan had a habit of waking me in the mornings with some inventive sexual escapade, but on Sunday, I awoke to a very different man. He was on his side facing me as he ran his fingers through my hair. He twirled the ends around his finger before laying the strands gently across the blanket. He repeated this motion with multiple strands until it appeared he was happy with the picture he had created.

"I like seeing you wake up in my bed."

Damn the no physical activity rule. I pushed his hair away from his forehead, but I must have brushed against one of the stitches because he winced.

"Sorry."

"S'OK."

"Let's get some food in you so you can take something for the pain."

"I'm feeling better this morning, like there's less of a fog, but that's probably a good idea."

I made us a breakfast of Denver omelettes and toast. Halfway through, Declan came and sat at the kitchen table. I felt his eyes following my every move.

"What?" I asked.

"I never thought I would get such satisfaction seeing you cook in my kitchen."

I nearly turned off the burners and said to hell with breakfast. If he hadn't needed his pills, I would have been content to let us starve. Instead, I plated the food and brought it to the table. "Eat first, Romeo. Talk later."

"There she goes ordering me around again. Wow, this is really good," he said after chewing the first bite.

I thanked him and gave him his pills. We chatted about the upcoming schedule, agreeing that he should take off the week from my class so he could focus on the play. The tentative plan was to have the understudy step in for a few days and have Declan return on Wednesday if he felt up to it.

Declan insisted on helping to wash the dishes, and afterwards, we took a nap on the couch as the Sunday news programs droned on in the background. We snacked on cheese, crackers, and fruit at lunchtime, and Declan called Dr Burrows to tell him what had happened. He agreed that Declan should step aside until at least

Wednesday. Declan insisted he come to rehearsals and sit in the auditorium, and although he originally was against the idea, Dr Burrows agreed once Declan convinced him that it would help to see the other actors from that perspective.

"It's been twenty-four hours," I declared after the conversation was over. I took his hand and pulled him down the hallway towards his bedroom.

"Damn, woman. If I had known you were hurting this much, I would've taken care of you this morning."

Then I realized what he thought I was leading him to do. "No. Not that." *Although I'd really love to.* "You need a shower, and I'm going to help you."

His look went from suave to horrified in a heartbeat. "Do I stink?" he asked, smelling his armpit.

I laughed at his gesture. I wouldn't have been caught dead smelling my own armpit in front of him. Such a guy. "No. You just don't smell like you, and it's freaking me out. I want to wash away everything that reminds me of what could have happened."

His face gentled as he put his arms around my shoulders. "You smell like my soap. Call me caveman, but somehow having my scent on you makes me hard as a rock."

"Hey, caveman. You get naked. Me get shower on. We meet in shower. Five minute." My cavewoman voice sucked, but he laughed anyway. He slapped my butt as I walked away, and I mocked a horrified look over my shoulder though my body's reaction was anything but.

I turned on the shower, stripped, and got in as the water turned from lukewarm to hot. The spray pounding my scalp and cascading over my shoulders soothed my sore muscles. I closed my eyes to wash my face and yelped when two large hands grabbed my breasts from behind. His hard arousal pressed against my lower back. "Someday I'll take your ass from behind. Would you trust

147

me to do that? Would you want that?"

More than I ever thought I would. "Yes. Maybe. But none of that today. Let's get you cleaned up." He grunted his dissent, but I wasn't going to lose this one.

I stepped to the side and guided him so the water would hit his chest but wouldn't pound on his sore scalp. I wet the washcloth, lathered the soap, and reached for his chest. "I can do this," he said, trying to take the washcloth from me.

I didn't let go. If he thought he was the only stubborn control freak in the shower, he was in for a surprise. "I know you can, but I want to do it. Please. Let me do this for you. And for me."

His eyes tested mine to see how firm I was. Seconds later, his hands released their grip on the washcloth and he hung his arms at his side, opening and offering his body to me. "Thank you. I know it isn't easy to let me take over."

The tick in his jaw agreed, but he stayed silent as his eyes followed my hands' movement. Soon, his muscles relaxed under my hands and his eyes closed as I washed his chest, back, and his shoulders, where I found a few small bruises forming.

There was no doubt this man was still virile and powerful, as evidenced by his arousal that brushed against my belly. Yet, the last few days had taken a toll not only on his body, but his mind too. He was like a race car that was used to running 220 miles per hour, and the accident had put a restrictor plate on him that wouldn't allow him to run over 200. I wanted to do something for him that would remind him of his strength, so I sank to my knees. His body shielded the spray from my eyes.

His eyes opened when he felt the washcloth brush over his erection. But he opened his eyes to where he thought my face was, and they snapped downward when he realized what I was doing. He bent over and tried to pull me up under my arms. "No, Jenn. You don't need to. I can't …"

"I don't want you to do anything to me. I just want to make you feel good."

A war battled inside him for a second, but then his grip on my arms loosened as he straightened and braced his arms on the sides of the shower. I memorized the dip and curve of each of his muscles before I turned my attention downward.

My hand guided his tip into my mouth. I sucked gently, letting my tongue explore the ridges and valleys. I concentrated on licking the sensitive underside that always elicited a groan from deep in his throat. His hips pumped forward, encouraging me to take more of his length. I sucked harder as I took all but the last few inches. I matched my rhythm with his hips' thrusts while my hand squeezed around the base. My other hand cupped and gently squeezed his sac, making him twitch against the roof of my mouth.

"Fuck, that feels so good." His breathing quickened. "Can you take it all?"

I popped off and looked up at him. "I don't think so. You're so big."

He grinned. "What guy doesn't want to hear that? But I think you could."

"How so?"

"You ever deep-throated?"

I shook my head. "No, but I'll try. Teach me."

His pupils widened, darkening his potent stare. His hand at the back of my head gently guided my mouth back onto his erection. "Do you have any idea what you do to me?" *Yes, if it is anywhere near what you do to me.* "Your mouth is so hot, and that tongue …"

He didn't finish his thought when his tip hit the back of my mouth. "Tuck your chin down. Breathe through your nose and relax the muscles at the back of your throat like you're swallowing a pill. Fuck, just like that."

149

I had everything under control until his hips inched forwards and pushed too far in my throat. I wasn't ready for it. I gagged and my eyes watered. He felt it and pulled out. "Shit. We're done. I didn't mean to push you." Once again, his hands went under my shoulders to pull me up.

I wiggled away and grabbed his length to put it back in my mouth. "Again."

He shook his head in protest. He was trying to be the gentleman, but I didn't want that. Not any more.

"I want to do this. I … liked it."

He studied me through the steam for the longest time like he was seeing a new woman. Maybe he was. Then he leaned down so our faces were inches apart when he asked a question to which I think he already knew the answer. "What did you like?"

I liked the feeling that I was being used for your pleasure. I liked being told how to please you, and I liked gagging on you. How fucked up is that? But I didn't have the guts to tell him, so I went for the safe answer. "I liked your hand at the back of my head."

His eyes darted across my face like he was trying to discover the hidden truth. "You liked me to take control."

"Yes."

"We already knew that. There's more. You're ashamed of it. Why?"

"Because I'm not supposed to like it."

"Says who?"

I answered with a shake of my head because I didn't know.

"We're done here. C'mon, Jenn. Get up." He sounded frustrated as he tried more forcefully to pull me off my knees.

"I don't know who, OK?" My frustration matched his.

"Then tell me what you liked." He punched each word like it was the last time he would ask.

The whole of it bubbled from me as I stood defiantly. If

he wanted the answer, he was going to get the answer. "I liked the feeling of being forced, OK? I *liked* choking on you. Hell, I wouldn't mind choking on you while you came down my throat. I wanted you to tell me I was a good girl, that I pleased you. I wanted you to hold me on you even if I struggled." New tears burned my eyes as I wondered what his reaction would be.

"*That's* the honest answer," he praised, as both his hands cupped my jaw. "Look at me, Jenn. You *never* have to hide your desires from me. There's *nothing* you could say that would repulse me. I want to hear your desires. Who cares what other people think about what we do behind closed doors if we both agree? If it's not my cup of tea, we'll deal with it. And the same goes for you. If you don't like something, everything stops. No questions asked. But that is the *last* time I want to hear you ashamed of what you *do* want. You hear me?"

I nodded "yes" as I wiped my cheeks and sniffled.

He turned around and reached for the soap. I caught his arm, and our eyes locked through the mist.

"Please. Don't stop now. I want to do this."

I felt the thousand drops of water pummel my skin as I waited for his response. He studied me, and it took all my strength not to look away.

Finally, he spoke. "OK, but we're going to do this right." He took my left hand in his right. "You're going to hold my hand and if it gets too much, you're going to squeeze. Got it?"

"Yes."

"You want this?"

"I have no doubt."

I barely caught his whispered command. "Then get back on your knees."

My clit pulsed at his command, and I sank to my knees, more sure of myself than ever. One of his hands held mine while the other guided my open mouth with gentle pressure on the back of my head. He had softened a little while we talked, so as my mouth pumped on his length to the rhythm he chose, I felt him harden against my tongue. Soon he was hitting the back of my throat again with inches yet to go. He lightly squeezed my hand as his other pulled me onto him with more force. I tilted my chin, breathed through my nose, and felt the tip of my nose brush his stomach.

"Fuck, yes. Right there," he hissed as he held that position. Then his hips started a slow retreat. "That's my girl. You like me taking control of your mouth, don't you?" I could only hum my assent. He already knew. "Well, here's a little secret. I love doing it." His hips thrust fast, catching me by surprise. I gagged once before I remembered to breathe through the instinct.

Don't pull me off. Don't pull me off. Thankfully, his hand at the back of my head pushed slightly harder. His voice was husky when he said, "Fuck. I can feel you swallowing around my cock. You squeeze me and you don't even know it. One more time. I can't hold it any more. You good with me coming down your throat?"

More than good. I nodded the best I could.

He retreated once more before he pistoned forward with a roar. But this time, I was ready. I started swallowing the second I felt the first hot rope of his cum hit the back of my throat. His knees buckled and the hand that was at the back of my head slapped against the shower wall. "Oh, hell. Take it. Take it all."

After he took another gasping breath, I was treated to the sweetest of rewards – the string of cuss words that told me he had lost all control. He pulsed for a few more seconds before he pulled out of me, and this time I didn't protest as he lifted me up.

His mouth connected with mine in a vehement kiss that said our thanks. I must have whimpered, because his right hand immediately went between my legs to rub my

152

engorged clit. "Your turn. Put your foot up on the bench. We're going to make this quick because I gotta sit down soon. I can't do to you what I really want, but I'm sure as hell not leaving you like this."

I thought about protesting. I really did. I hadn't led him to the shower thinking we'd get each other off. I had honestly wanted to get him clean and care for him. But I couldn't deny the ache that screamed for relief. I put my foot on the bench, opening to him. Two fingers penetrated my core easily while his thumb rubbed circles on my nub. He leaned in so our noses and foreheads touched. He closed his eyes and I followed. With my eyes closed, all the sensations my brain had been ignoring rushed into me. The steam swirled around us and the water prickled my skin as it pelted my back. The eucalyptus scent of his soap put me in a waterfall in the middle of a rainforest.

His fingers twisted while his thumb pressed hard.

"Yes. Yes. Yes," I chanted as my body twitched in pleasure. His hand continued to massage me as his teeth nibbled on the thin skin at the top of my shoulder. Despite its force, the orgasm was short and fled all too quickly. I felt my body chasing after the sensation as the intensity ebbed. Like a drug, I was addicted.

He pulled his fingers out and sat on the bench while I shampooed his hair, careful to avoid the stitches. As I gently massaged what I could, he wrapped his arms around my hips and laid his forehead against my stomach so I could feel his breath on my skin. Whether he was pensive or tired, I wasn't sure. Probably both. Every once in a while, his lips would reach out and peck the skin above my belly button. He didn't say anything as I used the washcloth to clean some of the dried blood from his hairline. A section of the washcloth turned pink as the water started to cool.

As I worked, I remembered that this whole thing in the shower had started as me taking care of him, but it had turned into a lesson about myself. Some of my tears mixed with the shampoo.

Those were happy tears.

After the shower, we dried off our bodies. Well, more specifically, we dried off each other's bodies, worshipping with the soft, white towels like something sacred had passed between us.

"Let's get in bed." He led me out of the small, steamy bathroom to a much colder bedroom. I crawled into the nook on his shoulder that seemed made for me as he pulled the covers over our naked, heated bodies. His fingertips trailed along my arm as he spoke. "I promised we would talk –"

"Yes. I want to say something first." I hadn't intended to interrupt him, but since the accident, I had things I needed to say and I didn't want to have them colored by what he intended to discuss. I didn't fear what he had to say. In fact, there was no mistaking in his eyes and his gestures the emotions he was feeling. But it was important for me to give voice to the hot air balloon that had been filling in my chest for the last few days.

"I'm not sure exactly what happened on The Maiden last weekend, but I feel like a different person."

His fingers paused almost imperceptibly before they continued on their trail. "You're still the Jenn I know."

His statement was true, but also false. "By name, yes. But maybe this whole time you knew a different Jenn than I did. It just took you and last weekend to … teach me."

"I didn't teach you anything, just like I didn't teach you anything in that shower. I just let you voice something you already knew."

"That's the thing," I insisted. "I don't think I knew it before last weekend."

"OK, then. What did The Maiden teach you?"

That was a question I wasn't prepared for. I was

prepared to tell him how *he* had changed me. I sensed there was an answer he was looking for, so I guessed. "To have more confidence in myself?"

"Maybe. But there's more. What's so amazing about The Maiden is that it takes you to some of the most amazing heights. But isn't it interesting that we spent a large portion of the climb downclimbing? In fact, we *had* to downclimb to get to the top."

He let the question swirl around me until I absorbed it. "You're saying that sometimes I have to go down to go up?"

"Sometimes there has to be pain overcome, conventional wisdom questioned, boundaries broken in order for there to be true growth. Isn't that what happened when I bolted you to the top of the mountain? Isn't that what kept your hands from breaking my strings in the tent? Isn't that what happened in the shower? You learned to overcome the shame of wanting something you had always assumed was wrong." After a pause, he continued, "I may have led you on that climb, but ultimately, you had to do it yourself. The ups *and* the downs."

His questions illuminated me like the sun moving to its apex. There were no shadows, only light. "The Maiden taught me to enjoy the downclimb," I whispered. He was right, of course. I had spent my entire life being the good daughter, the model student, the people pleaser, and the rule follower. I had never enjoyed anything that was taboo or considered shameful, never embraced anything other than order. I had become a product of expectations set by society, my parents, and myself. I had always thought of the downclimb struggles like pitfalls I had to overcome, not as things that should themselves be celebrated and embraced.

He silently let me work through that moment of understanding. Then he added, "Yes. I think you have realized the struggle is the most beautiful part of the journey."

Then I remembered the struggle and fear I'd felt yesterday and the accident that could have been so much worse. "Yesterday, I could have lost you. I just found you." *And myself.* "I don't want to lose you. Ever."

The tears were now flowing freely, and I couldn't have cared less as he shifted up on his elbows to look into my face. *Let him see.* His eyes lazily searched mine for a truth I think he already knew, so I gave it a voice. "I love you, Declan."

Although I knew he cared about me, I instantly worried what that four letter word would do to us as it floated and hovered between us like the steam in our shower.

His face registered no reaction at first. But then his eyes smiled. "I love you too, Jenn." The back of his fingers brushed against my cheek. "You're making me want things I never thought I'd want. After a lifetime spent witnessing the cruel jokes of relationships and marriages I swore I would never be in one. But you're the key to my lock. And you've walked through a gate I thought would never be opened."

The fire in my chest's hot air balloon torched again at his words, making it rise and expand with a warmth and a passion I'd never felt before.

"That gate has locked behind you. I don't think there will be anyone else that will ever open it." His thumb caught a tear that streaked to my hairline.

His brows furled. "But I wanted to tell you tonight that although I love you, I'm worried too."

A dark, sudden thunderstorm on the horizon threatened my cloudless sky. I sat up so we were perched on our knees, staring at each other on his bed. "What are you talking about?"

"Because we're in love, the stakes are *so* much higher. If this was simply a casual fuck, it would have been painless when it ended. If we ever caught a whiff that someone was going to expose our affair, it would have been so easy to walk away. But now I love you ..." He paused, scowling, like he couldn't put what he was thinking into words. He stared at the comforter for a while before his eyes darted to mine. "As much as it would kill me to leave you, I would bail if I thought we were found out. I love you enough to leave you, but for some reason I can't make myself do it now, when I should."

He was being practical with our hearts. This I could deal with. "But it's only for another month. Then you'll graduate, and we won't have to worry."

"If it's only a month, why can't we agree to cool it for a while so we don't have to jeopardize you?"

"What are you saying?"

"I'm telling you that one part of me wants to shield you from me, from a scandal, for the month. And if it takes a small downclimb to reach the peak, as painful as it would be, maybe it's the best choice."

It felt like someone was using a tweezer to tug hairs off my breastbone. "And the other part of you?"

"Wants me to say, 'Fuck it all. You're mine, and I won't give you up for anything.'"

I smiled through my tears. "I think I like that part better."

He allowed his face to register a smile through his worry. Then he took a deep breath. "There's one more thing."

Holy mercy. I can't take any more. The room was thick with tension, so I decided to use a joke to open the window and let it out. "You're pregnant?"

Declan's face blanked for a second with a bewildered stare, like he was looking at a piece of modern art that everyone understood but him. Then a sparkle of a smile blazed across his face as he put his arms around my neck and flopped onto his back. He brought me with him so my body lay over his. His belly laugh flooded me like rain

157

soaking a desert. He pecked my nose. "Thanks. We needed that. Getting too heavy, wasn't it?"

"Yep." I pecked him back.

"But in all seriousness, there is one more thing, Jenn."

"Go on."

"I've spent my entire life watching passionate, furious love burn bright then snuff out at the first sign of rain. I watched them fervently confess their love on sunny beaches, but it couldn't hold up when they got back to reality. I've seen how people use relationships to manipulate the person they're supposed to love, and it made me vow to never end up like my father. I guess what I'm trying to say is I'm not scared of love, but leery of commitment."

"So you're worried that commitment somehow taints love? Ruins it?"

Frustrated at his inability to communicate his feelings, he clarified after a long, heavy sigh. "It's just that I don't know what a healthy relationship looks like. I can fall in love, but I'm not sure I know what love looks like five years down the line. And I sure as hell have little confidence that it will burn so hot when I'm old and grey."

"Do you want it to? With me?"

He didn't hesitate. "Yes, but ..." His trailing voice sounded like a plea for help.

I drew small circles on his chest as I looked into his eyes, seeing a vulnerability that gutted me. "What do you need me to do?" I already knew what he wanted, but I wanted him to say the words, a trick he had taught me well.

He wanted me to show him that he was no more broken than I once thought I was.

In that moment, I vowed I would lead if he was willing to follow.

He whispered the first step on the journey. "Teach me."

Chapter Sixteen

I had always marvelled at the changing of the seasons in Colorado. Winter gave way to spring like there was a war waging for dominance. Winter would win one battle by dropping six inches of snow. Spring would win the next, melting the snow with a sunny, seventy degree day. But gradually, imperceptibly, the weather warmed so that one day we found ourselves complaining about the unbearable heat.

Declan's recovery was similar. On Monday, he left rehearsal with a nagging headache even though all he'd been doing was sitting in the auditorium. Bone-deep exhaustion circled his eyes with a black mask. Yet, on Tuesday, he'd stayed late to run through some troublesome scenes with Stephanie despite Dr Burrows's objections.

"We need you for the show, Declan. Focus on getting better. Don't push too hard."

"I feel good today," Declan had insisted, and he continued to run lines with Stephanie as Dr Burrows's worried scowl looked on.

But maybe Declan didn't understand his own limits because Wednesday was one of those bad days. He sat reclined in an auditorium chair next to me as he watched Stephanie and his understudy run through a scene. He would often groan and run his hands through his hair at a poorly-spoken line. He'd scrawl notes on my pad when he thought an inflection needed to be changed. His leg bounced next to mine in annoyance and restlessness. I had trouble focusing on the scene when I was so aware of the man sitting next to me. All I wanted to do was press up against his warmth, consequences be damned. But with Dr Burrows on my other side, our professional masks had to remain in place. Pretending there was nothing between us was becoming more exhausting by the day.

Declan left rehearsal early that day and I stayed late to work with Stephanie on some scenes in act four. I knew we planned to run the scene on Friday with Declan if he felt up to it, so I gave her advice on voice inflection, body language, and character development. Although she made some improvements, we wouldn't know if she could pull it off until Friday, when she stepped on stage with Declan.

After the extra rehearsal, I dragged myself back to my office to collect the papers I had to grade that night. In between some of the papers in the drop box on my door, I noticed a sealed envelope. I pulled out the handwritten note and smiled. Declan had continued to drop small notes to me, and, to be honest, I loved them despite the fact that it felt like high school all over again. He'd tell me he was thinking of me or that he missed the lunch dates that had, wisely, become fewer and farther between. But I loved them because sometimes his most honest and genuine emotions were communicated in those letters, and today's was no exception.

Sorry I had to leave early. Sitting next to you and not being able to touch you was torture. I'll call you tonight. LY

I tucked the note into my briefcase along with the students' papers and walked to my car in the fading evening light. I caved and grabbed some fast food on my way home and ate half of the large French fries before I pulled into my apartment complex.

I ate the rest of the greasy goodness at my kitchen table as I graded the papers written by my freshmen, all of which were predictably arguing for the legalisation of marijuana for reasons as compelling as "because this is what the world needs right now" or lowering the drinking age. *Ahh, to be eighteen and stupid again.* I smiled as I awarded another "C" and recorded the score in my grade book. My phone chimed with Declan's ringtone from where it was sitting next to me on the table.

"Hi. Thanks for your note today."

He groaned. "Ugh. Rehearsal was *awful*. Agony, I tell you."

I laughed at his over-dramatic comment. Such an actor. "Well, you won't be sitting next to me on Friday."

"Oh, yeah? What's Friday?"

"You're running act four with Stephanie."

Another groan. "That's one of our most difficult scenes."

"I know. That's why I stayed late to work with her on it. I think she's improving, but we'll test it on Friday."

"Thanks for that. We're going to need all the help we can get. What are you doing?"

"Grading. You?"

"Watching porn."

The Coke I had been drinking burned my nose with its carbonation. I had to clear my throat a few times to get rid of the sting. "Really?"

He laughed, and I heard his bed creak as he lay down. "No. Not really. I do miss you and that tight little body of yours, though. I wish I could see you tonight, but I'm really tired, so I'm going to bed early. I just wanted to call before I fell asleep."

"I miss you too, Declan."

"I love you, sweet girl."

"I love you too," I replied. We hung up moments later, and I finished the rest of my grading with a contented smile, even though I was still reading eulogies to marijuana and booze.

"Ah. The all-important act four, scene one," Dr Burrows said playfully as he took his seat next to me. He blew the steam off the top of his afternoon cappuccino, then continued. "Rosalind is disguised as Ganymede in order to educate our young Orlando."

"We all can hope," I played back.

He smiled, then continued like he was an over-dramatic narrator on a soap opera. "Will our dear heroine be able to challenge our starry-eyed lover enough to make him question his unrealistic dreams of for ever?"

I decided to play along. In a sensationalistic voice, I whispered, "Will she be able to convince our hero to take love one day at a time? To not get caught up in the magic of it?"

He allowed himself a hearty laugh before he added one more line to our farce. "And will she be able to dominate our hero with her quick wit? Will he hang on her every word? Will he beg to please her?"

I snorted laughter that echoed through the auditorium.

Dr Burrows's smile faded as he dipped his chin so our eyes met over the thick rim of his glasses. He unwrapped a finger from around his coffee cup and pointed towards the stage. "What are your bets that *that* is what we're going to see?"

I blew out a breath. "Fifty-fifty."

I knew we were in for it the moment Stephanie stepped onto the stage. Her steps were tentative, almost meek, and when Dr Burrows saw her, his groan matched my own.

The first run-through was awful, the second worse despite some encouragement from Dr Burrows in between. I slumped in my chair and watched the implosion I knew was coming. Like driving by an accident on the interstate, I couldn't tear my eyes from what I knew was going to turn ugly.

Gruesome was an understatement for the wreck on the stage. Any confidence she'd gained in our private rehearsal was obliterated in the first few seconds. She was supposed to reprimand Orlando for his tardiness to their lesson, but her attempt to gain the upper hand was laughable. To his credit, Declan tried to follow her lead, but soon I could see the muscles in his shoulders and jaw tense with frustration. It wasn't until I saw him act out the scene that I realized how different he was from Orlando – how much he had to fight who he was to play Orlando. Whereas Orlando had no trouble fantasizing about the happily-ever-after, Declan didn't believe in it.

It was in that moment that I realized both Declan and Orlando needed the same lesson. Though Orlando had to be taught how unrealistic his visions of forever were and Declan had to be taught to believe in forever, they both had to learn to live in the present.

To celebrate the everyday in all its potential ugliness.

To revel in the downclimbs and glorify in the peaks.

And I was going to teach them both.

"Dr Burrows," I leaned over to speak with him, "I think Stephanie needs to see how it is supposed to be acted."

He guffawed. "Me too, but do you have another Rosalind in your pocket?"

I gave him a sly smile.

"You?" he asked.

"Let me try. Just for rehearsal. I'll show her" – *and him* – "how it's supposed to be. I don't know all the lines, but the specific words aren't that important. How I say them is."

"By all means, have at it," he said with amusement. "Let's stop here for a minute," he said to the cast. I saw Stephanie bury her face in her hands while Declan held his arms out from his body and looking upwards like he was saying a frustrated prayer for help.

I rose to my feet and walked down the center aisle and towards the steps leading up the stage. The four-inch heels I had chosen this morning clicked on the old wooden floor as I took each step, the height of each one testing the seams on my pencil skirt. I had chosen the fitted blouse and tight skirt this morning for no apparent reason, but now I realized that maybe I'd known something like this was coming. I wore this sexier-than-normal outfit like a knight wears armour. The coat of confidence allowed me to straighten my shoulders, and with sure, measured steps, I met Declan's questioning gaze.

"Dr Lyons is going to step in for a few minutes." Dr Burrows answered the silent question. "Stephanie, come sit here with me and we'll chat about what we see. Everyone else clear the stage, too. Take five if you like."

Stephanie passed me with a small "thank you", but I barely heard it. My eyes were locked with Declan's intense stare from across the stage. He was challenging me already, and I welcomed it, basked in it. His eyes roamed up and down my body, and while the cast was distracted looking for seats in the auditorium, he mouthed, "I like it. Hot."

I answered with a confident lift of my chin and a siren's smirk. His answering sly smile showed his amusement. Game on.

I pushed my shoulders back and began part way through the scene. "Come, woo me, Orlando."

At first, Declan didn't move, testing how long I would wait for his compliance, but soon his feet moved steadily towards me. As Ganymede, I said my next line, "What would you say to me now if I were your very Rosalind?"

"I would kiss before I spoke." He leaned in to give me the kiss my body so desperately wanted. But it wasn't a kiss Ganymede would allow. There was a lesson to be had – she was not going to fold easily.

So I stepped back and reprimanded him. *Give me the weight of the scene, Declan. I can handle it.* His eyes blazed at first, like Declan, but then I saw an acceptance in them that was surely more Orlando. And as the scene went on, his shoulders lost their overly-proud tilt. His chin lowered in respect, and his voice lost the edge of control and authority. There was still a hint of carefully controlled power, which made him all the more convincing as a suitable mate for the strong Rosalind.

He relaxed into the role nicely until we approached the part of the scene where Ganymede tells Orlando to pretend he is marrying Rosalind, the woman he loves.

"Ask me what you will, and I will grant it," I said.

I saw the war between Declan and Orlando in his eyes. Every cast member would know his next line, but we were the only two in the crowded room to know how much weight it carried. "Then love me, Rosalind."

It wasn't the plea it was supposed to be. It was too much of a command to be authentic for Orlando, so I had to push him further. In order to gain control, I kicked off my heels and kneeled down onto the wooden floor. I sat back onto my bare feet and waited.

Waited for him to follow me down.

I was forcing him to make a choice. Did he remain standing as Declan, or kneel as Orlando?

Of course, these movements were ad lib. There were no stage directions telling me to sit, but many of the greatest moments in theatre happen when an actress takes the script and makes it her own. As I patiently waited on my heels, I imagined the green grass, twigs, and dirt under my knees in the Forest of Arden. I imagined how the audience would see two lovers sitting under a lush green tree, and the act of sitting would make this moment so much more intimate and authentic, like the audience were voyeurs.

Maybe they were.

Seconds later, Declan's knees bent as he folded his body down in front of me. He sat on his heels, facing me, similar to how we'd sat last weekend on his bed.

Rosalind praised Orlando in that moment, offering him the reward of her hand in marriage.

"How long will you love me?" Rosalind asked of

165

Orlando after they recited their vows.

Declan whispered his answer with a focused gaze that burned through me. "For ever and a day."

Oh, hell. I loved that answer, but Rosalind did not. She had to teach Orlando to love one day at a time, no matter how romantic, or unromantic, those days were. I didn't have Rosalind's lengthy speech memorized, so I used my own, more modern, words to communicate the gist of her harsh rebuke. I grabbed Declan's hands and held them between our knees. "Do not talk of forever when talk of the every day will do. Talk about how you will love me on the days when I'm jealous, overworked, and tired. Talk about how you will love me on the days I lose my patience with you when you've done nothing to deserve it. Talk about how you will love me in a shitty, one-bedroom apartment. When we have no money. No picket fences. No clean dishes. And piles of dirty laundry. We'll only have love. Talk to me about the worst of days. I want to know your love on those days."

He broke script with his next line as one of his fingers brushed circles on my palm. "You will," he vowed in a whisper only I might have heard. The sentiment was the same as Orlando's next line, but there was no doubt Declan spoke those words.

My eyes misted at his pledge, and I willed away the tears that threatened to give us away. Declan continued with the rest of the scene, and soon he exited, leaving me alone on a silent stage.

I felt every cast members' eyes on me, and for the span of what felt like minutes, nobody said anything. *Shit, was I too transparent? This was a terrible idea.* I peered into the darkened auditorium, trying to find Dr Burrows and Stephanie. Finally, I saw his darkened form stand and walk towards the stage.

"What a brilliant idea to kneel," he praised. "He had to lower himself to you."

166

"Thank you, Dr Lyons. I really needed that," Stephanie said.

"You're welcome."

"Let's take a five minute break, everyone, and then we'll run it one more time with Declan and Stephanie."

I noticed Declan hadn't returned to the stage, so I went to look for him after I slipped my shoes back on. He wasn't behind the curtains, in the hallway, or in any of the dressing rooms. Thinking that maybe he was taking a call or in the bathroom, I decided to go to the restroom. I splashed water on my face and steadied the breath I hadn't realized was racing. I opened one of the two stall doors, but before I could close it, a hand grabbed the door and wrenched it open. Another firm hand turned my shoulders a moment before a hard body slammed me against the tiled wall. A hand over my mouth muffled my instinctual yelp.

"Shhh ... we gotta be quiet, Jenn." Declan's nose was a centimetre from my own as we stared each other down. The only sound was the laboured exhalation that hissed between his fingers covering my mouth. His hips thrust forward, pinning me against the wall.

His scent circled me as he leaned forward to speak in my ear. "Fuck. You were so hot. When you were kneeling, at first all I could think about was the shower." He took his hand away, only to replace it with a kiss that blistered with its heat. The force of it pressed the back of my head against the unforgiving tile wall, which made me open my mouth even more. He ended the violent, almost savage kiss with an innocent and peaceful peck to my cheek.

"The way you took charge." His voice was reverent now. "I was amazed. You were so beautiful, so poised, so sure. My first reaction might have been heat, but the second was surely love."

"Oh, Declan ... you were such an amazing Orlando."

"I'll be able to do this scene now with Stephanie. I'll just act like she's you."

His voice when he spoke again was the most solemn and humble I'd ever heard. "I was honoured to kneel next to you. And what you said about those days where all we had was love."

"Yes?"

"I want a lifetime of days just like that. With you."

My heart was somewhere in my throat so I tried to swallow it down, along with the tears I had given up trying to contain. "Me too." I smiled. "But can I call laundry duties if you do the dishes?"

He smiled. "Only if you let me add one thing. A dog. I want a dog. Not one of those small, fluffy ones. A big, manly one."

I laughed, which caused more tears to spill from my eyes. "Yes. You can have your dog."

The door to the bathroom squeaked open and slammed closed as a set of feet entered the only remaining stall. Although we had closed and latched the door, it wouldn't be hard to tell there were two sets of feet in our stall.

"Oh, shit," I mouthed.

Declan's hand covered my mouth again as he shook his head sternly. "Don't say a word," he mouthed back.

The woman in the next stall flushed and walked to the sink. She washed her hands and walked towards the door. I thought she would leave without a word until I heard Ingrid's tinny voice. "Don't worry. I won't say anything."

She exited, but both of us remained unmoving long after the door had slammed shut.

Declan pulled away and cursed so loudly that it echoed around the stall. "Fuck. What was I thinking?"

My eyes followed him around the small stall as he paced, trying to get his attention, trying to get him to look at me. "Declan. Declan. Look at me. Please."

He stopped stalking long enough to say, "I said I would never compromise you, Jenn. And I did."

"Look. You gotta keep it together. Everyone else will

168

know if you don't go out there and pretend nothing is wrong. Do you trust Ingrid?"

"I don't know."

"Well, we'll have to." I wasn't sure where I was getting my moxie from. It was my career in the balance. "Go out there. I'll follow in a few minutes. I'll sit next to Dr Burrows and everything will be fine."

I could hear the clench of his teeth. "I don't like this, Jenn." He strode out of the stall without a second glance. The door announced his departure with a slam, and I stood with weak knees, thankful for the support of the wall at my back.

"I don't either," I said to the empty room. "But I won't give you up."

Minutes later, I walked back into the auditorium from the back entrance. Declan and Stephanie had already begun rehearsing the scene. Her actions were more purposeful, commanding, and Declan responded with a new sense of obedience.

"Much better," Dr Burrows said to me as we watched.

"Much," I agreed, although my mind was occupied with worry.

I did notice, though, that when it came to the wedding scene, this time Declan knelt on one knee before Stephanie.

I'll just act like she's you.

Yet she was still standing.

Chapter Seventeen

The end of semester was always hectic. Endless grading piled on top of my desk like the Empire State Building. The play didn't help matters either. The rehearsals the week before Friday's opening night performance were always in full costume and lights, which meant endless tweaking of stage make-up, costuming, entrance and exit points, and spotlights. The schedule I was keeping alone would have been exhausting, but pile on top of it Declan's edginess and I was drained and weary.

After Monday's rehearsal, I returned to my apartment, excited about the improvements the play was making. I tried to grade a few papers, but my mind drifted elsewhere. Declan had been distancing himself from me even further when we were in public since Ingrid had caught us in the bathroom. While I understood his concern, I missed the stolen kisses and dirty words whispered in my ear. Then I remembered something he said to me on the top of The Maiden.

I hope there will come a day when you learn to ask for what you want, that you take what you want. You're beautiful now in your triumph, but you'll be the most beautiful then.

As I sat on my new leather couch in the middle of a pile of papers, an idea came to me. I'd take what I wanted. I'd ask for it. And I wouldn't be ashamed of it.

I texted Declan.

Meet me in my office tomorrow at five. LY

I smiled when his reply came quickly.

Sure. What's going on?

My smile turned mischievous as I typed my reply.

You've been a bad boy.

This time, his reply didn't come as quickly.

You have no idea, Dr Lyons. So, we're going to see if you can lead, are we?

I didn't answer his question directly with my last text.

We're going to see if you can follow.

I let the conversation simmer there as I left my phone on the living room coffee table and walked to the bureau in my room. I dug through my everyday panties to the back of the drawer. I pulled out the lacy underwear I had once bought on a whim, and stripped so I could try it on. I wore it to bed that night as I dreamt about the promises of becoming even more beautiful.

Given how busy I was, Tuesday couldn't have dragged more. I watched the second hand drift over the numbers as the clock counted down to five. It wasn't that I was scared of what I had planned, but I wondered how Declan would respond. A few minutes before five, I realized I'd soon have my answer.

Through my second storey office window, I watched him park his motorcycle next to the street. He'd started riding his motorcycle when the weather allowed, and I loved it. I wanted to ride behind him despite the fact I'd never ridden before. Hell, I'd never *wanted* to ride before.

Now I wanted to feel the vibrations under my legs as I wrapped around him. I'd stroke his leather coat as the wind blew my hair into tangles. I'd lay my cheek against his back as he took us on long drives up Trail Ridge Road in Rocky Mountain National Park. I'd watch the towering pines zoom by in a blur, and we'd stop to feed the chipmunks sunflower seeds before we …

Knock. Knock.

I had lost myself in the daydream long enough that his rap on my closed office door startled me. After I closed the blinds, I ran to my desk, sat in my office chair, and arranged my curled hair over my shoulders.

I made sure my invitation was measured and professorial, like I hadn't been expecting him. "Come in, please."

The latch clicked when the knob turned. He opened the door, and I was treated to his full shoulders that filled out his leather jacket. He'd unzipped it so his tight black T-shirt peeked out from underneath. His jeans hung on his hips like just a small tug could pull them off. His heavy black boots thudded on my wooden office floor.

He closed and locked the door behind him. "You wanted to see me, Dr Lyons."

I propped my stiletto heels on the top of my desk, which exposed the warm skin above my knees as my skirt pulled tight. I felt the garter belt tug as I changed position. My core pulsed with emptiness as he stared, waiting for my answer.

And I made him wait. I leisurely took a drink of my coffee and pretended to rearrange the papers I'd been "grading".

"You've missed some classes lately." Of course he had – it was something we'd agreed on.

"Yes. I had an accident."

"Hmm … sounds like an excuse. You need to pass this class to graduate, yes?"

He stood next to the door, and didn't try to dominate the room. "Yes."

I knew what I wanted to say, but this was the point of no return. I paused, wondering if maybe he wouldn't play along. Then I remembered something else he'd said to me in the shower.

There's nothing you could say that would repulse me. If they're your desires, I want to hear them.

My feet left the desk and I walked across the office to where Declan stood. My heels clicked, and I could feel the extra sway in my hips. I stopped before him. "What are you prepared to do to pass this class?"

I saw the tick in his jaw as he scanned my face. Then he answered. "Anything."

I stepped forward so my silk blouse brushed against the heavy silver zipper of his jacket. "Anything? Now that's interesting."

A series of images flashed through my mind.

Ordering him to his knees.

Ordering him to fuck me on my desk. Where this need to call the shots came from, I had no idea, other than it was something that made my thong wet. I had thought about this moment the night before as I used my vibrator to bring myself to climax twice.

"There's strength in submission," I whispered.

He faltered at first as he tilted his head to the side, like a dog asking a silent question. His eyes hunted my face as he whispered, "Why?" It was the first question he'd asked that sounded like Declan, my lover, not my student. He had broken character, wanting to communicate with me about what we were doing.

So I answered as Jenn, not Dr Lyons, but this time, my voice didn't falter. "Because I've missed you. You told me to take charge of what I want, and this is what I want."

A graceful smile slid across his lips. "I was right. You are beautiful." His gaze roamed from my lips to my eyes before he added, "I love you, Jenn."

"I love you too, Declan. Is this OK with you?" I could see the desire that pushed against the zipper of his jeans, but I knew better than most that sometimes the body is willing but the mind is not.

He nodded as Declan before he said, "What do you want me to do, Professor?" Ever the actor, he slipped back into his student role with the last word.

If I had any doubt he wasn't into it before, there was no doubt in my mind when his knees bent, and he slowly knelt in front of me. His nostrils flared as he took in the scent of my arousal. His chin tucked against his chest as his eyes lowered, a sign of respect that made endorphins fly through my veins and settle between my legs. My nipples hardened to painful points under my lace shelf-bra, and goose bumps raced along my shins and forearms.

Here was this powerful, authoritative, dominant man, who could overtake me in a second if he wanted to. I felt like I had successfully managed to cage fire as I watched him kneel in front of me.

I reached around to my lower back and unzipped my pencil skirt. The sound of the zipper challenged my breathing for the loudest sound in the room as I let the material fall to the floor.

"Oh. Fuck," Declan cursed when he saw what I'd worn underneath. His hands reached up to cup the curve of my hips, while his thumbs brushed over the sensitive spot where the strings of the thong stretched over my hip bones. The only movement was his thumbs that skimmed back and forth, back and forth, creating a cadence that made me sway into him. Both the way he knelt and how he touched me were reverent, a moment that made me feel like I was being worshipped.

"Take them off," I instructed, and I widened my stance so he could slide my thong off.

I yelped as a rip thundered through the silence of the

175

room as Declan hooked his thumbs under the straps, tore the material from my hips, and threw it aside.

Well, you didn't tell him how to take them off.

The forceful way he'd taken off my panties reminded me of the man that lurked just below the surface of our charade, and that reminder only served to ignite a drum beat of passion in me so tribal, so feral, that my body couldn't remain stationary any longer.

In one motion, I grabbed his hair and tugged him to the ground. "You naughty boy. You ruined my panties."

I splayed the weight of my body on him and used my hands to push his shoulders into the wooden floor. I rocked my hips against his hard cock still caged in his jeans as I kissed him with a savage need. I pulled away a minute later, needing to draw breath. His gasping pants matched mine as I stripped him of his jacket and jeans.

As his clothes peeled off, I gave voice to my dreams from the night before. "You're going to be a good boy and lick me until I come, aren't you?"

He didn't answer with words.

I reached a hand under his boxers and stroked his cock. "Then you're going to fuck me just like I tell you to. If I tell you to roll me over, you'll roll me over. If I tell you to fuck me harder, you'll bang into me so hard my spine will ache. You'll come when I tell you to. You'll hold it for me, won't you, Mr Monahan?"

I felt him jump in my hand before he answered, "Yes."

I stripped him of the rest of his clothes and shoes so he lay naked on the floor of my office. He allowed my hands to roam where I liked, so I feathered my fingertips along his neck muscles and around his ear before I rose. With one heel on each side of his hips, I knew my nakedness was exposed to his fierce gaze that ran up from my heels, past my stockings, past the garter belt, and landed on my core. I slowly unbuttoned my top and exposed the small excuse for a bra underneath. The tops of my nipples peeked out from under the lace.

The drum beat's rhythm inside me sped up like the blood rushing through me. I walked to my desk in the muted darkness. Slices of late afternoon light slipped through the blinds and grew bigger as they scattered across the room. I sat down on the edge and waited for him. He stalked over to me, his arousal bouncing with each measured step. He might have followed my lead, but there was no denying the control he needed to do it.

I wanted to see what would happen when that control snapped.

I scooted back on my desk and hooked my heels on the edge of the old, polished wood before I lay down with my knees spread. The papers on the desk stuck to my sweaty back, and I heard Declan's growl as I situated myself and looked up at the ceiling. A single, large water mark stained the otherwise white ceiling. I stared at the mark as his hands drifted from my shoes, to my ankles, up my calves, over my knees, and along my thighs.

Where they stopped.

My eyes dropped to his, daring him to blink. Of course, he didn't, even when his tongue parted his wet lips. I closed my eyes, giving into the heady feeling of control as I gave myself over to him. Mixed with the exposed position of my body, I was walking a thin line between control and surrender.

His wet tongue parted me with a single, long lick. His hands on my thighs stilled me, opening me to him further as he licked one, two, three more times. Two fingers penetrated me, and I was so wet I could hear his skin slide against my sex. I rocked my hips, wanting to feel his knuckles bump against me.

"Fuck, you're so hot like this. You should see your clit."

"I feel it." I buzzed with an energy that made my skin hum.

"I can't wait any longer. You're going to come on my tongue." His mouth met my clit, where he sucked so hard I could feel his tongue move in waves against my bundle of nerves. The primal rhythm in me slowed as the room darkened and spun. My lower back lifted off the desk, wrinkling the papers underneath. My hands flew out as I tried to grab onto something. Something that sounded like a stapler or paperweight hit the floor, but my senses were so muted by then that I couldn't know for sure. All I knew was that my entire being was concentrated on a single spot as I floated.

I came with a scream that was cut short when Declan's other hand slapped over my mouth. The scream was muted, but that was the only thing that was subdued. His hand over my mouth rocketed my orgasm to another round of pulses that made my toes curl. When I became too sensitive, I closed my knees around his hand and tried to pull his mouth away with a handful of his hair. He protested as I pulled him away, but not before placing a short kiss on my clit like he regretted having to leave.

I sat up and licked my desire off his lips before I kissed him with the same reverence he'd shown me. My hands memorized the lean muscles of his shoulders. They were long, climber's muscles that were a product of days spent on the rock rather than dead-lifting in the gym. I raked my nails along his back, and his small nipples pebbled under my touch.

Now that the room had stopped spinning, I stood up, walked to the back of my desk, and pushed my chair out of the way. I bent at the waist so my stomach rested on the papers and I could grab the edge of the desk when I reached above my head. As my fingers gripped the wood, I felt Declan's thighs brush my ass.

"You're going to fuck me here," I said, laying my cheek against the wood.

He stroked my back so that I could feel his fingers

ripple along each vertebrae and settle at the base of my spine. "How do you want it?"

"Slow. Really slow. I want to feel every inch when you take me."

He grunted and pressed down on my back with one hand while the other lined himself up to my opening. His tip nudged me and slowly pushed forward, so slowly, in fact, that I felt my muscles trying to pull him in faster, deeper.

"Yes," he praised when I widened my feet to get a better angle. "You're so ready for me, Professor. How am I going to sit in your class now that I know what you wear under those suits? And how your ass looks when you're bent over the edge of your desk?"

I whimpered not only from his words but at the full possession he'd taken of my core. I was completely filled with his raw power that had been leashed for the last half hour.

Unleash it.

"You'll sit in class and not only think of my ass but remember what it feels like to pound me. Do it. Hard. Now."

His hips thrust forward before I had finished my command, and I scooted up the desk with each thrust that followed. His hips slapped against me like waves crashing against the rocks, again and again.

"Harder," I ordered.

He responded, and I heard the desk scrape as it inched across the wooden floor.

I peeked over my shoulder to watch as his muscles tensed with each strike. His hands gripped my hips to move me back onto him. Where he met me deep inside ached with his possession, a delicious combination of too much and not enough. I reached under me to rub my clit that burned with the need to release again.

He closed his eyes like he was in pain. His brow was

furled and his chin jutted out like he was concentrating. I felt him swell in me, and by this point, I knew him well enough to know he'd been on the edge for some time. Going this hard always made him come fast.

"Not yet," I chided. "I'm not ready."

His eyes opened, but he kept his punishing rhythm. His neck muscles corded with strain as sweat gathered along his hairline. "I can't ... I don't know if ..."

"You better do something to make me come then."

I figured he'd lean down to whisper something into my ear or take over rubbing my clit.

I had never anticipated ...

Smack. Smack.

He slapped one of my ass cheeks then the other with enough force that made my orgasm explode so unexpectedly and with such force that my knees gave out from under me. My ass burned in an outline that matched his palms and the heat melted, giving strength to the spasms of my core. His other hand covered my mouth, anticipating the scream that never came. This was a climax so powerful that every other part of my body refused to function as it absorbed the energy, and chased it for more.

The desk took my weight, and he pounded twice more before he growled, "Yes. Fucking take it." His fingertips dug into my hips as his balls slapped against me. He collapsed on top of me he entwined one of his hands with mine on the edge of the desk. He pried my fingers from the edge I hadn't realized I had gripped so hard. The only sound in the room other than our panting breaths was the rhythmic *beep, beep, beep* of the phone that had fallen off the hook when it landed on the floor. I laughed at the sound that usually jarred and annoyed me, and I wasn't alone. Declan's sweaty chest rumbled with laughter against me.

Then he sobered. "Sorry, Jenn. I should have asked before I did it. I just got caught up in the moment. You

OK?"

I knew he was talking about the spanking, but in that moment, I couldn't find words for how OK I really was. I closed my eyes, letting the sweet, slow tempo of peace float through me. I had never been better than in that moment.

"Jenn. You OK?" he asked again.

"Yes. Better than OK," I answered, and it was the truth I felt in every part of me, especially in the tranquil smile that spread across my face.

I knew that in the soft light of late evening, when I opened the blinds, I would still be smiling.

Chapter Eighteen

"What's wrong?" I asked Declan for the third time in the last ten minutes. He had come to my apartment with pizza after dress rehearsal on Wednesday night. We had cuddled and talked for a few more minutes in my office on Tuesday before we both dressed and he left. He'd been fine with what we'd done, at least he'd said so, but I could feel him simmering next to me as I graded and he typed his final paper for my class. I worried as I stared unseeing at his laptop that sat perched against his thighs as he propped his bare feet up on my coffee table.

"This witch of a professor is making me write this paper in order to pass the class," he joked.

"How dare she? What a wench!" I played along.

"Total drag. I could be out partying right now but, no, I have to be here."

I slapped his shoulder. "Easy, old man. I know what you'd be doing right now if you didn't have to write the paper."

He hit save on the paper and closed the laptop. "What?"

"Sleeping."

"No doubt." He stretched and yawned. "I'm getting too old for this shit. I've forgotten how terrible the week is before opening night."

The joking was fun, but it was masking the real emotions I knew he was attempting to hide. "No, really. What is going on?"

His head turned to look at me for the first time. "I'm worried. About you. About us. About my recovery. About the performance. About my dad. It just seems like the perfect storm."

"Well, I'm here for you. You don't have to question that."

"I don't."

"Are you wishing we hadn't met in my office?"

He paused before answering. "No. I don't regret what we did, but it probably wasn't the wisest choice we've ever made. Someone could have heard. And when we were almost caught in the bathroom …"

I tried to reassure him. "If Ingrid was going to tell anyone, she would have already."

"Maybe." His agreement wasn't convincing.

"And your Orlando is great. I've heard reviewers from the *Boulder Gazette* will be there, as well as representatives from Colorado Shakespeare Company. It will be great exposure."

He groaned. "For sure."

"And you said that your dad called and you had a nice conversation. He seems genuinely excited to see you perform. He even wants to have lunch with you before the performance on Saturday. Are you upset that he won't be there for opening night? Is that what's gotten you so wound up?"

"No. I'm *glad* that he won't be there opening night. Friday will already be hectic, I don't need his stress on top of it." He paused then added, "It's just all this stuff at once, I think, that has me overwhelmed."

I put aside my grading and moved his laptop to the other side of the couch. I wrapped my arms around his neck and straddled his lap. I coaxed a small kiss from his tentative lips, but I could tell he wasn't into it.

"Sorry," he said when I sat up. "Can I just hold you tonight?"

"Sure." I swung my legs over so I lay length-wise on the couch. He slid a throw pillow onto his lap to prop up my head and pulled a blanket from where it was hanging on the back of the couch. He spent a minute fussing over the blanket, making sure it was over my legs and tucked under my torso. He laid his head on the back of the couch as if settling in for a long night. One of his arms draped over my hip while the other held a remote. I could feel the small muscles in his forearm twitch as he aimlessly channel surfed.

"I still love you even though you're broody," I said after a while.

He patted my hip twice. "I still love you even though you're making me write a final paper, Dr Lyons."

That's the last thing I remember before slipping into a peaceful sleep.

Declan's ringing cell phone startled me awake what felt like hours later. He hadn't fallen asleep yet, so he reached for it quickly, trying to avoid waking me up.

"What time is it?" I grunted. "Who is it?"

He checked the caller ID, but from my angle, I couldn't read it. "Sorry, I gotta take this." He stood from the couch and walked into my room, where he shut the door.

I heard him murmur a "hello" before the door clicked shut, his request for privacy communicated loud and clear. At first, I bristled. *He's my lover, he's in my apartment, and I deserve to know who he is talking to.* My heart raced from a spike in adrenaline as my brain concocted scenarios of ex-lovers calling for another romp.

Luckily, I didn't act on my first instinct to rush into the room and plant my butt on my bed. He had never given me a reason to doubt him. He'd never gotten any calls from exes in my presence, and most importantly, I trusted him. I rationalized other scenarios. *He's probably talking to his dad or he's talking to one of his hiking buddies who he hasn't seen in ages.* I had never been the jealous type, and I made the conscious decision not to start now.

I tried to go back to sleep. Really I did. Then I gave up

and flipped through the channels with no real purpose. The longer he took, the more curious I got, so I idled away the time grading more essays and making a late-night snack of toast and milk.

I was chewing the last bite of toast when my door swung open and slapped against the door stop, announcing his anger.

Not good. Not good.

He strode into the kitchen, and from his heavy footfalls, I could tell he was troubled. If his deep scowl hadn't given him away, the tension in his shoulders surely would have. I had noticed that he carried his stress in his shoulders, and now they were practically brushing his ears.

I tried for nonchalance. "What's going on? Is everything OK?"

He stopped in front of me and placed a hand on the countertop on each side of my hips as I stood leaning against it. His grip turned his knuckles white. "Everything will be fine. But, I have to go."

"Declan, I'm starting to get worried. Why do you have to go? What is it that you can't tell me?"

I saw the moment he attempted to school his face into a smile. "Everything's fine. A friend just needs help. Sorry I can't stay tonight, but I'll see you tomorrow. Sweet dreams." He kissed my forehead before he grabbed his laptop and rushed out the door.

I locked it behind him and slid my back down it. I sat in the foyer for the longest time with my arms hugging my bent knees. I couldn't come up with any answers to the questions that swirled through my brain.

What can't he tell me?
Who is he going to go see?
Is he trying to protect me?
Is he lying to me?
Why do I feel sick?

around our table after she stated the obvious made me shift my legs under the table. "I've heard it's a full house tonight."

"Well, we all know why. They're filling the seats to see our Orlando." I didn't like her use of "our". He was *my* Declan, not our Orlando. "Once the press found out that Will Monahan's son was acting ..."

Declan's groan followed by a heavy sigh, the first sounds he'd made since Ingrid sat down, cut her off. "I wish that hadn't gotten out."

"Why the hell not? I've never understood why you don't want people to know who your father is," Ingrid said.

Because he doesn't want to ride his father's coat-tails, for one.

"I don't want to be a celebrity, Ingrid. Never have. Never will."

"You know, I heard a rumour –"

He cut her off again. "It's true. He's coming on Saturday."

"Oh, Declan." She covered his hand with hers on the table. "Will you please –"

"I'll introduce you," he said as he moved his hand away. His statement held a hint of annoyance to my ear, but for others who didn't know him well, it would have sounded polite and courteous.

"Thank you. Thank you. Thank you!" Each repetition squealed more than the one before it.

Sensing his growing frustration, I attempted to steer it away from Declan. "So, what are you doing after you graduate, Ingrid?"

I'm sure she answered my question, but I didn't really listen. In fact, she was practically talking to herself as Declan and I had a silent, private conversation between us.

"I hate this," his eyes said.

"Me too."

189

"I wish we could be alone."

"I wish we could finish our conversation."

When it was clear that Ingrid was there to stay, Declan finished his food, pushed the tray away, and stood up. "Thanks for lunch, ladies. I'm going to take a quick nap before we have to be ready for make-up and costumes."

There was no way I was going to sit alone with Ingrid. It would give her a chance to ask about the bathroom incident without Declan there to interfere. I stood up, threw my half-eaten food into the trash, and returned to the table. "I'm going to grade some papers in my office. Nice seeing you again, Ingrid. Good luck tonight."

"Thanks. Nice seeing you, too."

Declan strode out of the west exit while I left through the sunny south door. We went our separate ways with so much left unspoken.

Dr Burrows had relied on me heavily throughout the staging of the play. He relied so heavily, in fact, that many of the stage hands that worked on lights, props, and costumes came to me when they had a question. That was why I had only graded a few essays in my office before I went home, took a shower, got dressed, and drove to the theatre a full hour before my scheduled arrival time.

I chose a green shift dress with black lace accents for tonight's performance. It was modern and moderately sexy yet professional. I paired it with a black pearl necklace, matching earrings, and black, peep-toe heels. I styled my hair in loose curls that rested on my shoulders.

I entered the empty auditorium and took a seat in the back row. The house lights were dimmed, and the only light on stage was the ghost light, the single light left on when the theatre is locked up for the night. In that peaceful silence, I took a deep breath of the dusty, familiar air whose smell would always be connected to memories of Declan. The backs of my legs recognized the velvety seat under me. I had spent the last four months sitting in one of these chairs, first fantasizing about, and later remembering, what Declan's touch felt like.

Gradually, the stage came to life, first with more lights and then sounds of banging metal and wood. Drops were lowered into place as stage hands dressed in black scurried around the set.

The lighting director walked to center stage and shielded his eyes from the overhead light as he peered into the dark theatre. "Dr Lyons? Is that you? What are you doing here so early?"

"Just enjoying the calm before the storm. Do you need something?"

"Well, if you're not busy, I wanted to ask you a few questions."

"No problem." I met him in the middle of the auditorium so he could discuss with me some last-minute lighting changes he wanted to make.

"You know between acts two and three, I think we should use a crossfade. The transition feels too choppy."

"I agree. It will make for a quicker transition. But you'll want to run this by Dr Burrows, too."

"Sure." He spent the next fifteen minutes discussing the need for a Fresnel light, a softer diffused light, for Stephanie's final lines to the audience at the end of act five. Then he wanted a stronger followspot on Stephanie in act four, which would mean a more intense beam of light would follow her every movement on stage.

"I agree. The lighting can help direct the audience's attention on her, make her more forceful on stage. Just double-check with Dr Burrows," I reminded him.

He assured me he would and thanked me for my time. After he left, I thought I would be able to steal a few more minutes of privacy before the actors arrived, but word had got out that I had arrived early, so the few minutes of peace I'd thought I had were hijacked by the costumers and make-up artists who all bombarded me with last-minute questions.

Dr Burrows, to his credit, was also pulled in a million different directions backstage as he put out small cast fires and found missing props. He stole a minute of free time to talk to me near the dressing rooms. "Jenn, I just wanted to thank you for all your hard work. This production is so much better with your help. You have a great career in front of you, and I hope you'll work with us again on the next Shakespeare play."

"Thank you. I've enjoyed working with you, too. I would love to be a part of the next one."

"That's why I wanted to give you this." He handed me a copy of the program.

"A program?" I asked, confused.

"Look inside. You're listed as dramaturg *and* assistant director. Congratulations. You've earned it."

"Oh, wow! Thank you!" I searched through the program, found the crew page, and scanned for my name. Second from the top, under Dr Burrows's name, was mine, and seeing this brought proud tears to my eyes. *I love this job.* I might have stared at that page for a full minute to be sure it was true.

"I'll see you in the directors' seats at the five minute call," he said.

I wound my way backstage to the green room, where the actors and crew met to grab a quick drink or snack. I ate a few crackers and some cheese as I sat in a comfortable leather sofa. It felt good to get off my feet for a while, and I chatted with a few actors and crew who came in for relief from the mayhem of backstage preparations.

Half an hour later, the front of the house manager found me with my feet propped up on the couch as I chatted with James, the actor who played Jacques. "There you are, Dr Lyons," the house manager said. "There are five people waiting outside the auditorium for you. Are you free?"

"Absolutely. Thank you for finding me."

"House is open. I repeat, House is open. Half hour call," said the stage manager's voice over the backstage intercom, which meant that the audience could file into the auditorium to find their seats and the show would start in a half hour. Nervous adrenaline surged through me. I threw away my trash and walked through the dim hallways to the front of the auditorium where the sell-out crowd was already filing in.

I spotted my friends immediately. "Hey, guys! Thanks for coming!"

"There she is," I heard Nina say as I hugged Hannah and Beckett.

"Sorry, it's been really busy. But I'm so glad you're here. Both of us."

Hannah, Beckett, and Nina reflected my knowing smile. "Tell him good luck for us."

"I will. Hi, Tanner," I said, waving to the man at Nina's side. "Thanks for coming tonight."

Tanner's strong arm wound around my back in a friendly, chaste hug. He pulled away quickly and returned to Nina. "We wouldn't miss it."

"This is Ansley," Nina prompted, gesturing to a lithe, slender brunette with a shy, sincere smile.

"Nice to meet you," Ansley said. "I've heard a lot about you."

"It's nice to finally meet you too." I leaned in and whispered to her while pointing at Hannah and Nina. "Don't believe anything these bitches tell you."

Ansley laughed, seemingly grateful for the camaraderie. *I'll have to go out to lunch with her. She looks like she needs a friend.*

"Sorry I can't stick around longer. I need to get backstage for some last-minute stuff. Do you guys want to get together afterwards for some drinks?"

"Hell yeah," Nina said. "We'll text you where. Bring him if you want to."

"Great. Thanks again," I said over my shoulder as they found their seats and I made my way backstage. There was only one person I had left to find before show time and, thankfully, it wouldn't be unexpected for me to be talking to him before the show. But first, I stopped in the green room to grab my gift for Declan from my clutch.

Stephanie stopped me in the hallway to the dressing rooms. "Thank you, Dr Lyons. For everything. I'm a better actress because of you."

I returned her hug. "You're welcome, Stephanie. You're going to be fantastic." The backstage intercom announced the fifteen minute call. "Gotta go," she said, before she scooted into her dressing room.

Since only the two leads got private dressing rooms next to the stage, Declan's was next to hers. I knocked three times.

"Come in."

I cracked the door open and peeked inside. He was sitting in his make-up chair in front of the large mirror that was bordered by a single row of bright, naked bulbs. His feet were propped up on the counter in front of the mirror so our eyes met in the mirror first.

I saw Declan's smile through Orlando's make-up. "Hey. Just wanted to wish you good luck."

He turned, stood, and met me in the middle of the small room. As he came closer, I could see the heavy foundation, eyeliner, and brow pencils the make-up artist had used. "If you say one word about the make-up, I swear …"

I mimed zipping my smiling lips.

He stepped close enough so one of his hands gripped my hip while the other mimed unzipping my lips. "That won't do," he said before his mouth met mine in a tender, rolling kiss.

"I'm so excited to watch you tonight."

"I'll be thinking of you, Assistant Director."

"Ahh … you saw the program."

"I did. Congratulations. You deserve it."

"Thank you. I know that we don't have much time before places, but I wanted to give you something. A good luck charm."

"You didn't have to …"

I opened my palm between us.

His eyebrows lowered in confusion. "A chock?" he asked as he grabbed it.

"Yes. It's the last one that I took out on the top of The Maiden."

"You kept it all this time? Why?"

I shrugged. Sometimes I wasn't sure either. "For a week after our climb I wore it on a chain around my neck. Sometimes I still do, but other times I just carry it in my purse. It's a symbol of one of the greatest memories of my life."

His smile was rich in sincerity as he tucked the chock in the right pocket of his costume. "Thank you, Jenn. I'll always keep it."

"I have to go. I'll be in the director's reserved seating. Oh, and my friends told me to tell you good luck. They want to meet up with us for drinks after."

"I'd love to, but let's see how the night goes. Maybe we can swing it if we're careful where we go."

"I'll text you when I know when and where." With a short kiss, I walked towards the door. "I love you," I said over my shoulder.

He had turned to his mirror so he replied to my reflection in the mirror. "I love you too."

I closed the door with a slight click as the lights dimmed for five minute call. I was late, so I sprinted up the hallways and through the back of the house to the balcony seats where Dr Burrows was waiting for me.

"Sorry I'm late."

"No problem. It's a full house." He waved an open hand towards the floor seating below. I peered over the railing to see not one empty seat. The nervous energy buzzed in the dim room, adding to the feeling of expectancy and anticipation. A scrim, a thin drop at the front of the stage, didn't allow the audience to see the final preparations on stage. When a scrim is lit from the front, it's opaque, but when the play started, the scrim would be lit from behind, making it transparent.

"I always like watching the first night from above," Dr Burrows said as I scooted back in my chair. "It lets me see things we might have missed from below. Here, do you want these?" He held out what looked like an earpiece for an iPod.

I hadn't a clue what they were. He must have seen my hesitation, because he chuckled then explained. "These are wireless earpieces that connect us to the stage manager calling the show. We'll hear all of the lighting cues, actors' cues, and technical cues. If something goes wrong, we'll be the first to know."

"Sure," I said, taking one from his hand and placing it in my left ear. Right away, I heard the voice of the stage manager making calls for certain crew members. Then he called the actors. "Places." The single word rocketed adrenaline through me, and the skin on my back prickled with sweat as my body heated with the anticipation.

Listening to the behind-the-scenes workings through the wireless headset made me feel like I was in on a dirty little secret. Minutes later, I heard him call the first lighting and technical cue, which turned off the house lights and changed the lighting on the scrim so the audience could see through it.

Their eyes were treated to the love of my life.

His proud, stately shoulders commanded attention as he stood center stage with another character, Adam. His voice was clear and firm as Shakespeare's verse rolled off his tongue. The ebbs of the vowels and the staccato of the consonants lulled the audience into the scene, making them forget they were sitting in a theatre.

The stage manager called for the crew to raise the scrim, opening the play's sets to full inspection. It felt like the beginning climb of a rollercoaster. A little scary. A lot of anticipation. And some prayer.

At first I was distracted by the calls in the ear piece, but after a while, I got used to it. It was like watching a football game on TV with the announcers. Once you've experienced what it is like to watch football with the commentators, you couldn't imagine not having them. I could hear the occasional cuss backstage when a drop got caught or a prop was temporarily misplaced, but overall, the play ran smoothly. The stage manager called for the crossfade lighting cue change I had okayed between acts two and three. Dr Burrows leaned over to whisper in my ear. "I like that. Much better."

"Me too." His small praise lit a proud flame in my chest.

The play flitted along peacefully through the first three acts. The problematic fourth act loomed, and I could feel my heartbeat racing as it got closer. My foot tapped restlessly on the carpeted floor. Jacques began the scene, and I could hear Dr Burrows take a deep breath next to me. This really was the pivotal, make-or-break moment for our show.

Stephanie's control of the first half of the scene was believable, convincing.

Then she crossed the threshold. "Ask me what you will, and I will grant it." I might have mouthed the words when Stephanie said them aloud.

"Then love me, Rosalind." Orlando's plea resonated through the auditorium, vibrating with perfection. He reached his hand into his right pocket, which was upstage and shielded by his body from most of the audience's view. But from the balcony, I saw the little movement, one he hadn't made before, and I knew what he was feeling in his pocket.

I love you too.

They pretended to be married on their knees underneath a towering oak. The branches obscured some of the overhead lighting so that shadows danced across their faces. It was a beautiful moment, reverent yet playful. My heart felt the yearning of a love not yet fully realized.

The lengthy act five followed, bringing all the characters onto the stage for a series of four marriages. Stephanie ended the play with the epilogue that spoke directly to the audience, encouraging them to "like" the play, a tip of the hat to the title. Dr Burrows nodded his approval of the new lighting change as well. At the end of her speech, the stage manager called for a blackout, and the stage lights were rapidly extinguished. Dr Burrows and I left our seats quickly and made our way backstage.

The stage manager then called for a curtain call. We took out our earpieces and handed them to a crew member while we watched the actors parade onstage.

The actors with smaller parts went first. Rounds of applause thanked the actors for their performances, but the loudest by far was for Stephanie and Declan. Stephanie entered from stage right, Declan from stage left. They met in the middle, held hands, and walked to the front of the stage where they took their bows. Then each one stepped forward for an individual bow and motioned to the other one in a gesture of respect. A minute passed, and finally both of them stepped back into the middle of the line with the rest of the cast.

"Let's go, Jenn." Dr Burrows grabbed my hand and led me onto the stage. I'm sure my heels clacked on the wooden floor, but through the crowd noise, I couldn't hear them. Heavy applause and a few whoops (most likely from Nina and Hannah) filled the auditorium as we bowed once

Chapter Nineteen

Everyone arrived at my apartment with cases of beer and a few bottles of rum. We put the majority of the drinks in the fridge, but kept a beer out for each of us. We clinked them together in the middle of my small kitchen.

"Cheers." I twisted the cap off my first beer and guzzled half of it, thankful the first night had gone well. "Thank you for coming tonight, guys. It meant a lot to me. And Declan told me to tell you thank you."

"He's going to be here, isn't he?" Hannah asked.

"Yeah. Later, after he showers and changes."

"I don't know much about Shakespeare, but I thought he was really good. Like *really* good," Tanner said.

You don't have to know anything about Shakespeare to spot a born actor. I smiled. "Thank you. Speak of the devil," I said when the downstairs buzzer sounded. I went over to the control pad, buzzed him in, and waited at my door, giddiness making me bounce at the threshold.

Declan took the stairs two at a time like he was in a rush to get to me. His exuberant hug lifted my feet off the floor as he twirled me around. I giggled when he set me on my feet and went silent when his lips met mine in a desperate kiss. He pulled back his lips, but his hands stayed cupping my cheekbones. "I *hate* not being able to do that. You're. Mine."

I could tell he hadn't come down from his post-performance high. The endorphins still racing through his body were almost audible as we stared at each other in the dim hallway. "And you're mine." I kissed him again to stake my claim. "You were even better tonight than I thought you would be. I was so proud of you."

He rubbed my hand against the pocket of his jeans so I could feel the outline of the chock. He had transferred it from his costume to his street clothes. Knowing that he cherished the gift warmed me from within like a cup of hot cocoa. "I'm glad you like my gift."

He started to say something else, but Nina's call from inside my apartment interrupted him. "Hey, love birds. Get in here. We're doing a round of shots."

I led him by the hand into the apartment where he was greeted with a chorus of "bravos" and "encores". Declan mocked a dramatic bow then tentatively accepted a beer and a congratulatory handshake from Beckett. "Just one tonight, guys. I have to do this all again tomorrow."

They toasted the bottoms of their beer bottles like only guys can. Declan took small sips as he was introduced to Ansley, the only person in the group Declan hadn't met ice skating.

All of us settled into comfortable conversations in the living room. Between trips to the fridge for more beer and rounds of shots for everyone but Declan, it ended up with the girls talking on one couch while the guys stood outside on the small balcony. Given that this was only the second time Declan had been around my friends, I kept one eye on him to be sure he was comfortable and enjoying himself.

During a lull in our conversation, we found ourselves watching the men joke on the balcony.

Nina finished off her beer and pointed outside with the bottle's neck. "That is a fine group of men right there. Look at 'em. Each one of them is sculpted. Teeming with testosterone. The male species at its pinnacle. We are lucky bitches, ladies."

My body couldn't have agreed more. Declan was leaning up against the railing. His feet were crossed in front of him, and he held the beer bottle low near the waistband of his jeans. He'd been slow-drinking all night

202

between large gulps of water. He joined in rounds of laughter at a joke one of them made, and when Beckett made a good point, he tipped his beer to him in a shortened version of a guy toast before both of them drank. He oozed with a smooth confidence, which made me want to drag him into the bedroom right then, friends be damned.

"Enough ogling, ladies," Hannah said. "Let's do more shots." She filled four shot glasses with rum. She lifted hers, and we followed. "To hot men on balconies."

"Cheers!" we all chorused, although I could tell Ansley was less enthusiastic. She looked like I'd felt before I met Declan, like she had miles of uncertainty folded inside her. *She's probably wondering if she fits in with our group.*

After I swallowed the burn from the alcohol, I scooted next to her. "You OK?" If I had less alcohol in me, I probably would have been more eloquent. But as it was, the lack of food combined with the alcohol already made my head spin if I moved too fast.

"Yeah. I'm fine. I think …"

"We can be a little overwhelming, huh?"

"You could say that."

"Would you like to go to lunch sometime after my semester is over?" I thought maybe a one-on-one was more her style.

Her thankful smile told me I was right. "I'd love to. Thank you."

"You're welcome." We were exchanging phone numbers when the guys walked back in through the sliding glass door.

"Did I hear another round in here? Hannah, you're going to get drunk and I'll have to carry you home tonight," Beckett said.

"You say that like it's a bad thing," Hannah slurred.

Declan sat down next to me on the couch, slung his arm around my shoulders, and pulled me into his side. "What?" I asked when he gave me a strange, far-away look.

"I'm just happy," he whispered. "I really like your friends, and they haven't judged us for being together. I haven't had to answer one question about my dad. I can just be a normal guy with an amazing girl. I haven't felt this way in, well … ever."

The smell of beer on his breath made me want to taste him, so I closed the gap between us and swiped my tongue against his before he responded with a hum.

"When will they *leave*?" he asked against my lips, and I laughed at the desperateness in his voice. "I fucking ache. I want to take you now. Tie your hands to your headboard. Command you not to talk. Would you do that for me, Jenn?"

"Yes," I hissed as my body heated, an immediate response to his words that Pavlov would've been proud of.

Hannah popped the small bubble we were in. "Jenn, you have any games we can play?"

"Games? You mean like …"

"You know, board games. Like Scrabble."

Beckett immediately chimed in. "Oh, hell no. I already know how you play Scrabble, and I'm not going there again." Hannah laughed at their inside joke.

"No Scrabble. But I think I might have something in my coat closet." I peeled myself away from Declan and got a step-stool to look on the top shelf in the closet. As I climbed up, I felt Declan's hands steady my swaying hips.

"You're kinda drunk. Wouldn't want you to fall now, would I?"

"No, thank you." He helped me down from the stool and we returned to the living room with my plunder. "Will Pictionary do?"

"Fuck yeah." Nina bolted off the love seat with a clap of her hands. The guys followed us into the kitchen.

Nina, of course, took charge as she unpacked the game pieces and cards. "Guys against girls. This is a drinking game, ladies and gentlemen. The first team to correctly identify twenty pictures wins, and the losers have to take a shot."

Declan got everyone a new beer from the fridge while Nina continued the directions. "Each round will be three minutes long. One player will be the drawer and the others will be guessers. No numbers. No letters. The drawer can't talk. Try to guess as many pictures within those three minutes as you can. When time is up, the other team goes, and we alternate until one team scores twenty. Everyone got it?"

"Got it," we responded in unison. Nina sat down on one of the padded kitchen chairs, and I took one next to her, which meant that Ansley would draw the first round.

I ate a few pretzels and chips from the bowls in the middle of the table as Nina called time, and the girls' first three-minute round began.

"Damn right!" Nina yelled when our timer went off. She high-fived me, Hannah, and Ansley before taunting the men. "Beat ten answers, boys."

"No problem," Beckett promised. "We got this."

They nominated Beckett to draw, leaving Declan and Tanner to guess. Instead of sitting, Declan and Tanner stood up and feigned like they were stretching to get ready to play some sort of athletic game. They bounced up and down on the balls of their feet and swung their arms like they needed to loosen up. The fact that they were joking around in mock seriousness made them, well, hot as hell. Had they been grumbling about how silly this game was, it would have been a drag. But when they knuckle-bumped and told Nina they were finally ready for the timer to begin, us girls sported amused smiles.

The guys sailed through the first eight clues, but got stuck on the ninth. "What the fuck is that, dude?" Tanner yelled at Beckett.

"Orchard," Declan guessed.

"Forest," Tanner yelled.

Neither was right since Beckett kept drawing. The two kept guessing, but their annoyance was hilarious. Tanner was bouncing up and down in frustration while Declan was staring at the drawing from a distance, trying to figure it out.

While he studied the drawing, I studied him. There was a large casement doorway in between the eating area and the kitchen itself, and around the doorway was thick wooden molding. Declan's fingertips clung on to the top molding as his body rocked back and forth in thought with his ankles crossed underneath him. There was something so incredibly sexy about that. With his arms bent above his head, his triceps stretched his tight T-shirt, and his jeans rode so low on his hips that a slip of skin peeked between the shirt and his jeans.

But just as important as my body's reaction to him was my heart's. I realized in that moment that Declan fit in seamlessly with my friends like we had been hanging out for years. Although I might not have realized how important that was before, I did now. It was like we were weaving together our old lives with the new, and all the seams on our quilt were fitting perfectly. I felt my heart tweak in my chest and I fell in love with him a little more.

I had been staring at Declan so intently that when Nina called time, I jumped.

"Seriously, man. What the hell is that?" Declan asked.

"It's a grove!" Beckett yelled.

"Fuck that," Tanner said. "The girls get book, bridge, and engine, and we get grove? There's something crooked going on here."

The guys fell back into their seats as our second round started. "Ten to eight, girls are winning," Nina said as she turned over the timer and Ansley started drawing again. Whether it was because Ansley's drawings were starting to stink or because Nina, Hannah, and I were drunk off our asses, I'm not sure. But we only guessed four correctly. When the guys got another eight on their second round, they chest bumped like they'd scored a touchdown.

With the score fourteen to sixteen, we had to get six correct on this round to hit twenty first. When the timer turned over, Ansley began drawing, and we easily guessed candle and Saturn. But the third picture proved to be our undoing. Ansley drew two circles next to each other. Next, she added a long oval that ran horizontally with one end of the oval touching the middle of the circles.

The three of us girls busted out laughing at the same time. "Penis!" Nina yelled.

"Balls! Testicles! Gonads!" Hannah yelled when Nina's answer hadn't worked.

The guys simply tipped their beer bottles to their grinning lips.

Ansley blushed a bright red and shook her head, looking horrified. But now we had started yelling out obscene words, we'd happily decided to take our loser's shot if it meant we got to keep going. It was like a train rolling downhill without breaks, and we each tried to outdo the other.

"Cock!" Nina guessed.

"Twig and berries!" Hannah yelled.

"Boner!" I said.

"Pecker! Shaft! Prick!"

We were gulping air between our fits of laughter so we could wail our next obscene guess. "Schlong!"

"Big Johnson!"

Ansley looked like she was going to have a heart attack. She panicked and drew a man with a hat on standing behind the circles. He looked like he had some sort of wand he was placing on the top of the circles. If she thought her new addition was going to help, she was wrong. A new round of howling laughter rang through the room. Even the guys were chuckling at us as we wiped our eyes of tears.

"Holy shit. What is the creepy wizard doing to that guy's balls?" Hannah screeched.

"Kinky. I like it," Nina said.

The final nail in the coffin was when Ansley drew lines exploding out of the other end of the long oval.

"Oh my god, he just came!" Nina said.

"Splooge! Jizz! Spunk!" Hannah added.

"Stop! Stop! I can't take it any more!" I pleaded. I held my stomach as it cramped.

"Time," Beckett called.

"What the hell is that?" I asked.

But Ansley didn't answer. "It's a cannon," Tanner and Declan said at the same time. Beckett walked over to the drawing and pointed to it as he explained. "This is the cannon and wheels, and this is the little civil war guy wearing a hat, and he's lighting the fuse on the back of the cannon. And the cannon went off when he lit the fuse. You know, like ones you see in old civil war movies that back up when they shoot?"

The girls were silent for a solid ten seconds. "I liked ours better," Hannah said to Beckett.

"Let's show 'em how it's done, boys," Beckett said, rubbing his hands together and blowing on them. We turned the timer over, not expecting for this to be a game since they only needed four to win. But they got stuck on the first two, which meant they had little time left. The third one came easily, and with only about ten seconds left, Beckett turned over the last card.

"They'll never get this in time," Nina whispered in my ear.

Beckett drew a horizontal line and a long rectangle standing on the line. Nothing else. Right before time ran out, Declan yelled, "Skyscraper!"

"Fuck yeah!" Beckett hooted.

"No way! I call foul!" Hannah protested. "There's no

way that you could have gotten skyscraper from *that*. There aren't even any windows. That could have been a million things, like a door or something."

"It's *clearly* a skyscraper," Tanner added, as the guys poured the women our loser's shots.

"To wizards and boners!" Nina said as we toasted our shots.

The rum no longer burned its way down my throat. My cheeks were hot, and I was feeling no pain, a sure sign that I would tomorrow morning. "That better be your last one," Declan said as he wrapped his arms around my hips.

His nose was nuzzling my ear when I heard his cell phone ring in his pocket. His body went rigid behind me. One arm let go of my hips to retrieve his cell phone from his pocket. He checked the caller ID and cursed. "I have to take this." He walked through the living room, opened the sliding glass door, stepped onto the balcony, and closed the door behind him.

The screeching laughter of a minute earlier had been replaced by a silent, eerie stillness. A feeling of dread settled in my stomach and mixed with too much alcohol.

"It's getting pretty late, Hannah. We should probably think about heading home," Beckett said. Tanner, Ansley, and Nina must have agreed because they started picking up the empty bottles and bowls of food.

Declan entered the room a minute later, his face eggshell white. "I'm sorry, I have to go."

"Everything all right, man?" Beckett asked.

Declan stepped in close to Beckett, signalling that he wanted a private conversation, but given the silence in the room, I could still hear what he said. "Yes, but do you think you could stick around here a little while to be sure that Jenn is OK? She's had a lot to drink, and I can't be here to watch her."

"Sure. We can stay on the couch, I guess."

"Thanks, man."

"You OK to drive?" Tanner asked.

"I'm fine. Didn't even finish a beer," Declan said as he shook Tanner's hand.

Declan walked quickly over to me and grabbed my shoulders with a sure grip. He looked like he was struggling for the right words.

"Declan. What's going on? Please tell me." I was surprised I found the breath to speak.

He hesitated then kissed me on the lips. "Never doubt I love you."

I wanted to rant and scream, to tell him that he couldn't leave without an explanation. He couldn't walk out after that ominous command. But neither my feet nor my lips could move as he stalked towards the door. "Take care of my girl for me," he said over his shoulder before he opened the door and left.

Chapter Twenty

I'm not sure what my consciousness registered first. It could have been the glaring morning light coming through the blinds. Or it could have been the rolling nausea. But it most likely was the weight of worry that clung to each breath like I was wearing a suit of armour in the middle of the ocean.

When I went to the kitchen for a drink of water, my heart panged when I saw two sets of feet poking out of the end of the throw blanket on the couch.

Hannah sat up. "Hey. Do you feel as awful as me this morning?"

"Ugh. Yes. We're getting too old for this," I said. Hannah threw off the blanket and joined me in the kitchen. "Thanks for staying last night, but I was fine."

"I know, but Beckett promised, so I went in to check on you a few times. I was more worried *for* you than about you. Have you heard from him this morning? I hope everything is OK."

"Me, too, but I haven't heard anything."

"I'm going to go to the corner store and get us some donuts for breakfast," Beckett said, grabbing his keys. He kissed Hannah before he left, and she followed his trail out the door with a contented smile.

"I'm really happy for you," I said.

"Thanks. I'm happy too. And I think you found your happy. Don't you think?"

"I thought so, but this is the second time he's been called away late at night. Because of the performance yesterday, we didn't get a chance to talk about it. I trust him, but it's clear he's hiding something from me."

I poured three glasses of orange juice and tidied up the kitchen. "He doesn't strike me as the cheater type," Hannah said.

"I agree."

"So what could it be, then?"

I paused. "I don't know."

Hannah shifted the conversation to more comfortable topics. Fifteen minutes later, Beckett returned with a box of a dozen donuts. "Three chocolate cake, three vanilla, three glazed, and three raspberry crèmes. And one copy of the morning's paper."

"The paper? Why do we need …?" Hannah's eyes grew wide when she realized why Beckett had bought a paper. "Oh, the review should be in there."

"That was thoughtful. Thank you, Beckett," I said as I opened to the entertainment section of the *Boulder Gazette*.

On the front page of the section was the title, "As You Like It Shines" with a rating of five stars and a "must-see" label. I quickly read the article, my heart galloping more quickly with each new paragraph. The reviewer praised the sets, the lighting, the directing, and the acting, and he included a few quotations from our interview. The review ended with a final paragraph that left me speechless.

Another reason to attend is the acting of W. Declan Monahan, the son of famed Hollywood actor Will Monahan. Thankfully, this apple has fallen far from the tree. His portrayal of Orlando was fresh and innovative. Monahan's power vibrated under the surface, giving the audience the sense that they were witnessing a rogue that was tamed just enough to be the Orlando Rosalind needs. At times, he was truly exquisite, proving that at least one Monahan can actually act. The next performance is scheduled for 7:00 tonight. Tickets are limited.

I must have stared at the copy, reading and rereading the final paragraph, for some time. This was huge – for the college, for me, and most importantly, for Declan.

"Uh oh. Is it bad?" Hannah asked.

"No. It's the opposite." I handed her the newspaper and bolted down the hallway. "They loved Declan. I have to call him," I yelled as I found my cell phone plugged in on my nightstand. I scrolled to his number quickly and waited as it rang.

And rang.

And rang.

And went to voicemail. "Hi, this is Declan …"

I huffed my frustration, hit "end", and texted him instead.

Did you see the review? It's awesome! So proud of you!

I expected my phone to ping a response text, but it sat silent in my lap for minutes. The worry of the morning morphed into panic as I sat on my bed, willing my phone to ping.

Since it didn't, I called and texted again, willing myself to believe that maybe he was just too busy with his dad. Since he didn't respond again, I decided to take a shower to wash away the headache and the worry that caused it. When I got out ten minutes later, the light flashed on my cell phone, signalling I had a new text. I jumped soaking wet from the shower and slipped on the wet tile. I grabbed onto the counter at the last minute and wiped the water from my hands so I could swipe on my phone. I stood in a puddle of lukewarm water and read the text from Declan.

I did. Thank you. With my dad. I'll call when I can.

I battled between happy that he'd responded and pissed

at his terseness.

I deserved more than a vague text, didn't I? Especially after last night's departure.

I threw on some clothes and decided to make myself busy for the rest of the morning. Hannah and Beckett left after they finished their donuts, and I cleaned the apartment from one dust-bunny-filled corner to the other. I turned off my phone while I cleaned so that I wouldn't constantly be listening for a call or a text alert. If I was honest, I was a little – OK a lot – pissed. *Let him be the one not to be able to get a hold of me.* Yeah, it was childish, but it also wasn't healthy to sit by the phone for hours, waiting like a puppy for the next scrap of attention he threw my way.

Three hours later, my stomach rumbled with hunger, so I hastily made and ate a turkey sandwich. I was exhausted from the cleaning and the drinking from the night before, so I decided to take a nap, setting my alarm for three o'clock. My weary body welcomed the warm, flannel sheets, and I fell into a deep sleep with my dusty, dirty clothes still on.

I woke two hours later feeling more like myself. I needed another shower, but when I turned on the water, I realized that I hadn't turned my phone back on. When I powered it up and saw I had missed three calls and a text from Declan, I cursed myself for the foolish decision to turn off my phone.

His text read like a desperate plea.

I need to talk to you. Please call me.

I called him at least five times, and each time, I was directed to his voicemail, where I begged for him to answer. I must have called at least five more times during the hour it took me to shower, dress, and get ready for the night's performance. *The sooner I get to the theatre, the sooner I'll be able to see him.*

I drove faster than the speed limit, hoping he would get to the theatre early so we could talk. After I parked, I ran into the auditorium. When I pushed open the heavy doors, I expected to be greeted by the solitary ghost light on a quiet stage. Instead, the theatre was pure chaos.

"Dr Lyons, I'm so glad you're here." Dr Burrows rushed to the back of the theatre.

I'd never seen Dr Burrows so panicked. "What's going on?"

"You haven't heard."

"Haven't heard what?"

"Declan's left the university."

"That's impossible." I slumped down into the nearest chair as my knees weakened. "Why would he do that?"

"I don't have an explanation. All I know is that Dean Andrews called me this afternoon after he met with Declan and his father around three o'clock. Dean Andrews said Declan was no longer a student at the university, which meant he could no longer act in the play."

"Where is he now?" *Why the hell didn't he call me? Wait, he did, but you turned your phone off like a petulant four-year-old.*

"Dean Andrews said that he left with his father on his private jet, heading for Los Angeles."

Why would he go with a man he barely knows and hardly respects? He doesn't want that life. He wants this life with me, right? I had more questions than answers, but at this point, I had to remind myself that, for my career's sake, I had to react like the play's dramaturg, not his worried, possibly scorned, lover. No one could know that half of my heart was on that plane. I took a few deep breaths and schooled my face. I hid my shaking hands in the pockets of my pants. It would be understandable for me to be panicked, but not heartbroken.

215

"OK. Let's start running scenes with his understudy," I proposed.

"Yes. Steven is on his way. Thankfully, he's prepared since he had to take over for Declan when he was hurt. He'll do fine, but he's no Declan."

"We'll be fine," I reassured the director, but I was trying to convince myself more than anything. We spent the next hour preparing Steven. I was thankful for the distraction that kept my mind occupied, because during the lulls, my mind skipped from frantic worry to soul-deep hurt.

When Stephanie and Steven ran through act four, I remembered the way Declan's hand went to his pocket to touch the chock.

I remembered how regal he looked as he knelt next to me.

And I remembered the tilt of his shoulders and the look in his eyes when he asked me to love him under that sun-drenched oak.

When I felt tears of hurt and betrayal prick my eyes, I excused myself to the restroom. I ran with trembling knees, my foundation shaken. I made it to the stall, *our* stall, before I collapsed against the cold tile. Sobs wracked my body as I sat on the floor. I hugged my knees to my chest as I rocked back and forth.

He was gone.

"No. No. No," I chanted as I rocked, my falling tears staining my silk blouse.

Never doubt I love you.

"Why? Why?" I asked the empty room.

In my agony, I hadn't noticed that the room was no longer empty. Ingrid sat perched on the countertop next to the sink. Her legs, crossed at the ankles, swung casually as she watched me through the open stall door. If she was concerned about me as a friend in pain, she surely didn't show it. In fact, from what I could see through my tear-

216

blurred vision, she looked smug.

"You OK?" The lack of sincerity in her voice rankled.

I didn't say anything since my appearance answered her stupid question.

"The show will be fine with Steven."

"Yes. Fine," I agreed.

"But you're not sitting in this bathroom stall because you're worried about the play."

What is it with this girl's habit of stating the obvious? Then she said something that was the direct opposite of obvious. "I'm surprised you didn't know that Declan and I have been lovers for years."

"That can't be true." I tried to will it so.

"No? Am I not pretty enough?"

"You know you're pretty."

"Well, thank you." She accepted my compliment with a saccharine smile. "So why would you think it impossible that we were lovers?"

I searched my brain for a reason and couldn't come up with one. I knew Declan had had casual lovers before he met me.

Her face bent into a sneer that made her more ugly than pretty. "Oh, wait. Maybe it's because I'm not his *professor*. I bet that was one fun role play."

Anger straightened my legs, making me stand with a jolt. I stalked towards the bathroom door. "I've had enough of this. I don't believe …"

"You need proof? OK. Fine. I know he has a tattoo over his heart."

I paused at the door and spoke with my back to her. "Anyone who saw him with his shirt off would know that."

"True, but I know what it means." I spun around and was instantly greeted by a confident smirk that told me she wasn't lying. "He was with me last night. In fact, I think he left your place to be with me. He left just before sunrise

217

this morning. Said he had to meet his father."

I stood statue-still in the middle of the dim restroom at war with myself. I wanted to know more and less at the same time.

Ingrid continued, undaunted. "Oh, and he was at my place on Wednesday night, too."

I whispered, "You said you weren't going to say anything. Did you tell the university about us? Is that why he had to leave?"

"Me? Oh no, I wouldn't hurt Declan like that." I noticed she didn't show any concern for me. "And you know I'm telling the truth because if I *had* told, there's no way you would still be here."

She had a point. A good point.

She continued, "Some emergency, I think. In fact, he's called me since he met with the Dean. See?" She pulled her phone from her back pocket and scrolled through it. Sure enough, there was a phone call from Declan to her phone, around the time I had tried to get a hold of him as I was getting ready to come to the theatre.

In the span of that held breath, I realized that although he had tried to call me that day, all the missed calls were before the meeting with the Dean. After he'd left the Dean's office, he hadn't called. He would have had plenty of opportunity to call me on the way to the airport if he'd wanted to. Instead, he had called Ingrid.

Never doubt I love you.

When I didn't think it could get any worse, Ingrid turned the diamond-sharp blade in my chest. "He's even texting me. See, he's going to fly me out to California after the semester is over." She shoved her phone in front of my face, and, curse my curiosity, I read it.

I'll text you next week with the flight numbers and times.

"So, you see, you were just a temporary fling. He's always liked a challenge, so seducing the new professor must have been fun sport for him. You're just another notch." With that, she hopped off the counter, walked around me, and left. The door announced her departure with a bang.

I ran to the toilet and threw up everything in my stomach. All the hurt came with it until I was dry heaving on pure agony. I had opened myself to him. Trusted him. Climbed with him.

I'd been duped.

Duped by the man I thought I knew.

Duped by the man who tattooed his personal motto onto his chest.

Duped by a man who wanted to make pretending his life's work.

His T-shirt the first day I met him had told me what type of person he was, and I was stupid enough to forget it. I washed my face in the sink and scrubbed off the streaks of mascara from my cheeks as my stomach tightened like a knot being pulled at both ends.

Never doubt I love you.

"Too late," I vowed to my reflection and gave up trying to solve the Rubik's Cube of Declan Monahan.

Chapter Twenty-one

"Ladies and gentlemen, your attention please," the announcer started as the house lights dimmed. "Due to unforeseen circumstances, the part of Orlando will be played tonight by Steven Forsberg. Thank you, and enjoy the show."

At the news, whispers rolled through the audience where they reached Dr Burrows and me as we sat in the first row of the balcony. The scrim turned transparent, and the show started with Steven center stage talking to Adam. My mind's eye saw Declan standing there, commanding the audience's attention. I blinked away my mind's cruel trick. As I sat in the same velvet chairs under the same dimmed lights, I volleyed between nervous prayer for the show and seething anger for the man who had abandoned me.

Tonight was supposed to be the night he got to act in front of his father, and he'd robbed us both of the experience. I was going to get to observe his father from a safe distance like I was on some reconnaissance mission to figure out more about the man I loved by watching the man he didn't want to be. Would he come with a date? Would he walk in high-and-mighty like the Hollywood A-lister he was? Or would he wait to come into the auditorium until the last moment so that he didn't take away the spotlight from his son? How would he dress? And, most importantly, what would he think about his son's performance?

All those questions remained unanswered as the lights faded in and out, in and out. Stephanie's voice pulled me back to reality at the beginning of act four. Two hours ago during rehearsal, I hadn't been able to bear watching the scene that I thought meant something to us. Watching it then was like trying to rip a Band-Aid off a still-gaping wound. But now I watched it, recognising it for the charade it was. The scab had now formed over my gaping wound and my blood boiled in my veins. Fuming and simmering in anger, I felt the deception and lies in Orlando's measured words.

Fuck him, I decided as the stage faded to blackout. *Fuck the man who made me believe he wanted something more than casual sex. I've never needed a man before, and I don't now.*

Dr Burrows again led me to the side of the stage so we could take our bows. The routine was the same as last night's, and despite Declan's absence, the crowd's response still seemed positive. Dr Burrows held my hand as we entered from stage right and walked to the center. On our way out, I saw Ingrid respectfully clapping for us in the row of actors and actresses. Her pleasant smile betrayed none of the hateful words she'd spoken to me just hours earlier. The face she painted on now proved her ability to act went bone deep.

We bowed to a generous round of applause before the stage lights changed and the house lights illuminated. It was the same routine as last night, but the feelings couldn't have been more opposite. Whereas last night the applause had filled me with pride, tonight I was empty.

My feet felt like they were slopping through mud as I walked from the stage to the green room to grab my purse. I said goodbye to Dr Burrows and the actors and excused myself from a round of drinks with the cast. I couldn't make myself sit in a bar with the incomplete cast.

With my keys in one hand and my cell phone in the other, I thought about calling Nina and Hannah, but I wasn't ready yet to tell them what had happened. Was I embarrassed that I had fallen for his charm? Maybe. But telling them also made it more real, and that was the last thing I wanted.

I considered going home but decided against it when every room in that place was filled with memories of Declan. Hell, the sheets probably still held his scent. The couch, the shower, even the wooden casement to the kitchen would all remind me of him. So I decided to go to the one place that had always been my domain, the place where my sense of self-confidence had never waned.

My office.

I used the passcode to get into the Arts and Sciences building and walked down the hall to my office. On autopilot, I turned my key in the lock and pushed the door open to the darkened room. I flicked on the light, walked to my desk, and plopped down into my chair. Its leather squeaked as it took my weight in the otherwise silent room. I leaned back in the chair and stared at the ceiling. With my bare feet on the top of the desk, I swivelled back and forth as my eyes focused on the old water stain on the ceiling above my desk.

I'd thought for sure that when I got to the privacy of my office, the river of tears I'd been holding off would flood me, overtake me with its power. But as I sat there, all I felt was numb.

At first, I'd been angry.

Then I'd been pissed.

And now I was simply numb.

Dazed and detached, I floated, anaesthetized to the pain I'd allowed myself earlier.

It's the acceptance stage, my logical brain said, *the stage where you realize how much you don't need him.*

It's the deadened stage, my heart said, *the stage where you realize how much he took with him when he left.*

I let my mind drift aimlessly from thought to thought until one made me bolt upright and run to my door. I leaned around the door frame, suddenly realizing that my eyes had seen something that my mind had disregarded.

My drop box wasn't empty.

But I had emptied it late on Friday afternoon, and this was Saturday night. No student I'd ever met turned in a paper between Friday afternoon and Saturday night, so the box should have been empty.

I grabbed the large white folder and scurried back into my office. I tore open the sealed envelope and pulled out the paper, both dreading and hoping I'd find another note from Declan. My mind initially registered disappointment that it was just another late paper. That was until I saw whose name was at the top.

Declan Monahan.

It was Declan's final Shakespeare paper. He hadn't mentioned anything about the paper in my box last night when we were playing Pictionary. My mind drowned in a million questions and zero answers.

When had he turned this in?

Why would he turn it in to the drop box instead of just handing it to me?

Why would he turn this in if he simply planned on leaving the university the next day?

I dammed the flow of questions and began reading. My heart sank at his title.

Feigning Love: the question of real love in As You Like It.

I hung on every word of every line of every paragraph. He began:

Early in the play in Act 1 Scene 3, Rosalind makes the assertion that being a man means putting on a performance. She says that men have "semblances", meaning they put on pretences or veneers that are

*changeable according to the company they keep. In Act 3
Scene 3, Touchstone furthers this theme with the idea that
lovers are known for feigning or pretending their
emotions. The idea that lovers are somehow counterfeit is
an idea that even the famous Shakespeare scholar Frances
E. Dolan recognizes. In his introduction to the Penguin
edition of* As You Like It *he argues that the play asks the
question: "How is the beloved to tell whether one's love is
true or simply well played? How can one separate content
and form, truth and fiction, feeling and script?" While I
agree with Dolan that the play raises these questions, I
respectfully do not agree with his final assertion. He
writes, "Since, in the course of the play, both Orlando and
Rosalind plumb their 'true' feelings by means of
performances, the distinction between the true and the
feigned never emerges clearly." In contrast, I assert that
the play does, in the end, make a distinction between what
is real and what is not, and their love is certainly real.*

Although Declan's paper had all the trappings of a
formal, academic paper, I couldn't help but feel like he
was whispering it to me in the darkness of my bedroom as
we cuddled under the flannel sheets. He continued:

*One way we know that the love at the end of the play is
to be believed and not ridiculed is by the transformation
we see in Orlando. In the first scene, the audience learns
that Orlando has been denied the formal education his
station in life requires. He tells his brother that his lack of
education has "obscured" and "hidden" from him all of
his "gentlemanlike qualities". He sets out, then, to
"become a gentleman", and what he learns is that a
gentleman in spirit is very different to what he, at first,
thought.*

So did I.

225

I continued reading,

One of the lessons he learns is humility. Rosalind is right when she accuses Orlando early in the play that he loved himself too much to love another. His pride turns away the very person he needs to teach him what unselfish love is. The insecurities he masks as bravado ring hollow to the astute Rosalind. When she calls him on his arrogance, she has the ability to wound him far more than others who have levelled the same charges against him. Because her wounds cut deeper, we know she is different, and, eventually, we learn her wounds have the power to heal.

One example of this is idea when the lovers reunite in the final Act. Rosalind instantly notices the bloody handkerchief on Orlando's arm, proof of his bravery when he was injured saving Oliver from a lioness. What is more important than this act of bravery, though, is their discussion about it. Rosalind says she is pained to see the bloody cloth, because she is worried that his "heart" was wounded by the "claws of a lion". In a moment of honesty that shows Orlando's growth, he responds, "Wounded it is, but with the eyes of a lady." Orlando cherishes the wounds he has gained from Rosalind's education. For him, the pain has lead to a personal growth that allows him a deeper sense of authenticity in his love.

I had to wipe the tears from my eyes to keep the words from becoming too blurry. "Oh, Declan. This is the you I fell in love with," I said to the empty room. It was like we were back in my crowded classroom, having a conversation with each other that only we understood.

Reading his paper, I was unexpectedly conflicted. This was the voice of the man who I'd trusted so quickly, not the man who texted an ex-lover promises of plane itineraries. But it was so hard to believe that both could be the same man. Which was the real Declan? Then I remembered what he had said to me once.

I don't think there's a real Declan any more than there is a real Jenn. We all play roles. We all have our disguises and our defences. Some are just more authentic than others

His paper had stirred emotions in me I thought I had under control. The scab started to bleed again. I was exasperated with myself, feeling fickle and capricious. How could I say I loved him yet lose trust in him so easily?

I'd come to believe in a man who made me believe in myself.

I'd come to trust in a man that could take me to new heights by teaching me the value of a downclimb.

Most importantly, I'd come to know myself, and now I was again questioning who I was and what I was feeling. I felt like an unmoored boat, aimlessly drifting in open waters.

I read his final paragraph, conflicted. He finished:

All this focus on Orlando is merited, but one should also ask "How does the audience know that Rosalind's feelings are real?" She was a woman of rank, and she fell in love with a man she knew was estranged from his family and exiled from their prestige and money. She had no ulterior motive to fall in love with him, especially when the circumstances surrounding their meeting encouraged her not to. Most importantly, focus on the final scene where Orlando and Rosalind actually get married. They no longer come together with the disguises of Act 4. No masks. No pretences. No veneers. Rosalind no longer has to be the teacher and Orlando no longer has to be the student. They marry as the people they always wanted to be, individually whole in mind and spirit. But only together

227

are they complete.

Gasping sobs shook my shoulders. I cursed as I wiped my tears from the wet page, hoping that the words weren't too blurred to render them unreadable. Then I realized why he had turned in the paper even though he knew he wouldn't pass or graduate. It wasn't an academic paper, although it wore its mask well.

It was a love letter.

Chapter Twenty-two

I allowed myself one day. One day to feel sorry for myself, to mourn the loss. That was it. I had my Sunday mope in my frumpiest pajamas while I binge-watched Patrick Swayze movies. Halfway through *Dirty Dancing* and all the way through my tub of Rocky Road ice cream, I hadn't experienced any revelations, but it sure felt good to allow myself to drown.

Drown in my anger.

And drown in my confusion.

It was a confusion fuelled by the mixed messages and what else was in that envelope. After I reread Declan's paper in my office last night, I convinced myself that somehow he would make his way back to me. I had persuaded myself there were circumstances I didn't understand that had caused him to leave, and he would clear them up with a simple phone call on Monday.

Yet as I opened the envelope to tuck Declan's paper back inside, I noticed something in the bottom of the envelope. I turned it over, dumping the contents onto my desk where they landed with a clink on the polished wood.

The chock.

That piece of metal shattered the fairytale of a fix-it-all Monday morning phone call. He had no reason to give me back the chock if he planned on returning. Now I knew what it had felt like for poor Tommy Honeycutt in ninth grade when I had returned his silly pewter promise ring in an envelope I had stuffed through his locker grate between English and PE. After he had got that ring back, he hadn't bothered to call me. He knew.

The chock sitting on my desk told me everything I needed to know.

And if I was being realistic, so did the text on Ingrid's phone. With all the evidence against our happy reunion, I stocked my freezer full of ice cream and frozen dinners and settled in for a poor-me Sunday. The play wasn't running today. I had no obligations. That still didn't keep me from checking to make sure my phone was fully charged and on its highest volume setting. You know, in case I decided to drag my ass five feet from the couch.

I was putting on a strong front. Really, I was. That was until I received the phone call late Sunday afternoon.

"Hello?" I said, not recognizing the number. I mentally tried to calculate what time it was in California, because, surely, it was Declan.

"Hi, is this Dr Lyons? I mean, Jenn," the voice corrected himself.

The man's voice was vaguely familiar, but since it wasn't the one I was hoping to hear, my brain was short-circuiting. "Yes. This is Jenn."

"Ah, good. I wasn't sure if you'd pick up given the circumstances." The voice paused, then added, "And it being Sunday and all."

Oh shit. I recognized the voice. "Hi, Dean Andrews. What can I do for you?"

His heavy sigh turned my gut ache into a sharp cramp. *I'm getting fired.* "I need you to come to my office first thing tomorrow morning. Let's say eight a.m.?"

"Sure. I'll be there." I didn't have to ask why he wanted me to come. The churn of my stomach made me run to the bathroom.

But if you're found out, you'll lose everything, Jenn. Nina's warning echoed through me as I tried to swallow the bile.

"Thank you. I'll see you then." He disconnected seconds before I wretched until all the crap I'd eaten throughout the day was purged. I sat against the bathtub and panted, unable to catch my breath. Not only had I lost Declan, but I had lost the job I'd come to love, the only job I'd ever wanted. After Friday's opening night and the promotion to assistant director, I'd dreamt of years working alongside Dr Burrows, moulding Shakespeare's plays for the modern audience. That dream was dead, and now I had nothing.

No lover.

No job.

No career to hang my hat on.

Nothing to be proud of. And, in truth, I was ashamed – ashamed I'd been so stupid as to risk everything.

I might have slept Sunday night, but I wasn't sure. It didn't really matter, though. Nothing was going to help the dark circles under my eyes or the weight in my chest. I slunk into Dean Andrew's office, wanting the meeting to be over at the same time I never wanted it to start. He stood behind his desk and shook my hand like he had three months before, on that fateful day I'd first crossed paths with Declan.

"Thank you for coming in early, Jenn. Sit, please." He motioned to the leather chair in front of his desk. He didn't wait for me to get settled before he started. "I wanted to make you aware of a situation involving one of your students, Declan Monahan. On Saturday, I met with Declan and his father, Will."

I wanted to turn to ashes right there in the chair. He continued, "They told me that Declan would have to withdraw from the university. When I asked if there was an explanation they were willing to share, Will informed me that Declan's mother had passed away unexpectedly."

Wait. Wait. Wait. That was not what I was expecting to hear. I thought for sure our affair was the reason for the visit. Plus, Declan had told me that his mother had died when he was young. Was Will talking about Declan's step-mother, a woman he'd never met? Surely Declan would never leave the university because of her death. My mouth protested before my brain had a chance to tell it to shut up. "But his mom …"

"Died on Friday." Dean Andrews finished my sentence in a way I hadn't intended. But in that moment, I knew something, and it was profound. Dean Andrews sat back in his chair with his fingers steepled together in front of his wrinkly mouth. He tapped his lips with his joined first fingers and looked at me with a stare of a thousand words.

He knew.

He knew of the affair.

He was pretending not to know.

"How? How did you …" *figure it out? Did Declan tell you? Did Ingrid tell after all?*

"The circumstances were suspicious. Deaths in families happen all the time, and I've granted numerous requests for delayed grading. Usually, the student will finish the final papers or tests a week later than everyone else after the funeral and burial. When I offered Declan that option, he flatly declined."

"Why would he –" I began to ask, then stopped myself.

The Dean continued with a nod. "Naturally, I asked what his mother's name was. As Declan said 'Adele', Will said 'Lauren', who I later learned was Will's new wife. One of them must have panicked, and with that slip, everyone in the meeting knew I was aware of the lie they were telling."

"Lie? Why would they lie?"

"I wondered the same thing. There were only a few explanations, and since I knew you were his only professor this semester and that you were working closely with him on the play, I mentioned your name. His face paled and he couldn't meet my eyes. It was in that moment that I knew."

"Why? Why would you ..." *not fire me? Why would you give me another chance?* I couldn't speak the questions out loud.

"Forty-seven years ago, my now grey-haired wife was the most gorgeous brunette I'd ever seen. Her voice was prettier than a cardinal in spring, and I wanted to know everything about her."

Where is he going with this? "She sounds lovely."

"She is and was, but she was also my student." He paused as if he was reminiscing, then continued. "Falling in love with her was something I didn't choose and couldn't have avoided even if I had tried. Which I didn't."

Sounds familiar.

He blinked out of his whimsical, far-away look. "Jenn, I have to tell you, I've sat on countless advisory boards concerning professors who have chosen to break the anti-fraternization policies. While I've almost always voted for full expulsion of both student and professor, I can tell you that what I saw yesterday has changed my mind in this case."

In the last five minutes, my emotions had ping-ponged between miserable and elated and every emotion in between. "What you've seen?" I asked.

"Yesterday, I saw a man who, surprisingly, wasn't at war. He was willing to give away a degree and a chance to act in front of his father for a love that he knew he'd have to walk away from. He knew he'd lose *everything*, and he was choosing to walk away so she didn't have to."

Tears I couldn't control filled my bottom eyelids as he continued, "That's not an infatuation. That's not a drunken binge at a fraternity party. That's unselfish, honourable love, and I'd be a hypocrite to censure it."

"Thank you," I sobbed. "Tha –"

He cut me off with a wave of his hand. "But I must tell you that I have to maintain the public perception that the anti-fraternization policy is a good one, because in most

233

cases it is. Thankfully, it appears that this relationship has not become public, but I will warn you like I warned Declan yesterday. If this does become public, I will have to take a hard stance against it. You will go in front of the advisory board, and you will most likely lose your job. I will also give you the same advice I did to Declan. I think it would be wise for there to be no contact between you for a full month at least. Give it a chance to cool down. No emails. No texts. No phone calls. Give no fuel to the fire and no evidence for a committee to sift through later."

I prayed that the Dean's advice was the reason why Declan hadn't called. "I understand. I will take your advice. But, may I ask one thing?"

"Surely."

"What happens after that month is over? If we wanted to get back together, would that even be an option?"

"Neither I nor the university can dictate your private life. You are free to date anyone you like as long as it does not violate the anti-fraternization policy. If he is no longer a student at the university and there is no hard evidence that you were together before he left, you would be free to be together."

This meeting had gone so differently than I thought it would that my mind couldn't bend itself around what had happened. I wiped the tears off my cheeks. "I'm not sure what to say."

"You don't need to say anything. Just heed my advice. Go on with your classes. Go on with the play. Turn in final grades. Do nothing to spark the gossips. Know that my door is always open."

"I'll never forget your kindness."

He slowly stood from his chair, shuffled over to the sideboard, opened the cabinet, and poured himself a finger of Scotch. He lifted up his glass of "afternoon" Scotch as he said, "Remember that when I'm not able to offer you a raise this year."

He dismissed me with a wave of his hand – it just wasn't the type of dismissal I had expected.

Chapter Twenty-three

I spent the next month taking Dean Andrews's advice. The play ran for three more shows on Thursday, Friday, and Saturday of the following week, so my time on those days was, thankfully, occupied. A week later, I finished both of the semester's classes, graded the final essays, and turned in grades on time.

All of these commitments happily distracted me from the questions that still remained unanswered. What had prompted Declan to meet with Dean Andrews? Surely it wasn't Ingrid, because the Dean had mentioned there was no hard evidence, that the affair hadn't become public. Why did Declan feel he couldn't continue hiding the affair for two more weeks? Why had he given back the chock? And most importantly, why had he invited Ingrid to California?

I knew the reunion was still happening because on Friday night, Ingrid cornered me in the restroom before the seven o'clock performance. "It's supposed to be wonderful weather next week in California." Her voice was victorious and righteous, so I didn't acknowledge it. I washed my hands and pinned up the hair that had fallen from my casual chignon. Before I could escape, she branded her cell phone like a light-sabre. "See," she said as she held the cell phone in front of my face. If I wanted to read the small text I had to walk a few steps forward, and damn my curiosity, I did. The text message exchange was clearly with Declan's cell number.

Ingrid: *Play's last day is Saturday, so Sunday tickets*

work fine. I don't have any money, so where should I stay?

Declan: *You will stay with us at my father's house.*

Ingrid: *U R so sweet.*

Declan: *We'll go to the movie set on Monday.*

Ingrid: *Can't wait to see you!*

There might have been more, but I'd had enough. I vowed to never let my curiosity get the better of me again when it came to Ingrid. I turned around and opened the bathroom door.

"Is there anything you'd like me to tell him?" she asked.

I vacillated between "I love you" and "Go jump off a cliff," but I settled for "No. Nothing."

Her triumphant smile fell a little as I turned to leave the room.

Although my professional life served as a wonderful diversion, there were still times that being in the theatre without Declan felt like I was a link short of a chain. One of those nights was closing night. Saturday's performance concluded with final bows and subdued joy, the sense of ending anything but subtle. As Dr Burrows and I hugged on stage after the final bows, I mourned the loss of the play and the joy it represented.

It was in this somber mood that I reluctantly agreed to attend the post-show cast party. I drove to the bar near campus and was greeted by the familiar smell of beer and too much cologne. White, modern light fixtures hung from the high ceilings, accentuating the light birch woodwork. The only bold color in the bar was on the canvases that covered most of the walls with contemporary splashes of paint like someone had played a few games of paintball in the room before it was a pub.

I walked up to the concrete countertop that served as a bar and considered my order. Although I wanted to order enough shots to dull the ache, I opted for water. When the bartender scanned me quizzically, I thanked him for the water and escaped to the small room at the back that had been reserved for our group.

Most of the cast had already ordered their celebratory shots, which made me feel out of place and, well, old. I chatted with the director and the cast as best I could, but my mind was thousands of miles and two time zones away. That was until Stephanie pulled me aside.

"I wanted to thank you again for all your help, Dr Lyons," she said.

"You're more than welcome, Stephanie. I enjoyed seeing you develop into your character. Your confidence grew with each performance."

"Speaking of confidence, I wanted to tell you that I really admire your strength. You're a really strong woman."

No, I'm really not. Not strong enough to stay away from my student. Not strong enough to move on from him when he left, apparently with another woman. "Thank you for your kind words."

"There they are," Ingrid interrupted. "I have to leave because I have to catch an early flight tomorrow. It was great working with you guys." She air-kissed our cheeks like we were European and pranced out of the bar with a final wave.

The air was colder around us after Ingrid's interruption. "No, really," Stephanie continued. "Sometimes I think you don't see your strength, but you should know everyone involved with this play admired and respected you, including Dr Burrows."

It sounded a lot like what Declan had once said to me. I

allowed my shutters to unfasten just slightly, opening up a window of myself to Stephanie I usually hid from almost everyone. "You're right. Sometimes I do doubt myself."

"Don't we all?"

"I guess, but sometimes I wonder if maybe I do more than others."

"Why do you think so?"

I answered honestly. "I don't know."

With each day that passed, I was more able to answer that question. After the play and academic semester ended, I had two weeks that lacked any plans. And no plans meant no distractions. And no distractions meant that I could no longer avoid the work I really needed to do on myself.

Because of the end of the semester, I hadn't had much time to talk with either Nina or Hannah, so the following weekend – three weeks post-Declan – we decided to have a girls' night in at their apartment. "I'll make the food and you bring a bottle of our favorite Cabernet," Nina said as we made plans on the phone.

When I walked in the following night, Nina had a boiling pot of spaghetti on the stove. Her made-from-scratch sauce was a treat I'd always looked forward to in our days of grad student poverty.

She pulled back from our sisterly hug in the middle of the kitchen and eyed me suspiciously. "Uh-oh. I can't wait to hear this story." Her gift of reading people was uncanny.

"It's a doozy. Let's wait until after dinner."

She started to protest, but the loud, incessant banging on the front door interrupted her. Since Nina was stirring the sauce, I went to the door and opened it to a flailing Hannah who was trying to avoid spilling the four sacks of groceries she had in her hands. I lunged for the one that was most in danger of falling. Back in the kitchen, I helped her unpack and prepare the meal.

An hour later, with a plate of spaghetti and two glasses of wine in my stomach, I pushed back from the table, carried our dishes to the sink, and followed Nina and Hannah to the living room. Hannah tucked her legs under her as she sat in a recliner, and Nina sat to my left on the familiar couch. I hugged a worn throw pillow for protection like a baseball catcher wears pads. *Here it comes in three ... two ...one ...*

"So, out with it, Jenn," Nina instructed, not even bothering with a formal question.

I grabbed my full wine glass from the coffee table and turned it in my fingers as I told them everything, including my confrontations with Ingrid. "... so it seems that Ingrid is now in California with Declan touring Will's movie sets."

Nina didn't hesitate. "The bitch."

"No doubt," Hannah agreed. "But there is something really curious going on here. None of this makes sense. Why would he write you that paper then invite Ingrid to California?"

"That's what I've asked myself every day for the last three weeks."

Nina grabbed her laptop off the coffee table and typed in a few words.

"What are you doing?" I asked.

"Reconnaissance. Let's find out what our buddy Declan has been doing in California. There has to be at least a few paparazzi pictures." Hannah and I scooted next to Nina so we could all look at the screen.

"Bingo," she said, as the Google search netted thousands of results. She clicked on the most recent picture of Declan in an expensive-looking black tuxedo. He was smiling at the camera like he'd grown up on the red carpet. He was nothing but suave, polished, and sexy, but he didn't look anything like the Declan I knew. He

241

posed with his hand in one pocket, and behind him the screen read *Glorious*, the title of his father's latest movie. Nina clicked on another thumbnail, and when the picture loaded, I think I swallowed my heart. It was another picture taken at his father's movie premiere, but the only difference was that he had a gorgeous blonde on his arm.

Ingrid.

She leaned into his shoulder, moulding her full chest to his arm like they'd been a couple for years. The caption simply stated that Declan Monahan had recently made amends with his father and was supporting his most recent movie along with "an unknown woman". I leaned back against the couch, not wanting to see more. I vowed I would hate him forever, although I knew it wasn't true.

I was fighting to let go and fighting not to at the same time.

Thankfully, Nina closed her laptop and set it on the coffee table.

My two normally talkative friends were speechless as they watched me stew in a pot mixed with a pinch of anger, a teaspoon of shock, and a big dose of hurt. "What are you going to do?" Hannah finally asked. "Do you still love him?"

I gave voice to the conflict I'd been feeling for three weeks. "I wish I didn't. I wish I could wash my hands of him, say without doubt that if he called me next month I wouldn't rush to answer his call. But I can't. I think *that* troubles me more than any of that," I said, gesturing towards the laptop.

"So you're questioning yourself," Nina concluded.

"Exactly. What pisses me off the most is that I feel fickle, like I can't make up my damn mind. I've never been the type of woman who blew with the wind. Not when it came to the latest fashions, the latest boy band in high school, and, least of all, in relationships. That's not how I'm wired. I crave stability and predictability. I look

242

for people who can give me that. Hell, my parents' thirty-year marriage is the postcard for stability. That's why I was so skeptical of Declan when I first met him, because he was the opposite of everything I'd always wanted. Every time we talked, I couldn't tell if he was putting on a performance or if he was being real. He didn't scream stable, and he surely wasn't predictable."

"And you fell in love with Mr Unpredictable." I didn't respond. She added, "Why? Why do you think you fell in love with the *very* type of man you thought you didn't want?"

"I don't know. Why did you fall in love with Beckett? He was the opposite of what you were looking for."

Hannah was reticent when she answered. "I fell in love with Beckett because a part of me realized that my previous judgments had to be challenged. Veering away from my comfort zone made me stronger. It allowed me to come to him as a whole person."

"And changing what you believed in didn't make you feel like you were giving up who you were?"

"Not in the least. Changing your mind about something doesn't make you weaker. It shows your strength. Only idiots go through their whole lives without changing their beliefs. But I think the hardest part was the point at which I questioned everything about myself. It felt like the ground was falling out from under me and I couldn't grab onto anything solid."

That sounds exactly like my past three weeks. "So what did you do?"

Hannah shrugged. "I rode out the earthquake and, when it ended, I rebuilt what mattered to me most."

"Your relationship with Beckett," I whispered.

"Yes."

"So you think I should get back with Declan? That is, if he actually ever does come back and wants to start again?"

"I don't know about that. Only time will tell. And he'll

243

have a lot of explaining to do if he does. But what I do know is that in the meantime, in this month of limbo, the best thing you can do is work on yourself. Make yourself whole. Come to peace with who you are and why you fell in love with the man you did."

"Thank you, Hannah. You two mean the world to me." I hugged them, and as I wiped away the few stray tears, I finished what was left of my wine.

The rest of the night's conversation meandered through easier and safer topics until just before midnight. My buzz had worn off, so I decided to drive home. "Thanks for having me. This was exactly what I needed."

Five minutes later, I started the thirty minute drive to my apartment in Longmont. On the dark and deserted drive, I ran through everything Hannah had said after dinner. One thing had stuck with me. She had called this my month of limbo, and while this month definitely was filled with uncertainty, I didn't want it to be defined by it. Instead, I vowed to make it a downclimb, a purgatory where I would spend the coming weeks in this temporary place of suffering, working on myself so that I'd be ready when the next peak came.

When I got home, I changed into my pajamas and dug to the back of my closet for my briefcase. Inside, I found the envelope that contained Declan's paper. I reached in, grabbed the chock, and got into bed. I held it tight in my hand as I fell asleep to memories of my highest peaks.

Chapter Twenty-four

For the next week, I took long, peaceful walks, read books I'd had the intention of reading for months, went to lunch with Ansley, and continued to climb at the gym. While it might have appeared to everyone that my life hadn't changed much, the reality was very different. For weeks after Declan left, I had merely survived. The pain, the confusion, had consumed me. While I still thought about him a lot, I didn't have the raw sense of panic or unease any more. It was like I'd come to terms with the downclimb, and I didn't worry every waking moment if the next peak included Declan.

The hardest part was when the month-long hiatus of communication Dean Andrews had suggested came and went in silence. It was like we had stepped over a threshold and I could no longer pretend that the lack of communication was due only to Dean Andrews' advice.

That Thursday, I drove to the Boulder gym to blow off some energy on the treadmill and stair climbers. I hummed along to the new workout songs I'd downloaded as the twenty-somethings around me worked out, staring at screens filled with *SportsCenter* or soap operas. Ninety minutes later, my legs were jelly, and sweat ran down my temples. Had I been wearing make-up, I'm sure it would have been ruined.

I considered stopping my workout and heading for the shower, but since I had scheduled a session with a club belay in five minutes, I realized it would be rude of me to cancel.

I found the club belay, Jonathan, waiting for me when I

walked in. I'd been working with him on the climbing wall for the past few weeks, so we'd become friendly. I had told him about The Maiden, and he had talked about his recent climbs, all of which were much more impressive than mine.

"Hey, Jenn. I thought you were going to stand me up," Jonathan said.

"Nah. Just got into the workout and lost track of time." We double-checked our harnesses and ties while we chatted about his upcoming attempt to climb his first 5.11.

I was about to start my climb when another club employee came running in. "Jonathan, Zeke needs to see you in his office. It's an emergency." I knew Zeke was the club's daytime manager, so I told Jonathan he should go.

Jonathan seemed reluctant. "Who's going to belay for you?" he asked.

"I'll wait until you're done. Or twenty minutes, whichever comes first. I'll climb some boulders with the crash pads while I wait, and if you don't come back, I'll pack it in. I'm tired anyway."

"OK. Thanks for understanding." He untied his harness and rushed off. The climbing room door slammed shut behind him.

Since the universities were on break, the college students were off campus, which meant the room was vacant. I laid down foam mats under one of the free-standing boulders and started my climb. I'd chosen a fairly difficult inverted face that tested my arm strength. I attempted to put as much weight on my legs as I could, but my fingers and wrists ached with each new grip.

"You're gripping too hard." The voice below me was unmistakable. I let out a startled yelp as I lost my grip. I managed to land on my feet, but my momentum made me roll onto my back on the crash pad. I'd only fallen five feet, but I landed with an oomph that stole the breath from my lungs.

Or maybe it was the man standing over me – with an amused smile, no less.

"Holy shit. You scared me. What are you doing here?"

He tried for a nonchalant shrug, but I could see his Adam's apple bob with a hard swallow. "Just wanted to do some climbing. You need a belay?"

His mischievous smile told me that Jonathan had no "emergency". "You set this up? Let me guess, Jonathan isn't coming back."

He squatted next to me. "And if I did?" I read his non-answer loud and clear.

I wanted to drag him down on top of me and kiss him senseless at the same time I had to fight the urge to shove his shoulders and scream a month's worth of fury at him. But then I noticed the dark circles around his eyes, the gaunt hollows of his cheeks, and a body that was most definitely leaner than it had been a month ago. There was no doubt my body still heated in response to his, but I also couldn't overlook the differences.

As I took him in, his eyes scanned me, and I could see flashes of vulnerability and pain. "Where have you been?" I whispered.

"Oh, Jenn. Not now. Not here. Please. We'll have all the conversations we need to, but I need this from you. Let's climb. Please trust me. If you don't trust me with your heart any more, at least trust me enough to know that I'll keep you safe."

He kept you and your job safe even when it meant he wouldn't graduate. He offered me his palm as he stood. I didn't question whether or not I'd take his hand. My hand gripped his and he tugged me up, careful to keep space between our bodies.

Screw that. I stepped into him so our chests brushed against each other. I took a deep breath, filling my nose with the agar wood scent that would forever be attached to this man. I laid my cheek against his collarbone.

"And *I* need this from you," I said.

His chest expanded as his arms hugged me tightly to him and he let out his breath in a single, shaky exhale.

Of course, over the course of the last month, I'd thought a lot about this moment and what it would be like. Never had I imagined myself sweaty and stinky, with no make-up and my hair in a ratty ponytail. I smiled as I heard him breathe in the smell of my shampoo as his hands drifted over my hair, to my neck, to my spine, and to my hips like he was cataloguing my parts to be sure nothing had changed.

While nothing he could feel with his hands had changed, there were plenty of parts of me that had.

"God, I've missed you." I could feel the vibrations of his vocal cords against my forehead. "I couldn't stay away for another hour."

I lifted my head from his chest so I could look into his eyes. "Are we going to talk tonight or do you have to leave to go back to California?"

His hands brushed stray hairs from my temples. "I'm here for good, Jenn. I'm not going anywhere. Nice T-shirt, by the way." The corners of his mouth rose in a knowing smile.

I'd practically lived in the Estes Park T-shirt I'd bought during our weekend getaway. "Did you bring your climbing gear?"

He pointed to his stack of gear a few feet from the wall. "Hmm ... was I a foregone conclusion?"

The smile dimmed from his eyes as a crease crossed his forehead. "Never, Jenn. I'll never take anything about you for granted."

I leaned in to kiss the worry from his face. Our lips barely met, but the skin that did sparked with a month's worth of built-up static electricity.

We walked to the climbing wall where he put on his harness. We tied our knots and double-checked each other's work. When he found everything satisfactory, he patted my butt and said, "Up you go."

I turned towards the wall, swallowing hard as the next words caught in my throat. There were many times when I didn't know if I would ever say them again. "Climbing, Declan."

His breath hitched before he responded. "Climb, Jenn."

I smiled at the familiarity. In some ways, it felt like it always had, and in others it felt like we were two very different people with pounds of unspoken baggage between us. I climbed the route quickly while practising some of the advanced moves I'd been working on with Jonathan. I got to the top and yelled, "Take!"

"I've got you, Jenn." Declan slowly lowered me to the ground. The second my feet hit the spongy mat, Declan's hands turned me around and his body shoved mine against the climbing wall. The uneven surface poked into my back.

His eyes burned with something that looked like jealousy. "It kills me he taught you those things."

I laughed at the Declan I'd come to love because I knew exactly who *he* was. "He only taught me a few moves." *You've taught me so much more.* What I left unspoken rang through the room with a chime like church bells on a Sunday morning.

He must have heard it. "Good," he said, pacified.

I reached my hands to his cheeks in an effort to comfort him. "It's only you. I might have been madder than a hornet, but you have to know it's really only ever been you."

I untied the rope from my harness as our eyes stayed connected. "Off belay, Declan."

"Belay off, Jenn," he whispered back.

Chapter Twenty-five

We met in the hallway outside the locker rooms after we showered and changed. "Where do you want to talk?" he asked.

"Nowhere public." I'd come to peace with a lot, but there was still a part of me that felt the need to rant and scream.

He quickly agreed. "Let's go to your apartment. We'll make dinner then talk. I'll pick up some groceries."

He walked me to my car, shut my door after I got in, and watched me drive away. He stood like a statue in my rear view mirror for quite a while before he turned to walk towards his motorcycle.

Forty-five minutes later, I heard the roar of his engine cut off. I buzzed him into my apartment and helped him unload the small sack of groceries he had put in his backpack.

"What are we making?" I asked.

He greased one pan and added water to a large pot before he answered, still concentrating on the stove in front of him. "Blackened chicken Alfredo."

The same thing he made for our meal in Estes.

I wrapped my arms around him from behind and laid my cheek on his back. He stilled for a moment before his hands met mine at his stomach. He squeezed them twice before he resumed cooking. I clung to his warmth, the softness of his cotton T-shirt, and the strength underneath it. He didn't say anything, but neither did I. It felt good to simply exist in the same room together, both of us lost in thought and somehow found.

Ten minutes later, I prepped the garlic bread and placed it in the oven. The chicken sizzled in the pan and I watched him work much like I had in the cabin in Estes. Then I set the table with plates and forks while he uncorked the wine bottle and gave us both generous pours.

He plated the food and we sat down to dinner at my kitchen table like we were some old, married couple who had just come home from a hard day's work.

Declan was the first to break the half hour silence. "Does it taste good?"

"Really good." If the room had an awkward alarm, it would have been blaring. The clumsy silence was unbearable. "You look good, Declan ... but you look like you've lost weight."

His eyes closed and opened in a long blink before they met mine. "It's been a really hard month. But let's finish dinner first."

"OK," I agreed, although the last thing I wanted to do was fill my nervous stomach. I thought about asking how his dad was, deciding it might not be a safe topic. Then I considered asking what he was going to do back in Colorado, but that wasn't a safe topic either, since his plans were most likely derailed by his decision to leave the university – a decision my behavior had caused him to make. I scanned my brain for anything that would yield easy conversation. I was compelled to fill the pulsing, clumsy silence with something. "It's ... going to be a hot summer, I think."

His hearty laugh rumbled like the thunder I'd always loved during a summer storm. With one hand, he squeezed mine on top of the table and pushed his full plate away with the other. "Look at us. Sitting here like we're on our first date talking about the weather. C'mon, Jenn. We weren't going to eat, were we?" He grabbed another bottle of wine and led me to the living room couch.

I pulled the throw blanket over my legs as I sat against the armrest, facing him. He took a long drink from the bottle and offered it to me. I smiled and put my lips to the smooth glass and took a drink of the fruity sweetness.

My nervous swallow was audible as I passed the bottle back to Declan. After he placed it on the coffee table and leaned against the other armrest, he pulled half of the throw blanket over his legs. His foot brushed back and forth on mine as he began. "I need to start at the beginning."

"You mean the day you went to talk to Dean Andrews?"

"No, before that." He sighed and tilted his chin towards the ceiling. "Before I met you, I had no problem with casual sex." I started to tell him that this revelation wasn't a surprise, but he stopped me with a raised palm. "You know that, but what you don't know is that one of the women who I shared a bed with was ... Ingrid."

"I do know. She told me."

"Do you remember that day that you overheard a woman in the bathroom talking about me and the fact I blew her off?"

"Yes." *Where is he going with this?*

"That was Ingrid."

I sucked in a breath. "How do you know?"

"Because I had met her in the hallway on the way to leave that note in your drop box. She'd been trying to contact me, and I was hoping that she'd take the hint that I wasn't interested any more. After you asked me about the conversation you overheard, I talked to her the next day. I told her in no uncertain terms that I was interested in someone else and that she needed to move on. I never promised her anything but sex. At that point in my life, I couldn't have."

"But she knew about your tattoo and what it meant."

"Ugh. I hate this." He ran one hand through his hair. "I

did tell her one night about the tattoo because she had opened herself to me, although I hadn't solicited it. She was and still is a very needy person. Without going into too much detail, she's had some drug problems, and I'm not just talking a casual habit. She's gotten help for it, and one night when she was really low, I was the shoulder she cried on. I regretted it every night since."

"Because it encouraged her to think of you as more than a casual lay."

"Yes. I know I should have told you about my past with her, but I thought it was over. I really did. She didn't contact me for a few months. So you can understand why I was panicked when she overheard us in the bathroom. Although she *said* she wouldn't tell anyone, I didn't believe her."

"So what happened on the Wednesday before the play opened?"

He took another drink from the wine bottle before he offered it to me. I declined with a shake of my head. As he sat the bottle back on the table, his tongue licked a drop of liquid from his bottom lip. I shifted my legs against his under the blanket, liking how his coarse leg hair brushed against my skin.

"That Wednesday night, she called me, drunk and probably high, although I couldn't say what on. She said she needed me to come over because she was really depressed. That alone probably wouldn't have been enough to get me to come to her apartment, but because she knew of our affair, I couldn't risk turning my back and having her do something rash. I went over there to smooth things over, make sure she didn't need medical attention, and left an hour later."

"What made you leave so quickly on Friday night?"

"You know that Ingrid called again, but this time, her manipulation was obvious. She was using her knowledge of our affair to blackmail me into coming back to her. She told me that we had to resume our relationship, as she called it, or she would tell the university about our affair. I told her to wait for me at her apartment and not do anything stupid before I got there. That's why I had to leave so fast."

"What happened when you got there?" My chest tightened as I silently chanted a prayer. *Please say you didn't have sex with her. Please say ... Please say ... I don't think that is something I can forgive.*

"She was dressed in a little scrap of lace, so I told her to cover herself up. She moped like a toddler but she did, and then I told her there was no chance that I would have sex with her again."

"Did she try to ... persuade you?" *Why do I want to know this?*

Declan's legs shifted under the blanket as he sat up and reached for me across the blanket. His hands were warm as he grabbed my wrist. "Yes. She did. But I'm telling you the truth. Nothing happened."

I wanted to believe that. But the reality was that she had spent the last few weeks in California with him. Something didn't jive. "So she just accepted your refusal?" I couldn't help the skepticism that trickled from my words.

"No. By this point you know her well enough to know that she didn't take no for an answer. Since I refused her advances, she threatened to call Dean Andrews the following morning, and I couldn't take the risk she was bluffing. You mean too much to me to allow that."

The couch felt like it fell out from under me. "You *did* have sex with her. She said you stayed until the morning."

"No. I told her that on Saturday morning I would meet with Dean Andrews myself and leave the university. With me no longer a student, the school wouldn't take action against you."

"That's not true."

"I know, but she didn't know that. She hadn't expected

me to refuse her, and she certainly hadn't expected me to leave to protect you, so she was caught off-guard. She didn't have a back-up plan. Had she thought about it, she would have realized that she could have still gotten you fired because the affair happened before I left. What it comes down to is that I don't think that she thought I would really quit the university, and me leaving meant she didn't get what she wanted."

"You back in her bed," I finished.

His stare acknowledged I was right. "To some extent, yes. Even as I left her apartment on Saturday morning, I got the feeling she thought I was bluffing. She thought I'd never leave the play after the successful opening night."

My heart was sprinting. "Can we stop here for a second? I need some fresh air."

"Sure. Let's go out on the balcony." He grabbed the wine bottle and followed me onto the balcony, where the last few rays of sun were protesting the darkness. Thankfully, the air was cool on my heated skin. Declan stood next to me as we both leaned our elbows on the railing and looked out over the courtyard below.

The story he'd told had crushed me. I knew he had chosen to leave the university to protect me, but hearing the story from him made my heart break and my conscience ache. He said that he hadn't had a choice, but he had. He could have slept with her. He could have convinced himself she was bluffing in an act of self-preservation. He could have acted for his dad and then left the university. And he could have decided to let me lose my job. Lord knows I wasn't innocent in this whole thing either.

I felt Declan's arms wrap around me from behind as he rested his chin on my shoulder. "Hey. Why are you crying?"

"I'm so sorry. So sorry, Declan. I knew what I was doing with you was against university policy. I deserved punishment for what I did, and instead of getting what I deserved, you fell on your sword. It's not fair that I get to continue at the university and you got to face the consequences. You didn't get to graduate. You didn't get to act for your father. You didn't get to finish a play that you had worked so hard on. What about your acting career? What are you going to do?"

His words were measured and careful when he spoke. "*Both* of us were at fault. *Both* of us could have stopped it and *we* chose not to. And even knowing how it turned out, I wouldn't change a thing."

"How can you say that? She manipulated ..."

He interrupted me. "I would rather me get manipulated than you get fired."

How he could be so calm and logical about this was beyond me. "But you had to give up everything."

His arms squeezed around me. "Not everything, Jenn. Not near everything."

We stood on the balcony so long that I started to get cold. Declan rubbed his hands up and down my arms. "Let's go back in and finish this."

I grabbed the bottle of wine from the wooden decking and took a big swig. "Yes. Let's."

When we got situated on the couch again, he resumed the story. "I left her house early Saturday morning after I told her I was going to leave the university, and I could tell that she didn't believe I'd follow through. I slept a few hours, called the Dean to schedule an emergency meeting at his office after lunch, and met my dad at a restaurant."

"How did that go?"

He shrugged. "We hadn't seen each other in years, so it was awkward at first. Yet I could tell that he was really excited to see the play and to support me. He told me he was sorry for being an absentee parent when I was growing up. He wished he could take back how much he tried to shape my life because he said losing his relationship with me was the single biggest regret of his life."

"That's a really nice thing to say."

"Yes, especially since I know he has a lot of things to regret in his life," Declan joked, then turned serious. "From a man who rarely showed any emotion, I was ... stunned. I sensed that although he may have a bevy of women at his door, he was suffering and alone. Chasing fame hadn't fulfilled him like he thought it would, I don't think. So when he opened up to me, I decided that he deserved to know the truth about why he wouldn't see me act on Saturday night. I told him about you, our affair, about Ingrid and her blackmail, and about how much I loved you."

"Oh, Declan ..."

"He told me he supported me in my decision. That I had to make the decision I thought was best. He said he wanted to go with me to meet with the Dean because he made me realize that I had to concoct a cover story for why I was leaving the university so quickly. Of course, I couldn't tell the Dean the truth, so we decided it would make sense to say I had a family emergency. I tried to call you a few times as we drove to campus, but you didn't answer. I wanted you to hear from me that I was leaving the university."

"I know. I got your messages."

He smiled. "You turned off your phone, didn't you?"

"Yes. How did you know?"

He shrugged. "I know you. Anyway, we met with the Dean, and everything seemed to be going fine until he asked what my mother's name was. Instinctively, I answered with 'Adele', the only mother I've ever known, and my father said 'Lauren'. The Dean knew something was up then, and he had surmised the truth, because he gave me a warning that if what he suspected became public, he would be forced to fire you. But implicit in that warning was the idea that if it didn't become public, he wouldn't pursue disciplinary action. Then he gave me some advice, although it was more like a command."

"He told you to avoid any contact for at least a month."

"Yes. How did you know?"

"He gave me the same advice."

Declan looked surprised. "So you met with him too?"

"Yes. He asked me to come to his office Monday morning and told me what had happened, what he suspected, and what he expected me to do for the next month."

"So you knew about all this?"

"Some of it, but not all. What I definitely don't know is why Ingrid was in California with you."

"I'll get to that. I promise. After we met with the Dean, I called Ingrid to let her know that I hadn't been bluffing. She'd obviously spent the morning thinking, because she had realized that she could still get you fired just to spite us. I had no doubt that she would, too."

"I still don't get it."

"I had to come up with a way to silence her since my leaving the university wasn't enough. From what I knew of Ingrid, I decided to bribe her. The perfect idea came to me, but I had to run it by my dad first. I told her I'd call her back in five minutes and hung up. You see, ever since I met Ingrid, she's wanted to be an actress in Hollywood. She's always dreamt of getting discovered and becoming a movie star, so I decided to exploit that dream. My dad agreed to fly her out to California and let her stay in his mansion. We decided to take her to the set of the movie he had just started shooting and introduce her to the director. With my dad's clout, he could almost guarantee that she'd get some small stand-in role. She probably wouldn't get a speaking role, but getting her foot in the door would be something she couldn't have gotten on her own. Of course, when we called her with this plan, she readily agreed, and we made it clear that these favours were buying her perpetual silence."

"When she showed me the text that said she was staying under the same roof as you …"

"I know. I wanted to call you so badly to tell you, but I couldn't go against Dean Andrew's advice. Having such a powerful man in our favor was invaluable. I couldn't risk it. But know that the roof she stayed under was a really big one. She stayed in a separate wing from me and my dad, and I made sure to lock my door each night."

"I trust you, especially now that I know the whole story. But why did you have to take her to that premiere? God, you looked like a couple in those photos. I think I died a little when I saw those."

"As much as I knew those photos would hurt you, we had to do them."

"Why?"

"Insurance."

"I don't understand."

"Ingrid did end up getting a small part, and Dad agreed to pay her rent on a studio apartment for three months to help her get on her feet. After that, he plans on washing his hands of her. Yet, my dad and I still didn't believe Ingrid when she agreed to never report the affair even after everything we'd done. So we deliberately took her to some high-profile venues, knowing that the paparazzi would take pictures of her and me together and would assume we were a couple."

"Why would you want that?"

"Because if she did decide to go back to Colorado and testify against you, her credibility would be damaged beyond repair. She'd look like the jilted, vindictive ex-lover who was getting back at me after our 'relationship' went sour. Plus, she'd have no explanation for why she waited at least a few months to report an affair she 'allegedly' witnessed."

"You did all this for me?"

"I did this for *us*, Jenn. You have to know that."

"But I hate the feeling that Ingrid came out ahead. She got what she wanted by threatening you."

"If I learned anything in the month I spent in Hollywood, it's that there are a million Ingrids. And when I say she got a small part, I think she literally asked the main character if he wanted fries or tater tots. Not exactly Oscar-worthy. It is highly unlikely that she'll make a career in acting, and where she goes from this will all be on her. It was a small price to pay for a future with you."

"But you paid an even bigger price," I said, reminding him of the degree he would never gain.

"Not really. I've already talked to another local university, and it seems like I'll need to take one semester's worth of classes in order to graduate with them. In the scheme of things, it's nothing – it's only four more months of work. But with school and work, I'll be busy."

"Wait. Work? What work?"

"Oh, I didn't tell you?" he said in mock surprise. "You know a representative from the Colorado Shakespeare Company attended the performance on opening night."

I sat up. "Yes."

"The director of the company contacted me a few weeks ago and asked if I would be willing to take on some small roles for them in hopes that someday I could come on as a full company member."

"Holy hell! What did you say?"

"I told him I'd think about it." He burst out laughing immediately and I playfully slapped his shoulder. "I told him I would take his offer! It's what I've always wanted to do."

"I'm so proud of you. You deserved it."

"Thank you."

We talked a little more but soon I yawned, exhausted

both physically and emotionally from the long day. The bottle of wine on top of the reunion had taken its toll.

"Let's get you to bed." He offered his hand and tugged me from the couch. I led the way down the hallway to my bedroom where I threw some dirty clothes off the bed and onto the floor. I pulled back the sheets and got in as Declan shut off the light. I heard his footsteps round the bed, and in the darkness, I could see the outline of his body as he stood next to the side of the bed. He bent down and kissed my forehead.

"Thanks for listening. I –"

"Please stay," I interrupted.

"Jenn, I don't have to. If it's too early …"

"No, please. You don't know how many nights I've lain here, wishing that you were with me."

"Yes, I do," he said as he pulled up the sheets and climbed in. The mattress dipped with his weight as we both lay on our sides facing each other. I could make out his eyes and a few features on his face. "If you were anything like me, I dreamt it every night."

His chest expanded next to me as he took in a deep breath. His lips ghosted mine as he exhaled. My hand at the nape of his neck pulled him to me as I deepened the kiss. He responded with a groan before he levered himself off the bed and rolled me onto my back. His lips gentled as his hips pushed me into the mattress.

His mouth pulled away seconds later, and I sucked in much needed air. "I missed you, Jenn. Every second of every breath. This month was absolute torture. I hated doing all the Hollywood premieres, granting pictures I'd knew you'd see. To be away from you was bad, but not being able to talk to you, to explain, was even worse. Parts of me were missing in California, Jenn. You're the place I store my heart."

"And you're the place I store my dreams. Even the ones I wouldn't have allowed myself to dream months ago. I want them to come true with you."

"I love you, Jenn. You're the one place I don't feel restless." His hand covered his heart where his tattoo only scarred skin-deep. I, and more importantly our love, was much deeper.

"I love you too."

He kissed me again and pulled away seconds later. "Did you like my essay, Dr Lyons?" he asked.

"Dr Lyons did, but Jenn liked it even more. When did you put it in the drop box?"

"Right before I met with the Dean. It was all the communication I was willing to risk. I couldn't leave without telling you how I felt."

"I used to bring it out in the middle of the night when I couldn't sleep. I'd lie here wishing you were here to whisper the words next to me."

My eyelids started to close, but then I remembered something that had constantly bothered me. "There was one thing that confused me."

"What?"

"Why did you give me back the chock? It felt like what someone does when he breaks up with someone for good. I didn't know what to think: the letter made me hopeful, but the chock made me hopeless."

"I'm sorry. That's not what I intended. Don't get me wrong, I appreciated you giving it to me. It was a great way for me to feel connected to you when I was on stage. But it didn't feel right taking it with me to California. That chock is *your* strength, *your* triumph. I'd never take that from you. I wanted you to have that chock with you while I couldn't be to remind you just how strong you are."

Maybe on some level, I'd felt it too, because I'd slept with it next to me for the last week instead of burying it in the back of my closet.

I thanked him with a soft kiss, and minutes later, he rocked into me, carrying me away on gentle, rolling waves.

Chapter Twenty-six

We spent the next few weeks reconnecting. We agreed that the silver lining of the month spent apart was Declan's chance to reconnect with his dad.

"We're a lot closer now," he said one day when we were getting ready to climb at the gym.

"I noticed he calls you a lot more."

"Yes, we talk every week. He's excited to come out and see me act." Declan had been cast as Claudio in Colorado Shakespeare Company's summer performance of *Measure for Measure*. "I can't wait for him to meet you."

"I feel the same. He helped us out a lot with the Ingrid situation, and I'll forever be grateful to him for that."

The peace that Declan had with his father bled into our relationship, making it easier for him to open up emotionally. And, for that, I was also grateful.

Other days, we went on hikes and planned our next real climb up East Slab in Boulder Canyon. Since we no longer had to hide our relationship, and since there was no communication from Ingrid, we were able to relax in public. We could hold hands without looking over our shoulders in worry. We'd go out for dinner on a Tuesday night and then head to one of our apartments for a movie followed by love-making that Declan made sure was slow and sensual.

He'd been more reserved and less dominant with me since our reunion, and when I asked him about it, he said he didn't want to push too fast. "We're building back the trust," he'd say. While I appreciated his care, I needed, craved, the man who'd taken me on top of The Maiden.

So one Saturday night after sharing dinner at a steak restaurant, I decided to take charge. I snuggled into him on my couch as we watched the first half of some action flick. I'd seen it many times, so my mind wandered to what I had planned for the night. Nervousness vibrated under the surface of my skin as I peeled myself off Declan's warm, sprawling body.

"Where you goin'?" he murmured.

"Just have to go to the bathroom." I walked down the hall as he continued to watch the movie. I slipped into my bedroom and closed the door. I opened the top drawer I'd recently restocked and found the lace lingerie I'd bought with Declan in mind.

I stripped, pulled the babydoll top over my head, and secured it tightly around my chest by tying the bow between my breasts. I slipped on the matching thong and gave my hair a quick brush before I walked back to the living room.

I felt his eyes on me as I turned the corner like I had the first day I walked into the classroom. Only tonight, I had far fewer clothes on, and, ironically, I felt much less exposed. Now I knew the man whose eyes burned through the scraps of lace loved me.

"Whoa. C'mere." He sat up and reached one hand towards me. When I apparently didn't come fast enough, his hand waved towards his chest like a cop directing traffic. He nuzzled against my neck when I sat down next to him. "You're so hot in everything, but this is just … wow."

He fingered the bow tied at my breasts. "What's this all about?"

"I'm glad you came back to me."

"I'm glad too …" he said, confused.

"But I need *all* of you back."

His eyes darted to mine and read them left to right like a book. "You sure? I've wanted this for so long, but I couldn't until you were ready."

"More than sure."

I squealed in surprise a second later as he bolted from the couch, threw me over his shoulder, and carried me down the hall with long strides.

A second after I heard his foot kick open my bedroom door, he threw me on the mattress, where I bounced twice and settled onto my back, the cold sheets a welcome greeting to my overheated skin.

His eyes catalogued every inch of skin, memorising and worshipping it. "Fuck. Look at you lying there like a present I'm going to unwrap." He climbed onto the bed and lay next to me. "Turn over."

I followed his command and turned my chin so that my cheek rested on the soft cotton sheets. My nipples pebbled against them, my thong soaked with anticipation.

"This is the last time I'll ask. You're sure?"

"Yes."

"You remember that day we had lunch for the first time?"

"Yes."

"We asked each other questions and we had to answer them honestly. No evasions. No half-truths."

"I remember." *Where is he going with this?*

"I have one question left, and I'm using it now. What do you want me to do to you, Jenn?"

Months ago, I would have stayed on my stomach as I ashamedly whispered my needs into the pillows, grateful for the way my long hair shielded me from his gaze.

But not now.

I turned over so that I lay on my back. I reached out my hand to feather my fingertips over his sharp cheekbones and jaw, to his neck where I could feel his thudding pulse as blood raced through the artery. I told him what I really wanted. "I want you to take me like you promised you would. I want you to take my ass from behind. I want to

267

give myself to you. Like that." I leaned over to the bedside table, grabbed the bottle from the drawer, and handed it to him.

He stared at the lube like I'd handed him a winning lottery ticket. Then his face heated as his eyes cut through me. "I'll take you like that. But you have to know, it's going to be my way. *My way*," he repeated.

"Yes," I confirmed.

He scanned my face for a second before he whispered his next command. "Bend your knees." Declan sat up on his knees while I bent mine until the soles of my feet rested flat on the mattress. He used one hand to splay open my knees, and the intimate act of simply opening myself to him, made even more erotic by the lack of touching or talking, made a whimper escape my throat. I licked my lips and begged for his kiss.

He knew what I wanted, but he shook his head while his hand found my center. He rubbed circles before he pushed two fingers inside, his thumb pressing into my throbbing clit.

The fact that we weren't in the heat of passion with flying limbs and biting kisses should have made this moment feel clinical; instead, his eyes bored into me, making it the most intimate moment I'd ever had. I couldn't hide anything from his stare.

And for the first time, I didn't want to.

My hips bucked as his fingers hit a nerve inside me. He fingered me to the edge, and just before I tipped over, he withdrew his hand.

Words of protest threatened until I saw him reach for the bottle of lube on the nightstand. He squirted the liquid onto the fingers of his right hand and rubbed them together before he turned back to me. His left hand found my clit again as his wet fingers circled me. We had played like this a few times before the break-up, but it had been a long time, and there was a lot of water under this bridge.

Why touching there took so much more trust, I might never know. Maybe it was the forbidden. Maybe it was the taboo. Regardless, my heart sped until I heard it pound a rhythm in my eardrums.

I felt his fingertip penetrate me, and I must have closed my eyes because he said, "Eyes, Jenn. Don't look away when I take you." My eyes snapped open and followed his as they descended.

"I have to taste you." His tongue darted out and replaced his fingers at my clit while two fingers pushed against my tight ring.

I rocked my hips at the dual sensations. "More. More," I chanted like it was my personal anthem. And he gave me more. His tongue entered me before it retreated and flicked wildly on my clit that now sizzled and burned. He repeated this pattern again and again. I concentrated on it so hard that my mind disregarded everything else. Soon I was full with his fingers and more desire than I'd ever felt.

He sat up and slowly pulled his fingers away. For the first time since we came into the bedroom, he leaned down to kiss me as his hands untied the bow on the lingerie, pushed the straps off my shoulders, and slid down my thong. When I was undressed, he kneeled next to me and grabbed his shirt at the back of the neck. He pulled it over his head, revealing his washboard abs and small, erect nipples. He used his wadded shirt to wipe the small beads of sweat that had collected on his hairline before he threw the shirt onto the floor.

He unhooked his belt, slid down the zipper, and pulled off his pants. His boxers followed, and he squirted lube into his hand and rubbed it on his jutting cock. "There might be a day when I ask you to take some pain for me, but this is not that day. If it ever hurts, you tell me and we stop. I can do things that will help you if it does, but I can't if you don't tell me. This isn't supposed to hurt. This isn't something you gut through for me. That's not hot.

Not at all."

"I understand."

He nodded. "Turn over."

After I followed his command and grabbed the headboard above me, his hands lifted my hips off the mattress. His fingers rubbed circles around my tight hole as he lay down on top of me. His weight pushed my chest into the mattress as he spoke softly in my ear. "You and I both know that I have the power to hurt you, yet you lay there. Watching you put your faith in me ..." He didn't finish his thought as if he couldn't find the words. He started again, "It's the ultimate trust you're giving me. I'll show you it's not misplaced."

"I know it's not."

"I know, or else we wouldn't be doing this. But I'll spend the rest of my life reminding you."

He lifted off me to create enough space that he could enter me. His left hand reached around to circle my clit as his right pumped himself twice and tilted his cock to enter me. I felt the tip of him probe before it penetrated. What felt like a mile was probably only an inch, and I gripped the headboard, suddenly worried that maybe I couldn't do it.

"You're gripping too hard," he said, and I smiled. I loosened my hands and along with it, the tense muscles in my arms, shoulders, and stomach. "Much better," he praised.

His left hand circled faster and pressed harder. "Push against me a little bit." I felt a firmness in his penetration that rode the edge of discomfort. I blew out a breath as his middle finger flicked my clit and he pushed forward.

Then he stopped.

His hand slipped out from under me, and still inside me, he pushed my thighs together, tucked a pillow under my hips to change the angle, and sat up, straddling me. "You gotta talk to me. How do you feel?"

Possessed. Cherished. "Full."

"Not yet, but soon. Rub yourself." My right hand snaked down the sheets and found my clit. It panged with my slightest touch.

"Move. Please. Move. Take me," I begged.

"No. My way, remember. You're going to do it." His palms grabbed a handful of my ass and squeezed. Then he circled his hands in opposite directions, which pulled me apart and pushed me back together.

"You're going to lift up to me. Your speed. My rhythm." I followed the cadence of his circling hands as I tilted my hips up then down, taking more of him into me each time.

"Fuck me. Look at your hips. The way they lift. I can feel your muscles lift yourself onto me," he said as he squeezed my ass again, this time hard enough for me to moan. My ass brushed his hips and his balls pressed against me.

"There. Stop." His breath hissed like he was fighting to maintain control.

I paused my hips, whimpering in a combination of frustration of uncontrollable need. "Why? I'm fine."

"I know. You've taken all of me. Now it's my turn. Be still."

He retreated slowly and paused before he pounded a steady pulse.

In.

Out.

In a bit faster. Harder.

Out more slowly.

His hot breaths floated along my back as he worked me. One of his hands peeled some of my sweat-soaked hair off my neck, exposing it to the cooler air.

His rhythm continued, slower now, although the once measured thrusts became more forceful. Out of the corner of my eye, I saw his lips purse seconds before I felt him blowing cool air up my spine and to my neck. My skin pebbled with the new sensation. A shiver shook my shoulders even though most of me was burning.

His hot, sweaty chest pushed into my back, and his voice returned to my ear as he lay down on top of me. His left hand squeezed between my hips and the pillow. Two fingers entered my sex, filling me to bursting.

"Turn your head and kiss me," he demanded.

I lifted my head as best I could, and his tongue took possession of my mouth in the same rhythm as his fingers and hips. The tempo was irregular as I bucked back to him uncontrollably. The tell-tale tension coiled at my center. I pulled away and panted for breath. "I'm close. Please. Please make me come."

I expected him to press a little harder or increase the rhythm, but he kissed me with a probing, insistent tongue, then spoke against my lips. "There's no place I'm not in you." His tongue darted in again.

My mouth.

My sex.

My ass.

All possessed.

All filled.

"Yes. Yes. Yes," I screamed as my body peaked and fell, peaked and fell. The coil in my core slowly lost its tension, leaving behind a feeling of sated peace.

"You're pulling me over. Fuck," Declan roared, and he fell off the cliff with two hard pumps. I took his weight as his hips stilled and he spasmed inside me, emptying himself. His hand covered mine in a fierce grip on the headboard as we sucked in air in silence.

He pulled out slowly and turned my shoulders so I lay on my back underneath him. I sank into the mattress, buried in trust, grounded in love.

His powerful body loomed over me and his eyes sparkled with the question I will never forget. "So how's the view from the top?"

CPSIA information can be obtained at www.ICGtesting.com
Printed in the USA
LVOW11s0218080216

474142LV00001B/23/P